Miss Newbury's List

OTHER PROPER ROMANCES
BY MEGAN WALKER

Lakeshire Park

Miss Newbury's List

PROPER ROMANCE

MEGAN WALKER

SHADOW
MOUNTAIN
PUBLISHING

Library of Congress Cataloging-in-Publication Data
Names: Walker, Megan, 1990– author.
Title: Miss Newbury's list / Megan Walker.
Other titles: Proper romance.
Description: [Salt Lake City]: Shadow Mountain Publishing, [2023] |
Series: Proper romance | Summary: "Rosalind Newbury has a list of ten things she
    wants to accomplish before she marries the duke. Falling in love with her best
    friend's cousin, Charlie, was not one of them."—Provided by publisher.
Identifiers: LCCN 2022027870 | ISBN 9781639930524 (trade paperback)
Subjects: LCSH: Courtship—Fiction. | BISAC: FICTION / Romance /
    Historical / Regency | FICTION / Romance / Clean & Wholesome | LCGFT:
    Romance fiction. | Historical fiction.
Classification: LCC PS3623. A3595516 M57 2023 | DDC 813/.6—dc23/
    eng/20220822
LC record available at https: //lccn.loc.gov/2022027870

Printed in the United States of America
Lake Book Manufacturing, Inc., Melrose Park, IL

10   9   8   7   6   5   4   3   2

For Sophie—

Wherever life takes you, I'll follow.

Chapter One

Ashford, England, 1820

I leaned over the trunk at the foot of my bed in a desperate, frantic search.

Liza would be here any moment, and I could not for my life find that sheet of paper.

I'd hidden it years ago after learning that little brothers were as keen as hounds to find their older sister's secrets. And while Jasper and Nicholas were away at Harrow, Ben at eighteen years of age still played his part exceptionally well.

Apparently, so did I.

I hadn't slid my paper in any book or drawer, nor under my mattress or in the little space beneath my armoire. It had to be in the trunk. My fingers met fabrics of all sorts, from a soft old dress I'd worn nearly to shreds to scratchy linen sacks filled with broken paintbrushes and pigment jars.

I seemed to remember a little green box with ribbons and pressed flowers . . .

Someone rapped lightly on my door, and my senses

seized for the second it took for my maid to poke her head inside. "Miss Newbury?"

I gave Molly wide eyes, and she pinched her lips closed. "Quiet. Right. You're in hiding. In your own bedroom." She slid inside, blonde curls poking wildly out of their proper arrangement, and closed the door.

"Yes, and you cannot call out my name like that." Mama would hear and know exactly where to find me.

Molly stood above me and raised a brow. "Forgive me. How shall I address you then, if not 'Miss Newbury'?" She made a show of ignorance. "Miss *Rosalind* Newbury? Just 'Rosalind'? Or we could practice using 'Your Gr—'"

"You *know* what I meant." I narrowed my gaze at her twitching lips. Ignorant, she was not. Clever, though, for she could tell me exactly what she thought without saying much at all. And I would miss her terribly when I left. "I've asked you to distract Mama, and yet here you are. You must have news."

"The Ollertons have returned home at last."

Finally! "Is Liza downstairs?" I started to stand, craning my ear for the sound of her footsteps pattering up the stairs. Liza had a knack for solving the unsolvable; she'd help me find my paper. And then, we'd get to work. "You cannot leave her with Mama. The two of them will gossip for an hour."

Molly cleared her throat. Her gaze settled on the pile of things I'd pulled out of my trunk. "She has not yet come to call."

"She's not . . ." I furrowed my brow and turned to peer out my bedroom window.

The fields between our two estates stretched on, separated

2

by a grove of oak trees that, lush with summer leaves, occluded my view. Liza had been in London for her first Season for months. I'd suffered horrible jealousy, mourning my loss and bristling at the unfairness of being kept at home, until one day, just like that, the contract was in front of me, a pen in my hand. I'd made my decision. Why should it matter that I'd met my intended in Father's study instead of a ballroom? I'd told Liza the barest of details in my last letter, knowing she'd be dying for more. She'd promised to visit as soon as her carriage rolled to a stop.

So where was she?

"Something is amiss, Molly," I said. "Perhaps I should sneak over."

I eyed my bonnet hanging loosely on my easel in the corner, but Molly stepped into view. "There are more pressing problems at present," she said. "Your mother asked me to find you and fetch you right away."

"What did she say?"

Molly braced herself. "Something about another appointment."

"Good heavens, how many appointments does one need to plan a wedding?" I sighed heavily and rubbed my temples. Could we not simply say our vows and be done with it?

"I've told her you are still reading Fordyce's sermons." Molly winced at the lie.

I snorted. "I am sure she loved to hear that." What would Mama say if she knew the truth? That I was chasing a promise I'd made to myself eight years ago. A promise I had three weeks left to fulfill. And I was failing. "I think I saved my list in a little green box. . . . Oh, *where* have I hidden it?"

I'd been searching for days. I needed to get started on it, for the whole point was to *finish* the thing before I married, but moments alone were rare since my engagement, what with Mama and her endless lists of dress fittings and menu changes, Father drawing up addendums to the marriage contract, and my brother Benjamin insisting I follow him around the estate on some grand last adventure. Did they not understand that these were *my* last days? There were so few of them left.

My skin suddenly seemed three sizes too small. "Molly, I need more time to search. You must distract Mama."

Molly placed her hands on her slender hips. "What am I to tell her this time? Fordyce was enough of a stretch. She's bound to catch on."

I waved a hand in the air. "Tell her that I am . . . writing a sonnet about my feelings."

Molly drew in a long breath and chewed at her bottom lip like she usually did when attempting to keep her thoughts to herself. Aside from Liza, Molly was my closest alliance. When she held back her cleverly disguised opinions, it was serious.

I kneeled again and dug my arm deep inside the trunk. "Free your tongue. What is it?"

Molly hesitated, watching as I pulled out a wooden horse and set it in the pile, then tucked a loose string of golden hair behind her ear.

"You do not wish to lie to Mama again," I mused. "You think I am being irrational. That if you were getting married, you would not care about something as silly as a list of hopes and wishes to complete beforehand. But I am not as good as you, Molly. I am a mess. I've always been."

"You do often smear your dresses with paint."

I only half heard her. My own words felt like a dam about to burst. I felt them in my bones and clawing up my throat. All my life, I'd worked for this moment. I'd polished my accomplishments, learned languages and hostess skills and more manners than I could possibly uphold in an evening. And yet . . .

I glanced up at my maid, who watched me with a serious gaze, waiting.

"Tell me," Molly said tenderly, kneeling down beside me. "What are you feeling?"

So many things. Nervous. Frightened of falling short for my family, my intended, and his family. But there was something else, too. Something hard to name. "I feel . . . incomplete. Like I have not lived enough to warrant such a major life change. To be a man's *wife*, Molly. To run my own household. Benjamin has experienced more than I have, and he's two years younger than I am."

"But that is the way of things, Miss Newbury. Your brother requires a more extensive education. More experience—"

"Because he is the heir, yes, I realize." That same familiar burning engulfed my chest. *I* wanted more. Was that so terrible? "I imagined my engagement would feel more satisfying." Immediately, I wished I could rescind the words. It was a mortifying thing to admit, especially coming from a girl who wanted for nothing. I had no reason to complain or wish or dream because I already had everything, and what I did not have, I was about to get. And all this spoken to my lady's maid.

Molly watched me with nothing but kindness in her eyes, so I leaned against the foot of my bed and continued, softer, "Where is the excitement?" I laughed at the notion, at my grand expectations, but the sound came out pained and mournful. "There should be *music*. I feel as if I have been robbed of something I never had. But I think it's more that I have not yet lived. I am not ready to give my life away."

Molly hesitated for what felt like an eternity, her blue-green eyes filled with compassion. Then she said, "If I may, miss. You have only been engaged for a few weeks. Even still, I wonder if anyone is ever truly *ready* for marriage. Is it not a choice that we make based on trust and hope for the future?"

Of course Molly would say something beautiful to make me feel like an utter shrew. "Is it?" I said as I considered her wisdom. Could I trust my intended? I wanted to. I wanted everything between us to be perfect, to fit just right. I wanted to feel as excited as Mama was for my wedding plans, and to revel in my success like Father did. A match as good as mine came once in a century, he'd said.

I could easily recall my aunt Alice's wedding, the first one I'd ever attended. At twelve years of age, I'd been enchanted by her beautiful dress, her perfect curls adorned with flowers, and how she laughed and grinned the whole day as though she'd never felt so free in all her life.

When I'd told her how I wanted to be just like her on my own wedding day, so happy and glowing and unafraid, she'd pulled me in close. She'd smelled sweetly of lavender, and she'd looked me directly in the eyes, and said, "Rosalind, my darling, wild girl. You are so free and full of adventure. But one day a man will come along and you'll want to give your entire life to him. Make sure you've lived it fully first." Then she'd tugged out a folded square of paper from her reticule. "I'd meant to give this to Marvin," she'd said of her new husband. "But I have a copy at home. This is my completed list of all the things I wanted to experience before my wedding. Use it to inspire your own list."

Wide-eyed and incredulous, and utterly *in*experienced in all things, I'd taken her list and spent the next few weeks creating my own, promising myself that when my time came to marry, I'd be as ready as she was.

"A sonnet, then." Molly stood, backed into the door and opened it, and I nodded my thanks. She offered a small smile and said, "Good luck, Miss Newbury." She shut the door behind her.

The lie would not hold Mama off for long. Soon, she'd huff all the way to my room to drag me downstairs herself.

I sniffed and wiped a tear from my eye, pushing my emotions firmly down and out of reach. Tears would not serve me now. I needed to find my list and escape to Ivy Manor to see Liza without Mama's notice. Wringing my hands together, I stood and circled the room. Where had I stashed that little green box?

I returned to my knees and again leaned over the deep wooden trunk. I pulled out each trinket, one by one, each memory I'd accumulated over my twenty years of living, until all that was left were the blankets that lined the bottom of the trunk. How could this be? That single paper was the key to alleviating all my discomfort.

Accomplishing everything on my list as Aunt Alice had instructed, everything I'd wanted for *myself*, would ensure that I was ready to share the next chapter of my life with someone. I needed to find it. I had to.

Would that I could remember my list from memory. There was a line about the ocean . . . something about a painting of mine . . .

Wherever could I have hidden it? I leaned over the side of my trunk one last time. As I reached in to smooth the corner of a wrinkled blanket, my hand hit something hard.

I froze, eyes focused on the spot.

In a flash, I yanked the blanket back, and there, pressed up against the corner, was a square green box with the word *Rosalind* painted in black along the lid.

I pulled it out; the box fit perfectly in my hands.

I unlatched the little hook and creaked open the lid. Faded ribbons lay on top. I carefully pulled them out and placed them in my pile. Underneath the ribbons sat a stack of pressed flowers, and beneath the flowers was a neatly folded paper.

My list!

I snatched the little square out of the box and placed it securely behind the ribbon tied tightly around my waist. The only other person I trusted to read my list was Liza. But if I had any hope of seeing her today, I needed to escape to Ivy Manor *now*, before Mama came looking for me.

In a flash, I tied on my bonnet and raced down the marble staircase as quietly as I could. I stopped on the last step, leaning on the wooden rail. The foyer was empty, but Mama would be somewhere nearby.

Slowly I stepped down the last stair. Should I take the

longer route and sneak out the back? Or run the few paces ahead out the front door to my freedom?

A footman walked out of the dining room, stopping next to the entry door. If he opened it, I could dash through like a mouse to its hole. His hand grasped the knob, and my feet decided before my mind had a second to—

"Rosalind Newbury, where on *earth* do you think you are going in such a rush?"

Drat. Mama stood just outside the drawing room, her hands firmly holding her hips. Had she literally been watching the door for me?

"Mama," I said sweetly. "The Ollertons have just arrived this morning. I wish to see Liza."

Her eyes bulged, and she shook her head, causing her silky brown curls to bounce on either side of her face. "You cannot spend all your time over there, Rosalind. Not this year. We have too much to prepare with your intended visiting in a fortnight to dine with us and finalize wedding plans. I pray he got the special license for the wedding to happen at our estate or all our work on the grounds will have been for nothing." Mama started counting on her fingers. "Flowers must still be ordered, menus finalized. The house needs polishing. As do you, Rosalind. And your dress! Your final fitting is this week." She shook her head as though the more she thought about it the more confined I needed to be. "My darling, lest you forget, you are marrying—"

"—a duke," I finished for her. "Yes, I know. And I dearly wish for Liza's opinion on the matter. She is the closest person I have to a sister. I will have her help me choose flowers to order this afternoon."

I lifted my chin. People often told me I was Mama's spitting image. Though my hair was a lighter brown, my skin a touch darker from the sun, and my features fuller than hers, I feared the truth of their opinions when Mama gave me that look and walked toward me.

She took a long breath and let her features relax before saying, "The Newbury name has spanned generations of wealth but has never had a great beauty to tempt a title. Until you." She smiled, then took my face in her hands. "We are all so immensely proud of you, my dear. You are making the right choice for yourself, for your children, and for Benjamin and our entire family."

I could not hold her gaze and looked instead at the ruby pendant on her dress. I hated when she said it like that. Like I held the future of our family name on my shoulders. But I knew the significance of adding a dukedom to our line. Benjamin and the boys would move in circles previously unheard of for our family. Doors would open. And soon, Father had said, we'd have it all.

"I am honored to bolster our family name, Mama. And with your help, the wedding will be fit for a queen."

Mama dropped her hands to my arms and cleared her throat. "Flowers *and* ribbon colors. Take the afternoon to choose," she said, though the strain in her voice told me she reconsidered her choice the moment the words spilled out. "But return in time for dinner. You shall act as hostess and guide our family through the motions. After this week, I want to feel confident that you can lead a household, Rosalind. Gossiping and running wild with the neighbors will not teach you to become a duchess."

My lips formed a happy smile, and I stepped backward before she could change her mind. "Thank you, Mama!" I called as I raced out the door and into the bright afternoon sunlight.

What I wanted—no, what I *needed*—was Liza's assurance.

Even as children, she always knew the proper way for a lady to behave. We could not play in the creek without Liza first securing our hats, lest we take too much sun. And that was if I could convince her to play in the creek at all.

Liza would assure me I'd made the right choice. She'd gush about how handsome the duke was, ask me details about the proposal and which items I'd chosen for my wedding breakfast, and I'd finally take a breath of relief. Because the truth was, no matter how many times Mama squeezed my hands or told me how beautiful I'd look or promised me my wedding would be everything I'd ever dreamed, there was still an aching pit in the bottom of my stomach that refused to fill. An ache that I was missing something important.

I'd felt a similar feeling when Liza left for London without me. Like any other girl, I'd imagined a Season filled with dancing and music, stolen glances and smiling lips, and secret rendezvous in the courtyard. Instead, while Liza made a hundred introductions, I only made one—the Duke of Marlow, a tall, handsome man ten years my senior. He was soft-spoken and intelligent, though perhaps a little curt. His family had long sought a parcel of prime farmland we owned that bordered one of his estates. Land so conveniently placed was hard to come by. Indeed, the duke wanted that parcel of land as much as we desired his title. So I'd made my decision. And my family was better for it.

But still, I wondered what it would have been like to dance with a dozen men and hope they would send me flowers or call on me the next day. Would I still feel this ache? Would I be any better prepared to marry the duke?

I could not change the past, but I could work on my future. Thanks to Aunt Alice, I had my list. With Liza at my side, boosting me with courage and confidence, I could not fail. I would be ready.

A cool breeze propelled me through the pasture toward Liza's house. Oak leaves fanned and branches swayed in the grove of trees to my left, shading a large, round pond. Much of the grass had been grazed recently by the animals, so my steps were unhindered and swift, and my eyes focused on the tall, gray stone house a half mile from my own, with wide windows on each side of the tall wooden door. I'd painted this scene from a dozen different angles, half from memory alone.

I focused on the window to the left of the main door, the drawing room where I assumed Liza would be, and when my feet finally hit the lawn stretching in front of the house, I wiped my brow on the back of my glove and let myself fully feel the exhilaration and excitement I'd been holding in all morning.

Three weeks left to live how *I* wanted, and all that was missing was Liza.

I knocked on the tall wooden door, and Derricks opened it. The man was as pale as white lace. I smiled in greeting, awaiting his usual bow and side step, but instead, the footman's eyes squinted, and his expression turned flat and reserved. He did not move, but he somehow seemed to fill the doorframe even more so. Then he straightened his back, like a soldier at duty. "Miss Newbury," he said with a raise of his chin. "How may I assist you?"

"Good day." I tried a smile, but Derricks stood firm. "Is Miss Ollerton home?"

He blinked and scrunched his brow like he was surprised I did not know. "Forgive me, Miss Newbury. The Ollertons are not accepting callers today."

Chapter Two

Not accepting callers?

"Is the family unwell? Has someone been hurt?" I craned my neck to look beyond the footman and into the wide foyer with black-and-white-checkered floors and framed vaulted ceilings.

"They are unharmed." Derricks moved his head to block my view, and I frowned at him. His countenance remained stoic, revealing nothing. "Would you like to leave your card?"

My card? As though I'd brought one to my dearest friend's house! An uncomfortable heat rose up my neck. "I hardly think it necessary." I crossed my arms and stared at the man. Mrs. Ollerton had enforced silly rules on Liza and me before, but keeping us out of the mud was different than keeping me out of the house entirely. "Derricks."

Despite the growing nervousness in his gaze, he lifted his chin, and said, "Yes, Miss Newbury?"

"My visit is of the utmost importance, I assure you. I must insist you grant me admittance and show me to Miss Ollerton at once."

"Forgive me, but I am under strict orders, and I must follow the instructions of my employer. I will tell the family you came to call. Good day."

And then he shut the door in my face.

I stood in utter shock for half a minute, staring at the wooden door like Derricks would suddenly reopen it and we'd all laugh at the ridiculousness of shutting me out of my second home.

But when the door remained closed, I stepped down the stairs and peered up at the tall gray stones that made Ivy Manor. This house—the little crack in the stone to the right of the door, the tiniest chip in the drawing room window, every groove and crevice—was as familiar to me as my own home.

Which is how I knew exactly where to go.

If there was something truly serious happening inside the house, especially if it involved Liza, I should be right in the middle of it. I'd been invited in even when Liza had been so ill she could not get out of bed; surely this was no different.

My feet carried me around the corner to the servants' door, through which sat a staircase that led straight up to the main floor library. I would sneak inside, find Liza, and then this huge misunderstanding would be made right.

A hand on the doorknob and a subtle push, and the side door creaked open easily.

Oh, I shouldn't. As close to sisters as Liza and I were, and though I'd walked right inside their doors countless times before, this felt wrong. What if the Ollertons had good reason for their seclusion? What if someone was ill—contagious, even—or upset or hiding something they did not want to share?

A horse whinnied from somewhere too close, its galloping hooves thundering. I swung around, and a rider came into view. Panic seized me. Which was worse—being caught in the act of sneaking into Ivy Manor or sneaking in and *then* being caught? Only one promised me Liza, so I slipped inside the door and promptly closed it.

The little space at the foot of the staircase was dimly lit by random strands of sunlight filled with dust motes. Servants' voices and the sounds of a bustling, working household carried from the kitchen and unfamiliar spaces beyond. If I stood here for too long, I'd risk being seen.

My mind raced, grasping for a plan. Up these stairs, I'd open the door and find the library directly to the right, which meant the grand staircase leading up to Liza's room would be adjacent and easily within reach. Perfect.

I took the worn wooden banister in hand and hurried up the stairs. Then I grasped the doorknob to the main floor and—

What the devil was wrong with my brain? *No.* Sneaking into someone's house was wrong, no matter how close our families were. I was not so desperate nor so mad. Was I?

I'd certainly felt mad since my engagement.

But no. Functional people sent notes or left calling cards. I'd go home and explain the urgent necessity of a visit, and Liza would come as soon as she could.

I released my hold on the knob, determined to retreat, when the door swung open, forcing me down a step. A figure pushed inside the space, and I held fast to the banister and drew in a breath of surprise.

His eyes were wide, jaw slacked, gawking. Terror seized me, for even in the darkness, I could tell something was wrong with his face. His right side was swollen, and the skin was darker, especially under his eye. But his clothes were finely tailored, and instead of a simple white cravat, he wore a patterned red neckcloth with gold spots.

He quickly held up his hands, palms facing me. "Please don't scream."

"Charlie!" someone called. Liza? "We must talk this through!"

The mysterious man gave me a pleading look, and then, in a flash, he stepped forward and closed the door quietly behind him.

My heart beat faster with each sobering realization. I was alone. On a narrow staircase meant for servants. With a fearsome-looking stranger.

"Who are you?" he whispered. The distance between us seemed to shrink, and I shivered. His eyes washed over me. "You're not a servant. What are you doing down here?"

I could ask the same of him. Was he dangerous? I took another step down and measured his reaction.

"Wait." He reached out a hand.

"Hiding is not going to solve your problems, Charlie," Liza called, sounding close. "We must make a plan. Like it or not, as soon as your face heals, we *will* be—"

Again, the door flew open, knocking the man in the back.

"Ow," he groaned.

"You deserved that," Liza said, wriggling through the

crack. Her blonde hair was pulled back elegantly, and she wore a slim blue dress with a white ribbon around the middle. Then she looked down at me, and her bright eyes widened. "*Rosalind?*"

I swallowed hard to find my voice, but she pushed the man aside and was already upon me, arms encircling me with the familiar scent of honey and lavender.

"Oh, how I've missed you!" She pressed her cheek against mine, then abruptly pulled back. "But what are you doing on the servants' stairs?"

I winced. The heat of humiliation crept up my neck and into my cheeks. "Derricks would not let me in the front," I admitted. "But I had to see you."

She groaned. "The nerve of that man. He was instructed to keep *visitors* out, not family. Here." She took my hand and pulled me up a step, and just like that, everything was right again. My tense muscles seemed to sigh with relief. "Move, Charlie. We are coming up. And you had better follow this time."

The strange man flattened himself against the wall as we passed, and we exchanged a glance. I'd never seen him before, but Liza spoke to him with such familiarity. Who was he?

Liza led us into the library and toward the cream-colored settee in the center of the room. "I must apologize for my cousin's appearance. As frightening as he looks, he is quite harmless." She took a seat and patted the spot beside her. "I should thank you for blocking his escape."

"That man is your cousin?" I could not hide the surprise in my voice.

"Yes. Though I hesitate to claim him." Her gaze flicked

sideways as he sat down in a velvet blue chair opposite us. "Ros, this is Mr. Charles Winston. Charlie, my dearest friend—"

"You must be the famous Miss Newbury I've heard so much about," he said. He twirled something between his fingers.

I stiffened at his forwardness and at the strangeness of meeting a cousin of Liza's who knew my name.

The light from the tall windows fell on the bruise on his face. I swallowed, mesmerized by the dark purple and deep blue that swirled together and spread from under his eye across his cheek. If it didn't look so menacing, I'd almost want to blend the colors on paper.

"Are you the reason Ivy Manor is closed to visitors?" I asked.

He watched me with his light-brown eyes. There was a subtle scar in his left brow, and a cut healing along his lower lip. "Too brutish to allow visitors." He motioned to his face. "Can't have my good looks frightening the good people of Ashford."

I could not blame them. In truth, I could not decide whether to fear this man—Mr. Winston—or pity him.

Liza drew my attention. "I meant to visit directly, Ros, but we were in the middle of a discussion on what to do while Charlie heals—and afterward."

Mr. Winston twirled the little something around and around listlessly. "There won't be much of an afterward. I simply need a plan."

"A plan?" Liza laughed. "You've no money and Uncle has cut you off, so unless he dies soon, you are without a home or resources. And last I checked, you are not qualified for any decent occupation. So unless you intend to live on the streets of London, you ought to consider reform."

Mr. Winston harrumphed and sat back in his chair.

When no one spoke for a time, I leaned toward Liza and whispered, "What has he done?"

"I am guilty of having too much fun, Miss Newbury," Mr. Winston answered. "That is all."

"Breaking the Earl of Langdon's arm is fun?" Liza asked. Taunted, more like. With derision.

"That wouldn't have happened had he been fighting fair. He wagered he could beat me at Jackson's, then he grabbed my hair and gave me this bruise. I had no choice but to engage him. And, as always, I left a richer man."

I looked at Mr. Winston. "You look like that on purpose?" I asked, and Liza snorted.

"One day soon, your fighting will catch up with you," she said with raised brows. "What will happen if you anger someone more powerful than you who wishes to strike back? Perhaps in a way that can truly harm you?"

Mr. Winston squinted. "Lord Langdon was not exactly pleased."

She groaned, and he laughed. "Come, Liza. Try to understand my perspective."

She shook her head. "I won't. I cannot. No one in this world will ever understand you, Charlie."

"Then I suppose we can agree on something," he muttered. Slowly, he stood, and though his lips smiled, his expression was tight. He stepped around our settee and moved to the little table and chair by the window where the newspaper waited.

We sat still, listening as he shook it out and smoothed the pages.

Liza watched me, and her whole countenance softened. "I'm so glad you're here. Someone sane to save me from all this madness. And you are *engaged*! Tell me everything, and don't you dare leave out one detail."

We settled in, angled toward each other. I wracked my brain for something interesting to tell her. Unfortunately, I had few details to share. "Well, after Father agreed to give Marlow the parcel of land he wanted—"

Liza gave me an exhausted look. "No, Ros. What is he *like*?"

I pictured His Grace escorting me into dinner, how he looked down at me with a small smile as he helped me into my chair. "Tall. Formal. He has the bluest eyes. And he smells like mint and oranges."

"You smelled him?" She looked intrigued.

"Oh, for heaven's sake. Not like that," I chided, and she laughed. "He took me for a walk after dinner."

"A walk?" Liza's lips parted. "Alone?"

"It was not all that exciting." I wrinkled my nose. Indeed, it was the first and only time we'd been alone together. I had felt awkward, and every word out of me had seemed to pinch my throat. "Your turn. What happened to that handsome gentleman in London you wrote about? Mr. 'Would you like more punch?'"

"Well, *he* smelled like bourbon and expensive leather."

"Stop that." I laughed. "Why is he not here with us? In your letter, you spoke of how kind and genuine he is."

"Yes," she said, frowning. "But he's a third son. And as soon as Papa got wind of it, I was forbidden from dancing with him, sitting near him, glancing in his direction, and even sighing thoughtfully in the carriage rides to and fro." Her lips twitched, and her cheeks grew rosier.

A bolt of hot jealousy shot through me. "Liza Olivia Ollerton, have you fallen in love?"

"Don't be ridiculous. I am intelligent enough not to give my affections to someone my father does not approve of." She rested her elbow on the back of the settee and propped up her chin on her fist. "You should have seen some of those mamas, pawing at every eligible gentleman and hissing at any petty threat. It was exhausting." Liza made an exasperated face, and I laughed.

We'd been dear friends for as long as I could remember, but change was swiftly upon us, and I hated it. That gnawing feeling roiled in my stomach, demanding attention, so I gave it purpose, and said, "There is something I need help with, Liza. A favor."

"Anything."

I hoped she meant it. My future happiness depended upon completing this list. I couldn't explain it, but somehow I knew that once I'd finished, that awful feeling would subside. I'd feel whole. I'd be ready.

I took a deep breath. "Do you remember my aunt Alice?"

Liza gave me an obvious look. "I remember being abandoned by you every time she came to visit."

I laughed. "She gave me some advice after her wedding. Before she left for Birmingham."

Liza furrowed her brow. "I don't remember *that*. What advice did she give you?"

"She created a list of ten things she'd always wanted to do but never had. Some ridiculous, some terrifying. And just before she married my uncle, she did them. *All of them.* She encouraged me to do the same."

Liza's eyes were bright, and she drew in a breath. "And you did. Have you finished it?"

Mr. Winston cleared his throat, and there was a rustling of paper.

I leaned in closer. "My list has been hidden for eight years, but I retrieved it this morning. Shall we read it together?"

I traced my finger along my ribbon, searching for the little square I'd hidden there.

But it was gone.

"'Number one, learn to swim,'" a deep voice read.

My nerves, my senses, everything seized, and I spun around in my spot.

Mr. Winston sat back in his chair, his newspaper tossed aside, my list in his hand.

Chapter Three

"'Number two, run away for a day.'"

My heart flew up into my throat. Those were my words. How did he have them?

His eyes kept reading down the page, and I tried to swallow, to speak, to make sense of how this could possibly be happening. The list had been tucked in my ribbon!

"'Number five,'" he continued with a humored edge to his voice, "'hang my painting in a public place.'" Mr. Winston laughed. "Liza, I've seen your artwork, and I would not recommend sharing it."

Liza blinked. Her cheeks were as crimson as mine felt. "Charlie, put that paper down at once," she begged.

"'Number eight, change someone's life.'" With that, he reared back and leaned forward in his seat. "What if they don't want their life changed? What sort of list *is* this?"

"It's Rosalind's!" Liza snapped.

Mr. Winston's gaze flicked to mine and turned thoughtful for the slightest moment, but he did not lower my list.

Instead, his eyes wandered the page as though reading it over again.

Humiliation turned swiftly into frustration, and with a few long strides, I crossed the room and tugged the paper from his grasp. "Do you have any manners at all?"

A wave of hair fell over the scratch in his brow, and he brushed it away. "I found it on the floor in the hall. I had no idea it was yours."

"And that gave you the right to read something not addressed to you?" I folded my list into a tight square and swallowed hard.

"No," was all he said before I turned back to Liza.

"I should go," I said, moving quickly past her. My face was so hot I could feel it sizzling.

Liza followed me. "But what about your list?"

I touched my cheeks. "Were you listening just now? Did you hear him reading? 'Learn to swim' and 'run away for a day.' What in the world was I thinking?"

"You weren't thinking. You were dreaming."

She said it so matter-of-factly, with such simple conviction, that my racing heart came to a stuttering halt.

Dreaming.

Hadn't that been the point all along?

"Will you help me?" I begged. I felt like I was falling, and there was nothing to hold onto. "I know this all sounds mad, but I . . ." I could not find the words.

Liza held my arms, waiting. Her eyes were serious and worried.

"I *need* this, Liza," I said, and I felt it in my bones. The aching. The hope. The surety that this was the key to everything that felt wrong in my life. I'd been so focused on my accomplishments that I'd missed my dreams. I had to claim them before it was too late. Before I gave my life, my time, my everything over to the people who would be depending on me to be the Duchess of Marlow.

Liza straightened, determined. "Let me see it. The list," she said.

"I cannot bear to hear it all again."

"Rosalind," she insisted.

Reluctantly, I gave her the paper square, which she promptly unfolded.

I held my breath as her eyes read down the page.

"Well, number nine is manageable—recording your childhood memories. You've likely already done number seven, considering all the painting you do."

Two out of ten. That was something. "And the others?"

Liza pressed her lips together, still reading. "You were quite ambitious at twelve, Ros. Learning to swim, witnessing a scandal, running away? Good heavens, even Prinny could not do all this by himself in three weeks, and he certainly stays busy."

I groaned. "Don't say that."

She folded the page and handed it back. Then she let out a breath through her nose and forced a smile. "Ros, it is completely normal to feel nervous before your wedding. But you must know that finishing this list has no bearing on your happiness. You are brilliant and beautiful and already have far more life experience than most women our age."

We faced each other in silent argument. "Will you help me?" I asked again.

She looked truly pained. "I want to. You know I would. But he's—" She looked over her shoulder. "I promised my aunt I would keep Charlie out of trouble. We're losing him, Ros. We're all terrified that if he runs off again, he won't return. And if I follow you, I cannot save him."

I sighed, and my shoulders hunched. How could I fault Liza for such loyalty to her family? Compassion for my friend's heavy burden warred with the pain I felt from her rejection. I needed her.

I looked across the room at Mr. Winston, that frustrating man hidden behind his newspaper.

But so did he.

I flipped the paper square between my fingers. Could I do it alone? Could I fight my instinct to shrink under the sheer weight of my future and face my fears? Those hills that felt like mountains too high to climb. Why, why had I let myself dream?

"The point is not asking *why*," Aunt Alice had said. "Ask *what*. What inspires you? What calls to you? What, when you look ahead, will you regret not doing? Those are the things to put on your list. Those are the things that will make you feel whole."

Aunt Alice had understood. She had known this same gnawing feeling, but she'd done something about it. And she'd done it alone.

With or without Liza, I had to try. I took a step back and moved toward the door. "I wish things were different, but I understand. And I'll visit you when I can."

I found the hall empty, so I opened the door to the servants' stair to make my escape the same way I'd arrived.

"Ros," Liza said, following me. "Don't do anything rash. Perhaps I should call for some smelling salts."

When I reached the bottom of the stairs, I looked up at her. Liza had given me the confidence I needed, just not in the way I'd expected. I did not need anyone to affirm my list or hold my hand through it. Aunt Alice had already done that for me. Now, alone or not, I had work to do.

"I am not ill, Liza. Give them to your cousin. At present, he needs them more than I."

Chapter Four

The best place to start was at the beginning.

I hadn't written the list in any specific order, though judging by what I'd listed first—learning how to swim—I'd chosen the most embarrassing activity first.

Perhaps going at it alone was for the best. No one would see me shaking like a pair of dice.

I'd gone over my plan a thousand times since leaving Liza. I'd hardly slept. The only way I could escape Mama's prying eyes and ever-growing list of appointments was to slip out of doors before she—and the sun—rose.

I'd decided on the pond located almost exactly between my father's estate and Ivy Manor. It was shaded by a grove of trees that would hide me well enough.

I would return before Mama even awoke, and with one less number on my list.

"Do you not think it too early for a walk?" Molly asked for the third time through thinly veiled suspicion. But if I confided this to Molly, she'd have to warn Mama, and that would put an end to my list before it even began.

"The lady of the house is the first to rise. As Mama says, I must practice." I clasped my trembling hands tightly together.

I can do this. Swimming will be fun and not at all scary, and if I hate it, I never have to do it again.

What would Aunt Alice say if she read my list? After her wedding day, we'd not talked further on the subject. It was as if she'd shared a massive secret with me, and then both of us had pretended neither knew. Her own list had been rather daring and fun. Among her numbers, she'd chosen climbing to the top of a tree, dancing the waltz, and catching a fish. If she could do all that, certainly I could manage a quick swim.

After helping me dress in a brown muslin, Molly handed me gloves (which I'd have to remove at the pond) and my hat (which I debated keeping on, since I needed to keep my complexion for the wedding).

She narrowed her eyes. "And you are sure you'd like your pelisse?"

"I woke up with a chill." And I'd need something to cover up my wet dress.

Molly pursed her lips as she watched me tie on my bonnet. "How kind of Miss Ollerton to join you."

"Indeed. She is a dear friend for accompanying me." I tried not to wince at my ever-mounting lies. The sacrifice of integrity for liberation.

I'd walked in the countryside alone before, but bringing anyone other than Liza to watch me flounder in the pond was unthinkable. Besides, the pond was no great ocean. One could see the edge as it trailed down to the depths. I was sure I'd be able to stand as I tried to float in the water.

"Perhaps if I am not back in an hour, send someone toward the grove."

"Of course, Miss Newbury." She curtseyed and left me standing there amidst my lies and deceit, with nothing but a list under my pillow and a towel shoved in a satchel waiting beneath my bed for me to retrieve it.

I understood the basic motions of swimming—moving one's arms and legs to stay afloat. I'd imagined it, I'd read about it, I'd even seen drawings of women in their swimming costumes bathing in the ocean. If they could keep themselves afloat in moving waters, surely I could teach myself to swim in the little pond in the fields.

The sun peeked above the earth as I walked through the tall, dewy grass toward Ivy Manor, carrying my satchel. Over an old pair of brown stockings, I'd worn my boots, but they did not keep the hem of my dress dry. My toes caught on weeds and clumps of dirt, and, while I was glad to have my pelisse for *after* my swim, before I knew it, I'd worked up a sweat.

Cool water seemed a welcome respite, until the pond came into view. A large oval, the water sat still and untroubled.

I set my course for a large rock at the water's edge. With fumbling, shaky hands, I set down my satchel, then unbuttoned my pelisse and laid it smoothly over the rock. Then my bonnet. I glanced at my surroundings, around the pond and beyond, for any sign of servants or travelers. I hardly knew what to expect, but I was nearly certain no one else would be out for a morning swim. Servants would be preparing the houses, the stables, the animals. And I would be quick.

I laid my gloves over my pelisse and crouched down to untie my boots, checking over my shoulder for any signs of movement. No one would find me here.

This morning I would enjoy the breeze on my skin, the smell of wet grass, moss-covered rocks, and sweet oaks from the grove. And I would swim.

Rising from my spot, I pushed off my loose boots and took one determined step forward.

My stocking-clad feet squished into the earthy bank, sending a wave of both delight and repulsion up my spine. I tiptoed near the water's muddy edge and watched the glassy top ripple in the light breeze.

One more step.

But shouldn't I have something to grip? Something to hold onto like a branch or a rope? Peering down, I could see the earth and mud underneath the water for a few feet ahead. If I stayed close to the shore, I'd be safe. I'd merely have to pay attention to my footing.

I flung my arms out for balance and slowly dipped my toes into the cool, shallow water, then dug them into the soft, cold soil underneath. A stupid smile lifted my lips, and I forgot to be afraid. I forgot that most grown women did not swim, especially on a whim at sunrise, and that Mama would be expecting me in the drawing room in a few hours.

As I took another step, I listened to the birdsong and chirping of insects, and with each step, the water grew higher. It touched my ankles, then soaked my hem and every layer up to my knees, where I stopped and ran my fingertips over the silky-smooth top, making new ripples. My own ripples.

My skin shivered with gooseflesh, and I crouched down

to settle in as though I were taking a bath in the shallow water. I sucked in a breath and forced my body to grow numb from the cool temperature. Water tickled my neck, and I splashed and stretched out my toes and kicked my legs and laughed, leaning back to be held by the water. But soon floating wasn't enough. So I stood and walked further into the pond until I was waist deep.

Then I turned toward the shallow end, and, arms stretched out in front of me, I crouched down and pushed off my feet, reaching out onto my stomach.

I kicked my legs and swung my arms, and for a brief moment—

I floated! I swam!

My hands fell to the muddy earth, and my knees followed, guiding my footing until I'd secured myself back on the pond floor.

Good heavens, that was fun! I laughed to myself and quickly set off back to the waist-deep spot so I could try again.

Again I pushed off, and this time, I kicked with greater force. My arms could not keep up, so I tried again. Once more, and then another, until my arms moved in tandem with my legs all the way back to the shore and I was breathless, my heart pounding with exhilaration and exertion.

How far below me did the pond go? Despite my growing confidence, I did not need to swim in deep waters to feel successful. When I'd reached my spot again, I took a few slow steps farther back until the water hit just under my chest. I would not try for any deeper than this. Safety was my first priority.

I splashed my arms around in the water, taking deep breaths to bolster my confidence, when something long and very much alive brushed along my leg.

I shrieked and flailed and kicked my legs, but when the danger dissipated and my toes reached for solid ground, there was no purchase beneath me.

I gasped, inhaling a full breath of air, and in the seconds before my head immersed below the water, I thought I saw the sun blink.

Terror seized me. Instinctively my arms and legs began to move. I needed air, for air was life, and without it . . .

Oh, what have I done?

Blinded by the murky water, I could not tell whether I was moving toward the shallow end or the deep, but I knew I was making little progress. Every exertion made me hungry for a breath. But no matter what I did, no matter how hard my heart pumped and my lungs begged, I was sinking.

Mama's face flashed in my memory, then a vision of Benjamin laughing as he tugged at my hair, my brothers Jasper and Nicholas, and Father.

Keep moving, they seemed to say. *Whatever you do, keep trying.*

But I couldn't. Not without first filling my lungs.

Suddenly my feet hit something—the pond floor?—and I pushed off hard with every ounce of strength I had left.

Moments later, my head broke free of the water, my hair everywhere, and I sucked in a loud, gasping breath, only to fall again into the depths.

No! Emotion welled up my throat and came out in bubbles. *Please, no.*

I flailed my arms, trying to reach the surface, when out of nowhere a firm hand grabbed my arm. Shocked by the sudden touch, I fell still as I was dragged upward and pulled close. Hope filled me with a last bout of strength, and I clung to the person's neck like a leech, barely registering a loose cravat and strong shoulders.

Ben?

The man hoisted me higher until my head broke the surface again. My eyes burned, as did my chest, and I sucked in air, coughing and choking and gasping for more. Then he tugged me along with sharp, measured breaths as he swam us both until my feet could touch the earth again.

Still, I hadn't enough breath to move. My jaw started to shake, then all of me. My mind whirled. I could not focus. I had no idea what to do, but I knew I had to get out of that pond.

Blindly, I started forward, but the hands took hold of me again. We were chest-deep in water, and the man brushed back his wavy brown hair, revealing a face still as bruised and beaten and unshaven as it had been the day before. For a moment, there was only him.

Mr. Winston.

"Are you all right?" he asked through labored breaths.

I blinked, and my eyes focused on his, which were round and worried and reminded me of Liza's. I stifled a sob. "Y-you saved me."

"I happened to walk by when I heard a scream." His hands were shaking too. "How did you get so far out in the pond?"

My mind went blank. My thoughts muddled. "I was . . . swimming."

His eyes searched frantically around the pond. "Are you alone?"

"Yes," I quickly assured him.

But his eyes grew frustrated instead of relieved. "Swimming alone? Even accomplished swimmers never swim alone. Accidents happen all the time. If I had not walked by . . ." His voice rose, and my heart ached with the truth.

I covered my face with my hands, and the impending sob broke free. I deserved his rebuke. Every second of it. I was a fool.

His hand touched my wet back, and I startled. Gently, slowly, he guided me toward the bank.

My dress clung to my skin, but to his credit, Mr. Winston averted his eyes as I stepped onto the bank and took in the scene before me. A man's dark-green coat lay abandoned in the grass by the rock where I'd left my pelisse, boots, and gloves. But a bit further away was a large, full leather bag and a man's satchel.

My legs trembled, and my whole body shook in the cool morning air. What had I done? I'd almost died. Had Mr. Winston not come along when he did . . .

He walked a few paces ahead, and I examined my rescuer. Drops of water trailed down his face, his neck, his loosened cravat, and sopping clothes clung all about him.

All about him. His shoulders were wide and firm, his arms thick and muscular from activities I did not dare consider. Mr. Winston brushed out his hair with a hand, which did his chest and arm and shoulders every alluring favor. My already racing pulse beat loudly in my ears. Never had I stood alone like this with a man.

He reached for my pelisse and walked behind me, then guided my arms into its sleeves.

"Are you hurt?" he asked.

"No," I said in a weak voice. I pulled my pelisse tight and moved toward the rock where my satchel, gloves, and boots awaited me. I needed to get home.

I felt his gaze on my back for a long moment, then he turned and retrieved his own coat from the grass.

Leaning against the rock, I tugged the towel from my satchel and quickly dried my face and hair. Then I squeezed out my skirts to keep them from stretching and sticking to my skin and stuffed my feet into my boots.

"Still, we should call a doctor," Mr. Winston called. He'd put on his coat, and then removed his cravat and wrung it out with his hands. His neck was bare all the way to his collarbone.

My fingers fumbled to finish tying my bootstrings. I cleared my throat. "Absolutely not. No one else can know what happened here." Mama would never let me out of her sight again, and rightly so. If anything happened to my reputation, my marriage to Marlow would be compromised. Everything my family had planned would be for naught.

He stuffed his cravat into his own satchel and moved closer. "Miss Newbury, you nearly drowned."

"But you saved me." I tried to lift my voice, to fill it with confidence and pride I no longer owned. I stood. "I cannot possibly thank you enough."

Mr. Winston furrowed his brows and took another hesitant step closer, studying me. Then he leaned in, beads of water still clinging to his hair, and searched my eyes as though something troubled him. "Do you know what day it is?"

I tried to hold his gaze, to not stare at the cut above his brow or glance at the bare skin above his collarbone, but my voice still wavered as I said, "Tu-Tuesday."

"And what is your name?"

"Rosalind Newbury."

He rubbed a hand over his face, seeming to continue some silent debate in his head. "It is my duty to see you well."

I'd only known Mr. Winston for half a day, really, but even I could hazard a guess that he did not pride himself on keeping his duty. "Then allow me to release you from any obligation you may feel."

A slow smirk lifted his lips, and he huffed out a laugh. "If only a man's honor was so easy to dismiss. The Ollertons would never forgive me if harm came to you because of my silence." His forehead wrinkled with thought. "Does this"— he motioned to the pond—"have anything to do with that list of yours?"

If my face had not already reached the color of a cherry, it now did. "Well—"

"'Number one, learn to swim.'" His voice was playful.

I swallowed down the last of my pride and faced him directly. "Please. I beg you. Do not mention this to the Ollertons." And then it hit me. "Do the Ollertons know you're out here—alone? Where *is* Liza?"

His eyes grew wise, then he reached down for his satchel and slung it across his chest. "On second thought, I should be on my way. And so should you. Shall we pretend we never saw each other?"

"Wait a moment."

He took a heavy breath, then crouched down and heaved what was obviously a very heavy leather sack over his shoulder and started off toward the grove. What the devil was in that bag? Flour? Stones? A human body?

My eyes widened at the thought, and I followed, my wet stockings sloshing around in my boots as I hurried after him. "Mr. Winston, what sort of trouble are you into? The Ollertons are good people, and if you are up to something, if your intentions are ill-founded, you will be hurting a family who deserves only your best."

Slowly, he turned to face me, his back to the grove. There was a sudden pain in his eyes that vanished just as quickly. "I saved your life. Can we not safely say my intentions are honorable?"

I shook my head, actively trying to pretend we were fresh from a normal morning in the drawing room and not the pond. "What is in that bag?"

He gave me a look that said *you won't really care to know*, and then dropped the bag to the ground and responded, "Sand."

It could not be as simple as that. Hands on my hips, I continued my interrogation. "And what exactly does one do with a bag of sand?"

Mr. Winston smirked. "Would you like me to demonstrate?"

My eyes widened. "No, thank you." I strained to see Ivy Manor through the trees, but there were too many of them, tall and full with summer leaves. "But perhaps your cousin would."

His smile dropped. "She thinks I am sleeping late. As everyone always does."

I drew in a breath of surprise and pointed my finger. "You *have* snuck out."

"So have you."

"Not so. My maid knows I have gone for a walk. If she asks why I am sopping wet, I shall say I fell in the pond."

His lips twitched. "Excellent excuse. Perhaps I should make my own should the Ollertons notice my absence."

I looked hard at him. "You are the guest of a very generous and loving family, Mr. Winston. Why do you insist on running away?"

"*You* are engaged to be married—and to a duke no less. Why do *you* insist on finishing that list? Is your engagement not everything you've ever dreamed of? I should think you'd be twirling about with stars in your eyes."

I scoffed and shook my head. Twirling! Of all the ridiculous things. "Indeed, our match is everything my family has wanted for years. The title will bring excellent connections for my younger brothers. The duke is intelligent, responsible, honorable, and handsome . . ." I trailed off, trying to think of more things I could brag about, but the truth was I hardly knew him. "*And* he smells delightful."

Mr. Winston blinked, and I realized I'd overshared.

"None of that matters," I continued, waving a hand in the air. "The point is, unlike you, *I* have good reason to be out here. I made my list of wishes as a girl, and I will see it through before I marry. Before my life becomes so busy I forget I had dreams at all."

He huffed, and his gaze flickered toward my father's

estate behind me. I followed his glance. The house appeared as tall as my thumb from this distance. The sun was higher in the sky, and Mama would be waking soon, and Father, and Benjamin.

"Your stubbornness will get you killed." Mr. Winston's voice was deep and serious. "Gads, woman, you nearly died today."

The truth hit me like bricks, and I blanched. He was right. Time had slowed in those moments I'd been without air and taught me how fragile, how fleeting, life could be. I would make the most of what life I had left.

"I should tell your father what happened this morning." He looked into the distance, undetermined.

"You won't," I said, and somehow, I knew the words were true enough to call his bluff. "If you wanted to, you would not be heading into the grove right now. You also do not wish to be found out. I can only assume that whatever you carry in that bag is of utmost importance to you."

He glanced down at the worn leather bag with a look of near reverence. How odd, that. "In a way, it is."

An idea wedged so perfectly in my mind, I could not hold it in. "I shall keep your secret, Mr. Winston. You can sneak out every morning if you wish. If you agree to help me."

"Help you?" He raised a brow. "With that list?"

"Well, *you* would not lift a finger. But with your presence, then *Liza* would come—"

He half laughed, half scoffed. "You offer your silence in exchange for my cooperation? No, thank you. I can endure another lecture if I am discovered." He shook his head as though he already anticipated one. "But I will not encourage you on some ill-fated quest to complete, in so short a time, ten irrational and potentially dangerous life experiences that you desired as a child."

"*Nine* experiences." I bristled. "I have nine left. And I was not a child when I wrote my list."

His lips twitched. "Why not ask your intended for help? He, of all people, should wish to please you."

Marlow? The only thing he cared about was Father's land, but I would not give Mr. Winston the satisfaction of that knowledge. In fact, I would not give the man anything at all. "If you will not assist me, then . . . then I *promise* I will walk straight to the Ollertons and expose your secret." I crossed my arms and gave him a look, daring him to test my resolve.

He gave me one of pity that made me feel as though I was twelve years of age again. "You won't. For I shall make you a promise as well. If I catch you doing anything remotely dangerous again, I will go straight to your father. Morning, afternoon, evening—I do not care if I am indicted alongside you." He narrowed his eyes, then he crouched down and heaved the heavy leather bag onto his shoulder again. "Forget about that list. You have the world and a lifetime in front of you. Perhaps you should open your eyes and appreciate it."

Then he turned his back on me and walked into the grove.

Chapter Five

I cursed Mr. Winston all the way home. The nerve of
that man, threatening to tell Father of my list! Why did he
care what I did with my time? All he had to do was accept my
offer and sit still while Liza and I took the run of things, but
instead he'd abandoned me and left me worse off than ever.

Well, perhaps that was not entirely true. He had saved
my life, and for that, I was eternally grateful. But why *him*?
Why now? Why couldn't Liza have brought home an amiable
cousin with an affinity for adventure? I'd have even settled for
harebrained.

Heaven only knew what Mr. Winston was doing in the
grove all alone. That was the worst part: the man was up to
something, but I could not expose him without risking my
own secrets. I gritted my teeth. I needed a number eleven on
my list that included Mr. Winston's deserved fate. Until then,
I'd avoid the grove altogether.

Swimming had been like nothing else I'd ever experienced. While I enjoyed the feel of the cool water, the early
morning quiet and complete isolation, never again would I

swim alone. Nor would I take unnecessary risks with anything else on my list. I'd come too close to losing everything. But that single taste of achievement and success made me hungry for more.

I needed a new plan going forward. A safer plan that would ensure Mr. Winston should never find me in a dangerous situation worthy of sending for Father. Then as soon as I finished my list, I could expose *his* secret to the Ollertons.

I made it home, and Molly examined me with long breaths through her nose. We let my hair dry for as long as we could before arranging it.

When I went downstairs, Mama raised a brow upon seeing me, but apparently she thought better of asking any questions. She kept her silence on the matter through breakfast and all the way through receiving callers, where everyone wanted to hear about my engagement.

What a handsome couple! What a fortuitous match! When will the duke arrive? By the time the last visitors had left, I was slumping in my seat.

"Posture, Rosalind," Mama corrected me for the twentieth time. "Grace. Poise. A duchess never slumps."

I stretched my shoulders and somehow managed to sit up straight. After endless conversation and my secret near drowning, I felt I could sleep for a decade. "I am exhausted."

"We all are. You mustn't let it show." A crease formed between Mama's eyes.

If she only knew. I started to laugh. "Yes, but I had an early morning—"

"As you should." Mama huffed a breath through her nose. Her eyes seemed just as tired as mine. "Rosalind, you must work harder to improve. A duchess is never tired. She never slumps or takes calls with *damp hair*! You will be watched every second. Judged, whispered about. You will be looked to as an example of how to behave, how to act. Even in something as simple as how your neck holds your head."

I rubbed my temples.

"I know you'd rather be at Ivy Manor with the Ollertons, but you must practice these skills. At least until the wedding is over. Then you shall rest with your husband for a time."

I sighed. "I fear I shall never rest again."

Mama laughed. "This—the wedding, this change—is overwhelming, my dear. As all magnificent things are."

I managed a nod, but my shoulders slumped again.

Mama's happy expression faded, and she watched me, her delicate features wrinkling. "How are you feeling about your choice?" she asked. "The duke."

Her question caught me off guard, and I sat up as straight as any proper duchess would.

Marlow. His name warranted power, distinction, grace, but to me he would also be "husband," and the very idea was still too foreign. I *wanted* to marry him. Any young lady would be mad otherwise. Like it or not, marriage was barreling toward me like a runaway hackney, and the only thing to do was brace myself.

I spoke slowly, choosing each word before I spoke. "Our union cannot come soon enough," I started. "And yet, I hope I have enough time to do all the things I wish beforehand."

Mama's scrunched forehead smoothed, whatever anxiety she harbored dissipating. "You *are* excited," she breathed.

"Benjamin insists you are unhappy, but your father is right. It is just your nerves."

She pulled me into a tight embrace, so I patted her back. "Nerves," I repeated, clearing my throat. "Yes, I have been rather nervous."

Mama pulled back. "But you are also excited, yes? Happy with your choice?"

"Of course," I assured her, wincing at the lie. Was it a lie? Or was I just inexperienced and ignorant on matters of the heart? "Though I wish I had more time with Liza."

Mama smoothed my hair. "You ought to spend your free time with your brother. Benjamin might be two years younger than you, but he feels as protective and affectionate toward you as your father and I do."

I gave her a doubtful look. "Benjamin? Leisure time with him usually results in a chunk of my hair missing or a snake in my slipper."

"Did I hear my name?" Benjamin entered the drawing room dressed in a cream-colored overcoat and breeches with a blue-and-white neckerchief tied doubly around his neck. He stopped to kiss Mama's cheek. "Whatever she is telling you about me is a lie. I never put a snake in her slipper, nor did I chop her hair with the gardener's shears."

"What a brilliant coincidence, then." I furrowed my brow at him.

"Come, Ros. You must forgive and forget. You named that snake Pious, if I remember correctly, and set him free by the pond. And, because I trimmed your hair—"

"Trimmed? You cut off five inches!"

"—you made handsome ornaments for your loved ones. So you are most welcome."

I pursed my lips to keep from smiling. Ben, my ornery little brother. Annoying, yes. But easily redeemed. "Should you not be reading? Or studying? Or something more responsible than meandering around the drawing room?"

Mama stepped between us and put a hand on each of our arms as though to connect us. "Dearest, Rosalind and I were just discussing Rosalind's feelings on her wedding."

"Splendid." Benjamin moved closer to me. "And how *do* you feel about having your wedding on our lawn, Ros?" His eyes narrowed, teasing me to tell the truth.

"I could not be more thrilled." I mustered a smile and glanced at the far-off oak trees outside the window. Marlow and I had agreed upon a small, private gathering. I'd mentioned in passing how beautiful our lands were, and he'd practically snapped his fingers and arranged it all. I hadn't known whether to be thankful or terrified that he held that sort of power.

"Excellent." Mama clasped her hands together. The greatest benefit to having the wedding on our estate was how busy the arrangements kept her. She turned to me. "The invitations are sent, the menu set—did you decide on ribbons and flowers with Liza?"

"Flowers, yes." I nodded, desperate to recall any flower in existence. Peonies? White or pink? Were hydrangeas in season?

But Mama did not wait for my answer. "The quartet! I almost forgot to write back the man Mrs. Ollerton recommended. I'm hiring them to entertain our guests while they wait. And chairs! We need a dozen more chairs!" With that, she left in a whirl of skirts, and I let out a heavy breath.

Benjamin chuckled. "She shall wear herself thin for you."

"For me?" I scoffed. "If she had any care for what I wanted, the decorations would be scarce and the music simple. Everything befitting a small ceremony."

"Ros, you're marrying the Duke of Marlow. Nothing about your life will be small anymore. You must adapt."

I stared hard at him. "Oh, how I shall miss you, brother," I said flatly.

He gave me a quick, wide smile, before looking over his shoulder. When he was satisfied Mama was truly gone, he hurried over to the hearth and rummaged through the bookshelves on either side.

I followed him a few steps. "What are you doing?"

"Lost a book. *Fertile Lands*. Father means to discuss it after dinner." He moved to the little table in the center of the room to continue his search. Over, under, around. "Have you seen it?"

I sighed. How many times had we found ourselves in this very state? If it wasn't a lost book, it was a document or a letter or a pair of gloves.

"Benjamin, you are eighteen years of age. You are the heir. And soon I will not be here to cover your tracks when you misstep." I watched him drop to his knees to peer under the settee. "You must be more responsible. It is your duty. Have you even read this book?"

"Halfway," he muttered, opening and closing every drawer he could find. "If I cannot find it, I shall have to run away to America. You'll come visit me, won't you? Jasper can manage the estate."

I snorted and shook my head. "You are not running away to America. And Jasper will stay at Harrow with Nicholas. Simply think on it, Ben. Where did you last read?"

Having upended the entirety of the drawing room, Ben groaned and sprawled out along the settee looking as forlorn as an eighteen-year-old boy of genteel upbringing could.

"I do not know, Ros. If I did, I would not be here." He lifted a finger. "And I haven't time for a lecture, so if you're thinking of speaking more on responsibility, no thank you. I shall have enough of that from Father this afternoon."

"What would I lecture you on?" I perched on the arm of the settee. "Losing Father's book? Or waiting until the last minute to finish it? Or perhaps," I mused, staring at his boots, "I should lecture you on proper manners, and how one should never lie upon the settee with their muddy boots still on."

He groaned and sat up, swinging his feet firmly to the floor. "At least help me come up with an excuse. Is that not what older sisters are for?" He flashed an innocent smile, and I was thrown back ten years in my memories. Ben, a little boy, chasing me, laughing with a gap-toothed grin and his hair flying wildly in the wind.

I sighed and looked up at the vaulted ceiling. "Bring a few other books to the discussion. Tell Father you enjoyed the first half of the book he recommended so much, you were distracted by research and that you'd like an extension to continue your study. Father will appreciate a studious mind, and you will have more time to find your book and finish it."

A slow smile turned up Ben's lips. "Ros, you brilliant, devious woman."

"Go on," I said. I stood from my spot and encouraged him up with a wave of my hands. "You must prepare if you are to be believed."

Benjamin nodded, jumping to his feet. He plucked two books from the bookshelves by the hearth, then turned back to me. "Have you any plans for this afternoon? I am charged with visiting some tenants about a pest problem. Could be fun if you wanted to come along."

I covered my yawn with a hand. "As intriguing as that sounds, I am exhausted. Perhaps another day. Good luck finding your book." I waved at him and headed toward the door.

"We are running out of days, Ros."

His words stopped me in my tracks. The only sound was the ticking of the clock over the mantel. I looked over my shoulder at Ben.

He shrugged with a sheepish look. "Come."

Part of me wanted to go. To let Ben tease and terrify me like he always did. I'd laugh the sort of laugh that made my stomach ache. Per my list, I owed him an adventure, but if Ben knew, he would not waste it on some pest problem. We could do better than that.

I shook my head. "Perhaps another time."

He nodded once with a serious look and gripped his book in his hands. "I shall hold you to that."

Back in my room, I locked the door behind me and plopped down upon my bed. *Finally.* My head met my pillow in a heavenly wave, with a slight crinkle as I settled in.

My list.

I tugged it out from under my pillow.

1. Learn to swim.

What a disaster of a day. I flinched, thinking about how I'd very nearly drowned. I'd learned how fleeting, how fragile life could be, and that there was still so much life I wanted to live. I would not endanger myself again. I simply needed to plan better. I'd choose the least dangerous thing next, for my sake, and for the sake of Mr. Winston's silence.

I mentally crossed out number one, then read down the page:

2. Run away for a day.

Admittedly not my safest option. I would revisit that one later.

3. Follow Ben on a grand adventure.

Also, potentially dangerous. But not necessarily. Ben had matured quite a lot since taking more responsibility on the estate.

4. Eat all the sweets I want in one sitting.

Now that would be fun. I'd need to order quite a lot of sweets, though.

5. Hang my painting in a public place.

Possibly the most dangerous item on my list. Or at least the one that would pose the greatest risk to my reputation.

6. Hide treasure out in the pasture.

7. Paint a self-portrait.

8. Change someone's life.

9. Write about my childhood memories in my journal.

There—that was the least dangerous item of them all.

10. Witness a scandal.

I folded the page and shoved it back under my pillow, then settled on my side. *I can finish this,* I repeated in my mind. Today had been an accident. The worst possible scenario. I would not take such risks again.

Tomorrow, I'd start with the easiest thing on my list: recording my childhood memories.

At the very worst, I'd risk a stab from the nib of my quill pen or a finger slice from my paper.

Chapter Six

The next morning Molly helped me into an old favorite dress of mine, a soft, plain heather-blue with ruffled sleeves, and quickly fixed my hair into a chignon. I tugged on my boots, tied on my bonnet, and snatched my journal and a charcoal pencil from inside my desk drawer. Mama planned to take me out to return calls in the afternoon, so if I wanted to complete number nine, recording my childhood experiences, I needed another early start.

Certain I was the first to rise, I took the stairs with quiet steps, and I was surprised to find Ben putting on his topper in the entry.

"Ben? Where are you going so early?" I whispered. His cravat was haphazardly tied and his light-blue overcoat unbuttoned as though he'd just slipped out of bed.

"I should ask you the same. Are you unwell?" His face was still puffy from sleep, a boyish frosting of freckles cast across his nose.

"Merely taking advantage of my time." I quirked my brow. What excuse did he have?

Ben nodded and started to turn away. "Very well. I am off to meet a friend."

I stepped closer. "For what purpose?"

Ben hesitated, looking around the room as though to make sure we were alone. "For a bit of . . . exercise."

His reticence was strange. Out of character. "What do you mean? A walk? And with whom?"

Ben took a few steps backward. "Want to come and see?" he taunted.

I shook my head and fought a laugh. "I have work this morning."

"Work?" He tsked, crossing his arms. "It is too early for work. Besides, you abandoned me yesterday. You cannot abandon me twice."

Yesterday? Ah, yes. The pest problem.

"One last adventure? For old time's sake." Ben ducked his chin and looked at me with round, pleading eyes, and his face scrunched in a whine.

I sighed and clutched my journal to my chest. In truth, I had neglected him since my engagement. Not that a young man of his years needed his sister, but Ben had been my closest sibling in both age and confidence, and I, his. I had not fully allowed myself to think on how different my life would be without him so near. Perhaps my engagement had caused him to wonder about his own future. Perhaps that explained his persistence yesterday, and now.

Number three *was* following Ben on an adventure. But this? I'd imagined something more planned and with purpose. Though following Ben on a whim and being surprised seemed a better option than dealing with tenant pest problems.

I could spare an hour to bolster his spirits and still have time to write in my journal. Two list items in one day. The opportunity was too good to let pass. "Very well. But I have only one hour."

Ben's eyes lit up, and his lips curved into a catlike grin. "Excellent! You won't regret this, Ros."

"Oh, I am certain I shall." I took a few steps forward and opened the door. Cool morning air flooded in. "You are always going on about how I never attend you." Ben followed me down the steps and onto the drive. But there was no carriage. I glanced over my shoulder. "Aren't we taking the gig?"

Ben smiled and lifted his brows as though he'd proven a point. "We are walking."

Oh, no. "Walking where?"

I slowed my steps, and Ben started to lead the way. "You shall see. Come."

I started to protest, but he grabbed my wrist and tugged me along. We walked around to the back of the house and into the field, where the morning sun had just risen over the horizon, lighting the fog that hovered above the pasture. My fingers itched for a paintbrush.

"Are you taking us to the Ollertons?"

He glanced sideways at me and returned my confusion with a mischievous grin. He had not yet shaved, which meant whoever we were meeting was either a close friend or someone he did not care to impress. "This will be a fun last hurrah for us, Ros. When you were not off with Liza and you deigned to spend time with me, remember what we'd play?"

I walked beside Ben, whose steps seemed to jump with a new lightness as he waited for my answer. Little Ben, running through the fields, throwing nuts and acorns at my head or fighting me with sticks.

"You loved to play the part of the monster, chasing after me while I screamed for Mama," I said pointedly.

Ben threw his head back and laughed. "Yes, that too. But I remember how you'd hide treasure and create a map for me to follow."

My heart softened. Of course. He'd beg me to play treasure hunt every day after his lessons. It was likely the reason I'd included "burying treasure" on my list. "I remember that. You were such a sweet little thing back then."

He grinned. "I will miss our games. But this—joining me this morning—will be a memory I will not soon forget. Promise me you'll see this through."

His eyes focused on the grove ahead. But certainly he could not mean to lead us in. I'd practically given Mr. Winston that territory after he'd saved my life in the pond. Heaven only knew the secrets he'd hidden within its shadows.

I scrunched my brow. What sort of adventure was Ben seeking?

"What are we talking about? Climbing trees?" I asked, but he pressed his lips together.

All too soon, we passed the pond on our left, its waters still and empty, and memories of elation and utter terror from the day before flooded my mind. Had I really swum only yesterday?

I clutched my journal tighter and searched the scene ahead. We drew closer to the grove with its expanse of full, tall oak trees. It seemed like a hidden oasis, creating a shaded home beyond the pond apart from all else. The wildlife that lived hidden in the grass and trees and skies created a hum of sound as they awoke for the day.

A grunting noise carried from just outside the tree line. Then thumping.

"Benjamin, what is that sound?" My muscles tensed, poised to run at any moment.

But Ben only smiled and looked ahead. The same smile he'd give me just before pushing me into a mudhole or throwing a bug carcass in my hair. Ben was hiding something, and this would not be the first time he led me into trouble. There was a reason I'd included him in my list.

I did not often *want* to follow him on his adventures.

But we were adults now. How much trouble could he possibly get into on his own?

Ben nodded for me to enter the grove first. As the oldest, I was always the one to test the grass for snakes. Apparently, that would never change. I straightened my back, then marched through the overgrowth and into the trees. I followed the sound—a *pat-pat-boom*—as it continued, winding around trees and saplings.

I had not been inside the grove in some time. Sunlight sparkled through the leaves, which danced in the wind that blew through my hair, pushing me toward this new world I'd just entered. I caught myself staring at the treetops and slowing my steps to appreciate its beauty.

The sound grew louder, and though Ben seemed unperturbed, I could not place the sound nor make sense of it. I turned around and around until the corner of my eye caught movement.

I stopped in my tracks. Ben grasped my arm.

Mr. Winston stood facing a tree. His back was entirely bare and glistening with sweat. His arms were tense with strength, thick and angled with muscles into his shoulders and down his back to where his breeches hung low on his hips. His wide shoulders drooped, and on his hands, he wore strange leather gloves.

I'd altogether stopped breathing.

I stared—indeed, I could not peel my eyes away from the sight—frozen in place, but feeling scorched all over.

He lifted his hand and pushed against a long leather bag shaped like a bolster hanging down in front of him. Then, in the blink of an eye, he pulled back and thrust his fist hard against it.

I sucked in a breath, dropping my journal and covering my mouth with a hand.

Mr. Winston spun around, and his gaze caught mine. "Miss Newbury." His voice rang with surprise.

My eyes took in the arc of his collarbone and the rise and fall of his bare chest that was flushed from heat and lined with shadows and curves over every inch of him. My stomach tightened and swirled and sent tingling waves all through me. "Mr. . . . Winston." I breathed, then rushed to clear my throat. What was wrong with my voice?

He let out a breath; his smile was almost shy, but that couldn't be. He was bold and brash and exuded nothing but confidence. "Let me just . . ." He motioned to his shirt and jacket hung over a low branch.

Blinking, I turned away, pulling Ben along with me. "Benjamin Nigel Newbury, did you know he'd be here half-dressed?" I seethed, leaning in.

"Here, yes. Half-dressed?" He smirked, mischief in his eyes.

"I thought it would be just the two of us this morning, Mr. Newbury," Mr. Winston said.

I looked hesitantly over my shoulder. He'd dropped his gloves and fumbled to get his shirt back on. He rolled up his sleeves as he walked toward me.

Ben shrugged with an innocent smile. "Ros insisted on joining us."

My lips parted, and my face was so hot I felt dizzy. "I had *no idea—*"

Ben laughed. "You've startled my poor sister to say the least. She is quite undone."

Mr. Winston's shirt clung to his chest and the waves of his muscles. I'd seen him in the pond, but drowning must have clogged my senses, for seeing him now, *truly* seeing him . . . I swallowed hard.

"I am not"—I cleared my throat—"certainly *not* undone."

Mr. Winston nodded with humor evident in his eyes as he watched me intently. He scooped up my journal and handed it to me. "Then you'll join us for your brother's lesson?"

"His what?" I choked on air, exerting every effort to focus on Mr. Winston's frightening bruises instead of . . . everything else.

Ben had removed his overcoat and started to roll up his sleeves like Mr. Winston had.

My attention wandered to the scene behind him. "What is that?" I asked, motioning toward the long bag Mr. Winston had hit only moments earlier.

Mr. Winston looked over his shoulder. "The ancient Greeks called these heavy bags *korykos*. They used them for training their fighters. I believe you've seen it before."

His bag from yesterday.

Then he picked up his leather gloves from the ground behind him. "And these are mufflers," he said, trailing back. "Have you ever seen a mill?"

My brows constricted, and my mind went to work puzzling out what on earth he meant. The gloves were unlike any I'd seen before. I glanced to Ben, who seemed entirely enthralled.

"No, I don't suppose you have," he said as he studied me. He patted the empty gloves together, one fist at the other. Then it all fell into place.

"A mill is a boxing match. This is boxing," I said as though I had a lemon in my mouth. "But you cannot be a pugilist."

Pugilists were not men of good standing. They were desperate men from the working class who risked their lives fighting for money and a moment of fame. Not gentlemen with dimples in their chins and eyes that brightened when they smiled.

"I'm not—exactly," Mr. Winston answered. "I value my teeth. But according to my father, I have a 'reckless obsession.'"

"You fought Lord Landgon. You broke his arm in a *boxing* match, didn't you?" I could not help the judgment in my voice. "Why do you do this?"

His easy smile faded. "Why not?"

My stomach twisted, and I took a step back. "Pugilism is illegal."

He squinted an eye and tilted his head. "Pugilism's legality is ambiguous as it depends on the judge and specific charges against those involved. It is also irrelevant since we are merely practicing in the woods. In truth, gentlemen like myself, Lord Langdon, and your brother do not box for more than sport, though many also sponsor professional fighters."

"Do you?" I asked bluntly.

"Rosalind," Ben warned.

Mr. Winston shook his head. "I prefer to fight my equals and learn alongside them so that, should I need my skills one day in earnest, I shall be ready to use them. That's not to say I have not wagered in favor of my winning a time or two." He winked at Ben.

I huffed. My understanding of Liza's cousin sharpened. *This* was why his father had cut him off. This was what he refused to give up, and what he hid every morning. Liza had said he was supposed to be reforming. "This is what you've been hiding from the Ollertons. This savagery."

He shrugged. "This is nothing more than exercise. An art of self-defense."

"Pugilism is not an *art*." Could he hear himself?

"Oh? Have you tried it?"

Ben snorted as he strode away from us to lay his coat over Mr. Winston's low-lying branch.

"Absolutely not," I said, folding my arms together. "I am a lady."

"And? Plenty of women have come to Jackson's to learn," he said. "One, whose husband abused her. Another, too old for marriage, who wanted to feel safe walking the streets. Even a woman who merely enjoyed the exercise. Honestly, Miss Newbury, *you* could use a lesson or two. You hold everything inside of you, don't you?"

"Pardon me?"

He lowered his voice. "Every time I see you, your shoulders are as tense as bricks. But what I can't determine is why a woman in your circumstances could still be so unhappy."

"I am happy," I argued. "Why shouldn't I be? I have money, status, my father's protection, and an excellent match on the horizon."

"To the Duke of Marlow, yes. I have heard you claim your happiness before." He studied me, seeming to deliberate a moment more. "And yet, I still do not believe you. There is something else. What troubles you?"

I let out a laugh that was more a scoff. "What currently troubles me is that my neighbor's guest dabbles in an illegal sport."

He grinned, tilting his head to the side. "'Dabbles' would mean I am not yet proficient. I'd classify myself as more a professional."

I furrowed my brow at his teasing. "You fit the part of a pugilist, don't you? Homeless and poor," I volleyed back. "Perhaps you should keep your hobbies to yourself and leave my brother alone."

He pouted, leaning in for only me to hear. "After your

rendezvous in the pond, I should think you'd be more open-minded to trying new things."

For a moment, I understood the desire to hit someone.

Ben returned with a skip in his step. "Are we ready?"

I faced him. "How do you know Mr. Winston?"

"I called on Mr. Ollerton yesterday to ask his advice on that pest problem. Then he asked if Winston could join me on the endeavor. And, well, one thing led to another and here we are."

"Ben, this is not a good idea. This man is troubled."

"Troubled?" Mr. Winston laughed. "Quite possibly the most accurate description of me yet."

Ben added his laughter, admonishing me with a look. "He is no more troubled than I."

I looked heavenward. "I shall leave you two alone then."

Ben's jaw dropped, and he gave me a pleading, desperate look. "But you agreed. You gave me your word for one last adventure, just for us. Something to look back on fondly."

Mr. Winston cast me a knowing look. "I see," he said. "Surely you wish to *follow Ben on a grand adventure*. Do you not, Miss Newbury?"

My mouth fell open. He'd quoted item number three verbatim. Did he have my entire list memorized after reading it once? Shock mixed with frustration from his taunting, and I crossed my arms and huffed.

He rubbed his growing grin away with a hand.

"Come, Ros. Just one lesson," Ben begged. "Mr. Winston can teach us both, together."

Chapter Seven

My pulse pounded in my ears. Me? Learn to fight? My fists were as delicate as porcelain. This had to be a joke. Only, no one was laughing. Indeed, Mr. Winston awaited my response with adamant curiosity, like there was a right and wrong answer and I would be judged accordingly. Not that I cared what he thought of me.

But I did care what he could tell Father.

"Is this some sort of test?" I asked, looking between both men. "I will not participate. I would not want my father to hear of this." I gave Mr. Winston a pointed look.

He drew back as though my insinuation wounded him. "I assure you, Miss Newbury, our lesson shall not endanger you in the least. Your secrets shall be safe with me." He winked and tossed his mufflers aside.

Somehow, I felt even less secure than ever.

Ben rubbed his hands together.

"You must learn proper footwork first. We'll start with the basics of fencing." Mr. Winston picked up a long stick from the ground and held it out to me. It was not unlike the ones Ben and I used to fight each other with as children. He shrugged and said, "You'll pick it up quickly."

Ben picked up a matching stick-sword and, before I could argue, walked a few paces ahead of me. He faced me with one foot in front of the other, his stick raised at the ready.

The serious look on his face, the same he'd held as a boy when he truly believed he wielded a real sword, brought back a time when the only thing I worried over was whether Mama would allow me an extra dessert after dinner.

My shoulders relaxed. A laugh tickled up my throat at his seriousness. I wanted to never forget this face. "You look ridiculous, Benjamin."

Ben straightened his stance. His face pinked, and his lips turned into a scowl. Suddenly he leapt at me, jabbing the stick toward my stomach, but the distance between us only made him look foolish.

"Let us see your skill, then, Ros. If fencing is so beneath you, it should be easy to best me."

I pursed my lips. It wasn't that fencing was beneath me. I was a lady. And there were certain things a lady mustn't do. Ben knew the limitations of my sex, same as I, and his adamancy to prove otherwise made me wish I *could* jab him in his stomach with my stick.

Mr. Winston held out the stick for me. "Hold tightly, about here," he said, pointing to a place where a handle would have been on a sword. The stick was heavy and gnarly. My thumb traced a knob on its side.

Just once. One go at Ben, for memory's sake.

Mr. Winston's rich brown eyes fixed firmly on mine. "One foot in front, one in back. Glide forward on the balls of your feet to advance a hit. Lead with your back foot to retreat. Always keep your sword at the ready."

"My stick, you mean?" I straightened.

But he did not laugh. "Imagine that you are cornered here. That whatever it is you are searching for, whatever you most desire, lies just beyond your opponent. To reach it, to find that happiness you seek, you must pass to the other side untouched."

"This is silly," I said, poking my stick into the earth.

"Sillier than a list of things to accomplish before one marries?" His voice was low, only for me, and his eyes held mine.

"No." The word burst from my lips, and I glared at him.

"Then show me." He held his hands up on either side of him, one toward Ben and one toward me. Then he stepped back and, with a whoosh, lowered his hands.

Ben slid toward me, employing some fancy footwork not unlike dancing in a ballroom. He thrust his sword forward, and fear pierced my heart. I stumbled backward, shocked at his intensity. This was only a game, after all. My brother would never meaningfully jab a sword at me.

"Good," Mr. Winston said to me. A slow smile crept upon his lips. "Your instincts are sound. Listen to your feet. They'll tell you where to go." He motioned to Ben. "Again."

Ben, whose attention had been entirely on Mr. Winston, snapped back at me. Standing with one foot in front of the other, he raised his stick again; I held mine at the ready. This time I wouldn't let him get so close to me.

Mr. Winston lifted my elbow higher, and I started at his touch.

"You know your brother." He spoke in my ear so Ben

could not overhear him, and my spine straightened. "Can you anticipate his movements? Where will he aim?"

Mr. Winston retreated, and all the while I kept my eyes on Ben.

Who started forward and glanced at my neck.

He wouldn't. Would he?

I moved backward, one foot following the other. Ben's stick jabbed forward, and I felt an overwhelming impulse to move sideways. But Ben was too fast. He bore down, and I shrank in my spot, crouching low. His stick hit my shoulder in a thud.

"Ben!" I whined, rubbing my shoulder against a sharp, though fleeting, pain.

Mr. Winston offered his hand to me and helped me stand.

"I should've moved left," I muttered.

He smiled kindly. "The instinct to protect ourselves is overpowering for a reason. We must simply retrain your mind to associate protection with your capabilities instead of your fears."

Mr. Winston strode over to where Ben stood. He muttered his approval and relieved him of his stick, then returned to my side.

He patted my leg with Ben's stick. "One foot out in front of the other," he said, businesslike. "You'll not need to learn en garde or fencing to defend yourself, but in pugilism—and fighting in general—your footwork is just as important."

"She's an accomplished dancer," Ben said. He'd retreated farther back to lean against a wide oak tree. He watched Mr. Winston with interest.

Mr. Winston grinned and looked back to me. "Very good. Let us use that skill here. Back and forth, just as you've done. Your feet should move in one-two steps. One-two, one-two in quick succession."

"We are stretching propriety paper-thin," I said. I had agreed to spar with Ben, not Mr. Winston.

He shrugged. "We're just having a bit of fun."

Is that not exactly what he'd said about the man whose arm he'd broken? I gave wide eyes to Ben, to the trees, to anyone or anything that would see reason.

Mr. Winston walked a half-dozen paces in front of me, stopped, and faced me.

"En garde!" Ben called, smiling stupidly to himself.

I stepped my right foot out in front of my left.

"Just lift your arms comfortably," Mr. Winston said. "I shall be slow to engage. We'll talk it through as we go."

I swallowed. My breaths came in rapid speed, and my nerves started to seize. I glanced nervously at Ben. How had he and Mr. Winston switched places so suddenly? And why in heaven's name was I holding a stick twice as long as my arm?

Mr. Winston took slow strides toward me, and I found myself balancing my body's weight between my feet as though my muscles were prepared for action in a most unladylike fashion. What would I do? Hit him with this stick? What if I hurt him? What if *he* hurt *me*?

His eyes were set, and his lips were a straight line. "On three, I want you to step forward just like we talked about and strike me," he said, still stepping forward. "One . . ."

I froze. My heart was thumping wildly in my chest. I'd

never used a weapon to injure anyone. But the pain from Ben's hit on my shoulder still stung, and I would not let Mr. Winston near enough to add to that pain.

"Two . . ." Mr. Winston raised his stick, and I winced. He would lash out and hurt me, and Ben was just standing there, doing nothing to save me.

Hit him, I thought. *Hit him hard, and this will all be over. All the nerves, all the fear, all the discomfort.*

My palm grew sweaty around my stick. He was right in front of me.

"Three."

I squeezed my eyes shut, took two steps forward, and swung my arm as hard as I could. The force of my weapon hitting his burned up my arm in waves, and I dropped my stick.

"Well done," Mr. Winston said. His voice sounded even, as though me hitting him with every ounce of strength I possessed had neither surprised nor affected him in the least.

"I missed," I argued, rising tall.

"Because I blocked you."

"I do not think I shall continue," I said more to Ben than Mr. Winston.

"You expect to be proficient after one encounter?" Mr. Winston taunted.

Ben strode to me. "What's this? You are fantastic, Ros. Do not dismay. Mr. Winston will have you sparring like the best in no time."

I rubbed my sore hand and took in a long breath to settle the frustration brewing inside of me from this ridiculous sport. I would not give the man another thing to laugh about.

"I do not wish to spar, Ben."

Ben shook his head, his eyes alight and merry. "You're learning the science of fighting. Your footwork is perfect."

How could I argue against that face? That boyish, innocent, perfectly happy face that I'd loved for as long as I could remember. One last adventure. One step closer to my goal.

"What is next, then?" I asked through my teeth. "The sun is halfway up, and Mama will be expecting me."

Mr. Winston tucked his arms behind his back again like a proper teacher addressing his student. But in truth he was a man cut off from his inheritance and cast out of his home. Clearly, boxing did little for a man's intellect.

Mr. Winston moved directly in front of me, an arm's-length away. "After footwork comes fighting."

"Oh, no." I laughed. "No, no. I simply cannot. Benjamin, be reasonable. I am your *sister*, and there are certain things you should protect me from. Shall we move on? Take me on a walk around the pond for frogs. I would even dig for worms with my bare hands—"

"I am right here, should you need protecting," Ben said with his hand to his heart. His eyes were full of mirth.

This. *This* was why I needed Liza by my side. She always knew when to abandon ship, even when her brother looked at her with such pure joy and enthusiasm.

Mr. Winston looked just as pleased with my discomfort as Ben did. "Tell me, Miss Newbury. What makes you angry?"

My eyes flicked to his. "I am a lady, Mr. Winston. I do not feel anger."

He lowered his chin. "Is that so?"

On second thought, *he* made me angry. Mr. Winston, with all his strength and pride, embodied every frustration I'd suppressed since my engagement. He thought my life was as easy to fix as his own. That if I waved my fists around, I'd suddenly feel whole and complete and successful.

My definition of success was marrying well. I thought I'd meet a handsome baron or a newly titled earl, and we'd dance and dine all through the Season. We'd take our time and fall in love. Instead, a match was found for me. A good one, yes. But not one of my choosing. I knew I should be grateful, and I was. But how I longed to scream out in grief for the experiences I'd never have.

Mr. Winston held up an open hand by his jaw and motioned for me to hit his palm. "Show me what you are feeling."

My fists tightened on instinct. I'd never seen a bout of fisticuffs in person before, but I had seen drawings. I knew that men raised their fists in front of them, that they leaned back at their waists to protect their heads from their opponents.

So I raised my chin. I thought of all the little things I loved that I would have to leave behind when I became a duchess. I let myself mourn my silly adventures with Liza, Ben chasing me through the fields with something slimy in his hands, and Mama calling from across the lawn for me to practice the pianoforte. My children would not have such memories. More would be expected of them.

In such a short time, everything would change. All my interactions would be forced smiles and conversations with people I would never truly understand. All for my family's legacy. For Ben and the boys. So my children would grow up comfortable in the upper crust of Society.

That was the life I'd chosen.

Success. Increase. Comfort.

Why, then, did I still feel so unsettled?

Why could I not flip a coin and remove every worry, every anxiety and uncertainty? A woman's engagement ought to be the happiest season of her life. But I felt as though I had been robbed, and I was suddenly *angry* in the most unladylike manner.

I stared at Mr. Winston's chin. Then I met his eyes. They were brazen under serious eyebrows. His full lips parted, and I again noted the cut on the corner of his bottom lip. He nodded as though to encourage me. I focused on his open palm, tightened my fists, and imagined the feeling of every frustration pouring out of me.

I reared back my arm, tensing every muscle within it.

At the same moment, Benjamin snorted.

Mr. Winston lowered his hand as he cast a silly grin over his shoulder at the same moment I pushed my fist forward.

Right into his jaw.

Chapter Eight

For a moment, I felt no pain, only shock and fear and a pang of guilt. Then came the burning and aching in my knuckles.

Mr. Winston held the side of his face, which had to feel even worse than my fist, and cleared his throat.

"Mr. Winston, forgive me," I rushed forward, breathless. Why had he turned? Why hadn't I waited? *Why had he dropped his hand?* "I am so terribly, terribly sorry. I aimed for your *hand.*"

Ben moved between us, seemingly unsure of who to aid first. His mouth formed an O, and his eyes were just as shocked as mine surely were. What had I done?

Mr. Winston stretched out his jaw and rubbed his cheek with his thumb. There were a million thoughts behind his eyes. "How is your hand?"

I stayed behind Ben and stretched out my fist. "Well enough. How is your face?"

He stretched out his jaw again and rubbed his left side. "Handsome as ever."

Ben chuckled, his eyes gleaming as though he was in the presence of some sort of hero.

"For one so small, you landed a heavy blow," Mr. Winston said with a sideways glance at me.

I looked down at my hand. "Truly?" The pleasure in my voice was all wrong. "I mean, very good, then. I've mastered it. We are finished here."

"Come, now," Mr. Winston said with a little pout. "You must give me a chance to retaliate."

Ben rubbed his hands together. "Yes! Excellent! Second round!"

"Benjamin!" I exclaimed.

"The sun is barely in the sky. We have plenty of time." He nodded toward Mr. Winston, who handed me a pair of gloves. The very same kind I'd seen on him before. Then he handed a new pair to Ben. There were no finger holes, save one for the thumb. They were padded and well-worn.

"Mufflers," I remembered.

Mr. Winston grinned. "You're a real pug now, Miss Newbury."

I drew in a little breath. "I most certainly am not." Though the sweat dripping down my back felt anything but ladylike.

"Bare-knuckle fighters sometimes use mufflers for training. They will keep those delicate hands safe. Make a fist, if you please."

I stepped back. I'd given Ben more than enough of an adventure to warrant a check next to number three. "Benjamin, it is your turn. You heard him. Make a fist."

"Ros." He pushed me forward. He'd started tying on his

own glove. "One last time, I swear it. You owe as much to poor Mr. Winston after landing him a facer."

"*Ben*," I said through my teeth. But it was no use. He and Mr. Winston had me cornered like a fox in her hole. Dreadful men. Thank heavens I was marrying up.

Hesitantly, I tucked the mufflers under my arm. I showed Mr. Winston my open hand, and then closed it tightly with my thumb tucked inside my fingers.

"May I?" He motioned to my hand.

I looked to Ben, who stood a few feet away, then nodded my permission.

Mr. Winston gently took my bare fist in his hand, which was rough and smooth and warm all at once. My stomach flipped, and all the anger and frustration boiling within me sizzled out as his fingers grazed along my knuckles and the back of my hand. He tugged my thumb from inside my fist and wrapped it around the outside of my fingers instead.

"There. Now you shan't break any fingers or wound your thumb or wrist." His voice was gravelly and deep. "Tighten your fist as much as you can inside the glove."

His eyes met mine, and I nodded, swallowing.

The mufflers were dense and heavy when I put them on, and Mr. Winston helped me lace them tightly. When he finished, I could hardly lift my hands under their weight. Then he moved to Ben and finished tying his.

Ben raised his hands in front of him, facing off against an invisible foe.

"Make your fists properly," Mr. Winston said, facing me. "Then give my leather bag your best, Miss Newbury."

"This is ridiculous," I muttered.

Both men watched me expectantly. If Liza found me here, she'd faint from the unsavoriness of seeing my hands in these manly things. But Ben—I caught sight of him once more—looked happier than he had in weeks. His bright, carefree smile was one I would carry with me.

How hard can hitting a bag be anyway? I extended my arm, putting my strength into engaging the bag. But the mufflers were too heavy, and the bag was heavier still. It barely swayed from my hit.

"Mmm," I winced, shaking out my gloved hand. "That will do."

Mr. Winston and Benjamin smirked at each other as though they shared some secret joke.

"Again," Mr. Winston called.

"What?" I almost laughed. "It is Benjamin's turn."

Before I could blink, Ben hit the leather bag with such great force, it swung hard like a pendulum.

"Very good. You win," I said dully, turning away and stalking off. I held up my mufflers, lace side up. How the devil could I get them off without using my fingers?

"Come now, Miss Newbury," Mr. Winston stepped to my side. "Don't you want to fight with me again?"

"You?" I let out a mirthless laugh. I half considered tugging at the laces with my teeth before shuddering at the thought. Instead, I held out my hands. "Untie me, please."

"This is even more fun than it looks in the papers," Benjamin called over his shoulder. That same *pat-pat-boom* I'd heard before reverberated off the leather bag as he continued without me.

"It is far better than sitting behind a desk, is it not?" Mr. Winston grinned.

Ben laughed in response.

"Please do not fill my brother's head with falsehoods, Mr. Winston. He is grateful for his inheritance and has worked hard for his success."

"Good," he said with a smile. "I hope it suits him. Just as I hope becoming a duchess suits you."

I narrowed my eyes. His words were kind, but his tone said something else entirely.

"I do not doubt," he continued, "after watching you yesterday at the pond and this morning with your brother, that you can do and be anything you want."

A sudden urge to defend myself and my choices overpowered me. "I shall."

"Good." He shrugged. "You deserve to be happy."

"I am." My shoulders tensed, and Mr. Winston's eyes dropped as though on cue to watch the motion. He smirked.

"What?" I clipped, forcing my muscles to relax. "What are you smirking about?"

"Nothing." He shrugged, looking back at Benjamin. "Raise your fists a touch higher, Newbury. *There* it is. Stay on the balls of your feet and put everything into your right arm."

I waited, feeling equal parts frustrated and unsure. He clearly had something to say. Why would he not relent?

He flicked me a glance. "You look like you want to strike me again."

"Why are you so smug all the time? You've been cast out of your family home. No allowance. Burdening your family."

"Oh, I am not this smug all the time."

"No?"

"Just when I'm around you."

I scoffed and looked heavenward, unsure if he meant to flatter or irk me. "I cannot imagine why."

He grabbed my muffled hand from my side and started unlacing it. "I was wrong about you. You do not see your successful match as a prize. You are willfully forfeiting your dreams—"

"I am *not*—" I tried to argue, but he silenced me with a knowing stare.

"—albeit *honorably*. For your family. Giving up a year or two in service to your ailing parents or grandparents would be one thing, but giving the rest of your life to a marriage you do not desire, all for the sake of your family's future . . . That is either selflessness or stupidity."

Cool air hit my sweaty fist as the muffler was peeled away. Mr. Winston took my other hand. His movements were natural, familiar to him, but gentle. *He* was gentle, which was so ironic, considering the fading bruises on his face and the scars and crooked nose.

Somehow, in the course of one ridiculous boxing lesson, he'd cared enough to determine the source of my anxiety. Whether he was right or not was another question entirely. But my voice softened anyway.

"I am the only one who can bring a title to the family. I am the only daughter."

"But why should your happiness be sacrificed to gain that?" He spoke with passion, as though there was some lesson I stood to learn.

"Who's to say it will be? I will live in luxury all my life."

"Yes, but what is luxury over—" He stopped his sentence. "Love?"

His fingers stilled on my glove, and his eyes met mine, curious and seeking. Somehow, I'd admitted the deepest worry of my heart to this man without any effort at all.

"I wouldn't know," I said with a forced smile. I would never know.

Mr. Winston slid my other glove off. "Yet still, you so easily forfeit the chance."

"I never said my choice was an easy one to make." Though I had made it rather fast. At the time, surrounded by Father's excitement for the title and Mama's romanticized wedding plans, the choice had never really seemed like a *choice* at all.

Mr. Winston nodded his head. "Well, it is your life."

"Thank you." *Thank you?* What in the devil did I need to thank *him* for? As though I needed his approval.

"Out of curiosity." He squinted his eyes at me. "What would you be doing with your summer if you'd chosen another path besides marriage? I've heard stories about you from Liza, but after meeting you in person, I wonder if they're true."

"Mr. Winston," I started to chide him. This was too familiar.

He crossed his arms over his chest. "Indulge me. I did save your life, you recall. And I shall truly keep your secrets from now on. No stipulations. I promise."

I raised my brow. That was quite a promise. I glanced at Ben, who was far enough away to not overhear us, not to mention his attention was entirely focused on the leather bag.

I did owe Mr. Winston for saving me. And for the hit. And I did not have to tell him *everything*.

"What would I do?" I mused, tilting my head back. "Well, I'd still be here. I have never loved any place more than I love our estate. And I'd prepare for my first Season."

"So you do *want* to marry."

"Yes, obviously. I want a family of my own."

"Here? In Ashford?" He looked back at Ben in a show of nonchalance, but I had a feeling he cared more about my answer than he let on.

But *why* did he care? "I loved my childhood, so, yes, if I had the choice, I'd place myself nearby, or somewhere similar. With a husband as committed as my father but as playful as Ben. Someone who loves me, who makes me feel as comfortable as I do when I'm alone."

"Without pretense," Mr. Winston added.

"Exactly." I nodded. "My time could be my own. Take calls as often or as little as I chose. Help our village or community grow and thrive. That sort of thing."

"You'd need a pond as well." He nodded his head, almost businesslike.

I pressed a finger to the corner of my mouth. "And a changing room like they have in Brighton."

He grinned. "Very well. Any pets?"

My lips twitched into a smile. "A few hounds for my husband. Cats for the field mice. And horses, obviously."

"A room for painting?"

I met his gaze, and my smile slowly faded. How did he know that I loved to paint?

"The list," he mumbled. Were his cheeks turning pink? "Two of your numbers were about painting. I assumed—"

"Yes," I cut him off. "I'd love a room for painting."

His gaze flicked back to mine, almost shy, and he raked a hand through his hair. "Well, those are brilliant dreams."

"Thank you," I said, and I meant it. "Your turn. Why are you really here?"

He scratched his neck, and for a moment, I wondered if he'd respond.

"My funds ran out. 'No allowance,'" he quoted my words back to me. "And my choice is to either seek work that I am not qualified for or go home."

"And why will you not go home?"

Lingering between us was the memory of my words *cast out* and *burden on your family*. He turned his gaze toward Ben. "Newbury, extend your arm fully and follow through."

Ben wiped his brow with his arm, panting. "Come and be a proper teacher, then. Ros, thank you for the exciting morning. A fitting last adventure indeed."

Mr. Winston nodded and looked back to me. He cleared his throat. "I meant it when I said you've a natural talent. If you ever wish to practice . . ."

"No, of course not." I furrowed my brow, rearing back dramatically. He gave me a—disappointed?—half smile and a bow, before jogging over to Ben.

"I hope these memories last you a lifetime, Ben," I called as I picked up my journal and gloves from their spot in the grass.

He laughed, and I heard the *pat-pat-boom* from behind

me. Just before I twisted around the trees, I shot one last glance over my shoulder.

Mr. Winston had tied on my mufflers—*his* mufflers. He faced Ben and started to round on him, using that same footwork he'd shown us earlier.

I turned back toward the house, shaking my head. How could one man be two people? A gentleman who cared about hopes and dreams and love as well as a brooding boxer who only sought a little fun.

Perhaps he wasn't two people. Perhaps one man was who he wanted to be, and one was who he truly was.

And perhaps—I looked heavenward at the sun—I should not be thinking about Mr. Winston at all.

Chapter Nine

All morning and through calls, I felt full of secrets. Had someone seen me out there in the grove? Had they passed by on the road with eyes that could see through the trees?

No, we'd been too far within, too hidden.

I stretched out my hand, the one I'd used to strike Mr. Winston. My forearm ached, and my knuckles, though they'd been padded with a muffler, felt tingly and sore.

"Why did you stop playing?" Mama asked, looking up from her writing desk set in the corner of the drawing room.

My fingers settled back on the pianoforte keys, striking a chord near the end of Mozart's *Fantasia No. 3* in D Minor and gliding along with effortless precision.

But before I could finish the song, Mama stood, shaking out her page. "Well done. I did not notice any flaws, Rosalind. I think you are ready."

Ready? I miscalculated and hit a sour chord right at the end. "I would not say that by any means."

Mama set down her page and strode to the pianoforte, her red floral open robe following. She took my music and organized the pages. "A perfect piece. Marlow will be pleased. As will his mother, the duchess, I am certain of it."

Her compliments mixed with that same strange, unsettled feeling in my stomach, and I sat on the stool with my hands in my lap.

"Now," Mama said, examining me like a teacher inspecting her student, "have you practiced a vocal performance?"

"No," I said with a sour face. I could sing, but I enjoyed it about as much as I enjoyed a headache. I much preferred playing. And Mama knew that.

"Do you need my assistance choosing a song?" Her tight smile gave little room to argue the matter. I wanted to groan and topple over the keys, but I'd worked so hard on my posture all day. I would not sag now.

But, honestly, was all this polishing necessary? Would I not be the same girl with Marlow as I was now?

"Actually, I know just the song." I tilted my head and smiled innocently. "How about 'The Irishman'?"

Mama practically flinched and grasped her neck as though to protect herself from all ungodliness. "I am trying to *help* you prepare. Once they hear you play, they will expect to hear you sing, and you cannot sing '*The Irishman*' in front of Her Grace and expect a warm acceptance."

I pressed my lips together to keep from laughing at the terror still evident on her face. "What, then, would you have me prepare?"

Her expression relaxed. "An Italian aria. From an opera."

She likely already had the exact piece picked out. "Mama, you know I cannot bear the opera. If Marlow wishes to hear me sing, he can do so in the privacy of my personal sitting room after we are married."

"Rosalind," she said my name in warning. "You were blessed with a beautiful singing voice. Go to the library and pick an aria and practice."

"I have already seen what we have."

"Then the choice should be easy for you."

We stared at each other down our respective noses. Any other time, I would stand my ground. But I had better manners than she clearly thought, and our time together seeped away like sand in an hourglass. I wanted to please her. But I also did not want to sing.

"Can I not *paint* him an aria?" I finally asked.

Poor Mama looked as though her nerves would burst through her ears. "Rosa*lind*."

I raised my hands in a show of surrender. "Very well. I will choose an aria. But not for Marlow. For you, dear Mama."

Her entire body seemed to exhale. "Thank you."

I stood up from the pianoforte, wishing I could escape the house like I always used to after calls. Then the grandest idea came upon me. "But in truth, I *do* know every page in our library."

Mama stared.

"I am certain Liza has come home with something new from London. Perhaps I could borrow something from her and surprise you?"

My innocent act was not lost on Mama. "That would require a visit to the Ollertons. How very convenient."

"The duke deserves my best," I said with passionate seriousness.

Mama squinted her eyes, likely trying to decide whether or not to believe my act. "You have worked hard today. But the standards of the aristocracy are hard to attain. We must continue working hard with what little time we have left. So"—she cleared her throat, holding my gaze—"be back well in time to practice before dressing for dinner. If I do not hear your voice carrying down the stairs at half past five, Rosalind . . ."

I grinned. "Thank you, Mama!" My mind whirled so fast, I had to get my bearings before racing toward the door.

She followed. "Do not forget the aria. Italian. *Apposito!*"

I flew out the door, half running toward the back pasture before Mama could stop me.

Figures moved on the expansive, manicured lawn rolling out in front of Ivy Manor. A woman in a thin yellow dress floating out in the wind faced a gentleman in a straw top hat.

As I drew nearer, they both turned.

"Ros?" Liza's enthusiasm carried on the wind, and I quickened my pace.

Seeing Mr. Winston again so soon sent a flutter of nerves to my stomach. His clothes were more formal than he'd worn that morning, his hair tamed, and he twirled a stick around in his hand. A few steps closer sharpened my vision, and I noticed a long head at the bottom of his stick. He held a pall-mall mallet.

"Liza," I called back, holding my arms out wide as I approached. "You are out of doors!"

She embraced me, then nodded surly to Mr. Winston, who picked up a wooden ball and tossed it in the air. "Charlie whined all afternoon about how terribly bored he is in the house. So here we are out in the sunshine."

I flicked my attention to him, and he acknowledged me with a small bow. Familiar, but somehow still foreign.

I crossed my arms and shook my head. "If only there was something meaningful he could do with his time." I raised my brows. Although, he had unwittingly aided me in two of my list numbers already. "He must be bored indeed with such a dreary schedule."

Liza's eyes filled with mirth. "Do not tempt his bite, Ros. He has only been awake for a few hours."

Mr. Winston grew smug. "I do like to sleep late," he said, then measured my countenance for my reaction.

Oh, to give up his secret! What pleasure I'd have. What fun. But it would cost me too dearly, and he knew it.

"Papa dug up his old pall-mall set. We thought we'd play. Join us?" Liza asked.

"Pall-mall is really only for two players. Or teams." Mr. Winston made a pained face that did not look very pained at all, then he shrugged. "Though you are welcome to follow along and watch me play."

Liza swatted at him. "Leave her *be*, Charlie."

"I am afraid an audience would give you too great a pleasure," I retorted, and he laughed, stepping so near that our faces were as close as they'd been while boxing. But his scars and bruises and scruff did little to intimidate me now.

He did not back down. Instead, he stepped one foot closer. "And what brings *you* out of doors, Miss Newbury? I imagined you more of a morning person."

I raised my chin. I would not react to his taunting. "I have actually come on an errand. Mama wishes for me to prepare an aria from an Italian opera for the duke, and I wondered if Liza might have something new that might suit me."

"Ros!" Liza cut in with wide eyes. "Did you hear? The opera is in session starting tomorrow. Our box is just begging to be filled!"

I frowned. She knew—

"I know you hate the opera—*hate it*—but *if we can convince Charlie*," she whispered at full volume, "the music would be so lovely. We could have an evening out, and things will be just as they once were!"

Mr. Winston blinked and flicked his eyes at mine. "No."

Liza deflated. "You are a miserable toad, Charles Winston." Then she turned to me with a sigh. "I have a beautiful new aria, Ros. I shall send it over."

"Perfect. Pall-mall?" Mr. Winston brightened, tossing his ball in the air. Several strides away stood a tall metal arch.

"Yes, thank you," I said, reaching out and relieving him of his mallet, then his wooden ball. I sauntered over the lawn, toward the metal hoop, and dropped the ball onto the grass.

Liza trailed behind. "Come and watch, Charlie. You can play the winner."

"Come and watch two gently bred ladies take fifty hits to arrive at the arch?" He did not sound intrigued.

"I can make it in four," I said, measuring my swing. "Easily." How hard could it be?

"I should give myself six hits." Liza squinted an eye. "No . . . seven."

Mr. Winston laughed. "I swear, if either of you makes your goal, I shall give you each whatever you want."

Liza sucked in a breath. "The opera?"

My list?

I glanced over my shoulder. Mr. Winston stood a few paces away. He took off his straw hat and fluffed out his dark-brown hair before replacing it.

"I shall hold you to that," I said sweetly. Then I turned forward and traced a mental line from where the ball sat in the grass all the way to the metal hoop. I would need a strong first hit with enough control to send the ball straight where I wanted it. My fingers wrapped tightly around the mallet. As though on instinct, I turned sideways to give myself ample room to swing.

"Steady, Ros," Liza whispered. "Steady."

I reared back slowly. My muscles seemed to know what they were about as they coiled up, focused on that invisible path I'd drawn in my mind.

One practice swing to test my trajectory, then another. Mr. Winston laughed, and I turned to scowl at him.

Focusing once more, I drew my mallet back, then with a *whoosh*, I swung it and sent my ball flying across the lawn. It landed and bounced, bounced, bounced, rolling a little to the left, but surprisingly, incredibly, stopping over halfway to the hoop.

Liza's jaw dropped. Then I realized mine had too.

"Good heavens," she breathed. "When was the last time you played?"

"I honestly cannot remember," I admitted. Childhood? With Ben?

"Well done," Mr. Winston said, still staring out into the distance.

Liza found her footing where I had stood. And after similar preparations, hit her ball nearly halfway to the hoop. She jumped and shrieked in delight before clearing her throat and straightening her skirts. "This is rather exhilarating."

We squeezed hands as I passed by, walking ahead to where my ball waited. Liza and Mr. Winston followed close behind. I'd need one solid hit to ensure that two more would be enough to see my ball through the hoop within four total hits. Then Mr. Winston would have no choice but to follow me along on my list of adventures, and with Liza in tow!

I crouched down low, measuring that same invisible line with my eye. This hit would need far less strength.

"Careful, Miss Newbury. You must temper your hits."

"Are you master of pall-mall as well as pugilism, Mr. Winston?" I made a show of ignoring him, rising from my spot with as much confidence as I could muster. I had this game nearly won.

The ball made a pop sound when my mallet connected.

But it was too loud. Too hard. Too fast! It flew past the arch and kept rolling. I dropped my mallet and covered my face with my hands. "Noooo," I wailed, crouching low. "No."

"Oh, Ros. What rotten luck." Liza rubbed my back. It was over. I'd lost. I could not recover from such a poor hit with only two left to spare.

Mr. Winston stepped beside me. "I tried to tell—"

I stood and pointed a finger at him. "You distracted me on purpose."

Mr. Winston reared back a bit and laughed. "Why on earth would I do that?"

"Perhaps you can recover and still beat me," Liza called to me, hitting her ball a few paces toward the hoop. But beating Liza wouldn't win me my prize.

"You knew if I won, I would ask for help with my list," I said to Mr. Winston in a low whisper.

A muscle popped in his jaw. "That list . . ."

Liza appeared between us. "Shall we start a new game? I rather think I have the hang of it now."

"*My* list," I corrected him. I swallowed back the raw emotion in my throat. "Liza would join me, but for some unfathomable reason, she will not abandon you."

Mr. Winston shifted his weight to one side. Then the other. "Do you truly believe that doing all those things on your list will help you move forward with your future?" His eyes seared into mine.

I thought of Aunt Alice, of her joy as she descended the steps of the church on Uncle Marvin's arm. I wanted that joy. "I do."

He swiped his face with a hand and looked off in the distance with what I could only imagine was anticipated regret. "Very well. You have your list on your person, I assume?"

I froze. "Yes, but—"

"Give it to me. I shall need a copy if I'm to be a part of this."

"The list?" Liza looked between us, and I wondered if I too had misheard him.

"I did not make my goal. I need more hits than I claimed to reach my hoop," I reminded him. "Why would you help me?"

Mr. Winston's eyes dropped to mine. He gave me a thoughtful, lingering look that seemed to connect us for a beat. "Because no one should be rushed into a life they are not prepared for."

His words seeped into me like warm tea, swirling and settling into my heart. "No," I agreed. "They should not."

"Where do we start?" he asked, clapping his hands together and shifting the air between us. "What new danger shall I save you from first?"

I heaved a sigh. "From now on, you shall need to be serious, Mr. Winston. On all accounts."

He nodded, tempering his smile.

"My list is not a cure for your boredom."

"No, indeed."

"For this to work, we shall need rules."

He ducked his chin. "Such as?"

"You cannot laugh at me."

"On my honor."

"Or try to change my wishes."

"When they are already so perfectly spelled out?"

I gave him a fierce look, and he smiled innocently. I bit back my retort and removed my list from its spot behind the ribbon at my waist. "All right, then." I held it out to him. "Make your copy."

He nodded once and started unfolding the page. "If we are to do eight more . . . Forgive me." He cleared his throat and sent a hesitant glance toward Liza, who had no idea I'd already checked off two numbers on my list. "*Ten* experiences, then we ought to make a plan." His eyes read down the page, then he folded it in half. "May I have your permission to ponder one?"

I blinked in surprise. I hadn't expected him to *ponder* anything. "That sounds . . . helpful."

"I am not so sure this is a good idea," Liza said in a small voice between us.

Nor I. But I finally had everything I wanted—everything I *needed*—to succeed.

There was no turning back now.

Chapter Ten

Right before bed, Molly brought me a bulky note from
Liza.

> *Opera tomorrow! (Can you believe Charlie*
> *agreed?) We shall come for you at 8 pm. Let me know*
> *if you like this aria. If not, I shall send another.*

I sat atop my white covers embroidered with white flowers and decorations and separated the papers into three piles:
her letter, my list, returned from Mr. Winston, and the Italian
aria. I tucked the latter away for tomorrow. Mr. Winston had
likely agreed to the opera just to spite me. But I could not
complain. Since my wish had been granted, so should Liza's.

I groaned. I could appreciate the music, and singing in
general, but hours of loud, constant vibrato took its toll on a
person.

I'd have to endure the opera, and Mr. Winston would be
there. Which Mr. Winston, though? The smug boxer or the
gentleman friend? Regardless, he'd given me Liza back, *and*

he'd promised to help me with my list. At present, I would take all the help I could get.

I continued reading the last of Liza's letter.

> *Also, Charlie has had his nose in your list all day. He is so dedicated and serious, I hardly recognize him. Ideas are brewing for better or worse, and he would like to be prepared. He asks that you kindly send along your favorite watercolor first thing in the morning so that he may decide how to best proceed.*
>
> *Love,*
>
>

My favorite watercolor? He was thinking of number four.

My mind whirled with the possibility of my painting hanging somewhere for anyone to see. I'd written number four because I loved to paint, not necessarily because I wanted to be recognized for my skill. But having a painting hung seemed to be the pinnacle of success in that field. And I wanted to succeed as an artist.

I knew immediately which painting I wanted to share. Jumping down from my bed, I tugged out a flat, rectangular case from underneath my bed. I unlocked the two clasps and lifted the lid, revealing pages of my favorite sketches and watercolor paintings I'd saved from my training. Flipping through the first ten or so images, I found it—my very favorite watercolor I'd done of the grove. I knew that spot better than any other on the estate. Liza and I had picked flowers there, hid away for afternoons long past, and climbed saplings as they grew.

Trees framed the painting as though the viewer was walking into the grove, sunlight sparkling through the leaves. Greens, browns, yellows, and specks of blue and orange filled the paper, creating almost a tunneling effect. It was, in my opinion, my best work. I could take one look at that painting, close my eyes, and feel like I was there.

I tucked my case back under my bed and rolled up my painting. Then I tied it with three strings, one around each end and one in the center.

I found a paper on my desk and pulled out ink and a pen. After dipping the pen, I started to write.

> *Liza,*
>
> *I trust you will keep my painting safe. I do wonder what plans your cousin is brewing. Any clues? I shall see you tomorrow at 8 p.m.*
>
> *Ros*

After the ink dried, I gave my letter and painting to Molly to deliver in the morning and snuffed out my candles.

I focused the next day on learning my song, taking calls, and drafting the perfect menu for Marlow's arrival, and before I could blink, it was time to dress for dinner. I picked out an emerald-and-golden sari gown and had Molly arrange my hair with a matching bandeau.

There were only two problems: I'd heard nothing back from Liza, and I'd yet to inform Mama of my plans.

"You look lovely this evening," she said with a happy sigh as I descended for dinner. "Chin high, Ros."

Father and Benjamin were waiting for me as I entered the drawing room with Mama on my heels. Father waved me over to join him. "I've had a letter from His Grace, Rosalind. I assume you'll want to hear what your intended has to say."

I wrapped my arms around Father's neck and kissed his cheek. "If he wants more land, tell him no."

Father laughed. "Negotiations are not for you to trouble yourself over," he said, and I pursed my lips. "His Grace wrote to inquire after your favorite jewel. I think he means to buy you a wedding gift before his return."

My eyes widened. "A jewel? That seems extravagant." Then again, as Mr. Winston had so prudently pointed out, I hardly knew the duke.

Father grinned, eyeing the color of my evening dress. "Shall I suggest an emerald?"

I could hardly imagine receiving such a lavish gift. It was much too generous. How would I thank him? "An emerald would be lovely. Did Marlow say anything else?"

"About you? No." Benjamin narrowed his gaze. "About the land . . ."

I huffed, reaching out to flick my brother, but Father took my hand and gave us both a silencing stare. "Just that he expects to arrive on the third Monday of the month, which shall be"—he tilted his head—"in eleven days, with the duchess."

"He could still be a day or two early," Mama said. "Men are always overestimating their schedules."

I sank into the ivory-colored chair opposite Father.

"Before we go in, I forgot to tell you both, I have promised to accompany Liza to the opera after dinner tonight."

Mama's brows knitted together. "You did not ask our permission."

"She is asking for the opera, Charlotte. And with the Ollertons." Father glanced at me. "I trust you will have a chaperone?"

"Yes, Father," I replied.

"Glad it's not me," Benjamin said, but I wondered if he meant it. Would he have liked for Liza to extend an invitation? Neither she nor I had felt it necessary before, but my little brother was growing older.

"I daresay she will need her rest, Frederick." Mama looked anxious.

Father gave Mama an exasperated look. "Let her go to the opera one last time without the social obligations of a duchess."

My stomach twisted. I hadn't thought of it like that. As the duchess, all eyes would be on me. I'd sit in a box and have visitors and one wrong glance could be taken as a snub. My every move would be calculated and weighed. It would be exhausting.

Our butler, Mr. Norris, stood in the doorway. "Miss Newbury, dinner is ready."

Mama raised her chin expectantly. We'd been playing this game for weeks now—me, running the house as though I owned it. I stood from my seat and straightened my dress. Then I cleared my throat and painted a smile on my face, like always.

"Mama, Father, Benjamin—shall we go in?"

Chapter Eleven

Horses clip-clopped up the drive just as the footman crossed the entry to open the door. Mr. Norris handed me my shawl, and Mama, through her frown, pinched my cheeks and walked me out of the drawing room.

"With your engagement still so fresh, you'll be watched by all of Society, without a doubt. Keep your chin high and your smile in place."

"Yes, Mama." I peered through the darkness, my heart beating like a drum. This was exactly how I'd pictured my summer—Liza and I out in the world together. The carriage rolled to a stop. By the dim light provided by lanterns and the moonlight, I made out Mr. Winston as he descended, then saw a servant placing steps for Liza.

I noted Mr. Winston's finely tailored brown overcoat, a handsome blue-spotted neckcloth, and polished, fashionable Hessian boots. But it wasn't until I walked down the stairs and onto the gravel pathway, watching as Mr. Winston walked toward me, that I truly saw his face.

His hair had been cut and brushed back—his face, his

square jaw, his full lips, all clean-shaven and fresh. Either the shadows worked in his favor or his bruises had healed immensely. Indeed, for the first time in our acquaintance, he looked every bit a gentleman.

"Good evening, Miss Newbury," he said in a gentle voice, his eyes locked with mine. He bowed so low I felt as though I'd already claimed my title. My legs could barely bend in return.

Good heavens. Was this the same coarse man from the grove?

Liza curtseyed to Mama. "Mrs. Newbury, might I introduce my cousin, Mr. Charles Winston, whose company we will enjoy for another few weeks."

If Mama questioned our chaperone for the evening or disapproved of Mr. Winston at all, she did not show it.

"I am honored to meet you, Mrs. Newbury," Mr. Winston said with another bow.

Mama smiled as elegantly as always. "What a pleasure, indeed." She offered a nod. "I trust you shall keep these two ladies in good company."

"They are my priority for the evening."

The man could sweet talk a mama, of that I had no doubt.

"Shall we?" I asked.

He offered me his arm and nodded to someone behind me. I glanced over my shoulder, where Benjamin stood. My brother nodded in reply.

"How is your hand?" Mr. Winston asked me as he led us to the carriage. How strange to think the gentleman at my side was the same man who'd taught me to fight in the grove.

I'd glimpsed this side of him in moments, but this? This was the real man under it all.

"Better," I managed, sneaking another glance. "You look . . . clean."

"Thank you," he said with a laugh. "Shaving wasn't as painful as I thought it would be. I might get a few stares, but I think I am healing nicely."

"Perhaps you will blend in after all."

"Believe it or not, I am capable." He gave me his hand and a playful look, then helped me inside the waiting carriage. Then he offered Liza a hand, and she scooted in after.

"I could hardly believe it when I woke up this morning to Charlie fully dressed and shaved and ready to repent of his wrongdoings. What did you do to get him so excited about your list?" She narrowed her eyes as Mr. Winston entered the carriage.

"I haven't the slightest idea," I said.

"He's kept watch over your painting like a mother to her pups."

I noticed a long cylinder in the carriage. My painting? Why was my painting here? No one had said anything about needing it for tonight.

"Are you nervous?" Liza asked, moving closer.

Mr. Winston took his seat opposite us and placed a hand upon the cylinder casing.

My hands fidgeted with the fingers of my gloves. I had the distinct impression that, like Ben and our morning in the grove, the most important details of this outing were being kept from me. "Why should I be nervous?"

A servant closed the carriage door, and Mr. Winston

knocked twice on the roof before stretching out his back against the taupe-cushioned wall. "That's the spirit. We shall be in and out before anyone notices, and then we can do whatever we please."

I quirked a brow, and Liza furrowed hers. Whatever Mr. Winston had planned, he'd done so alone. "I do not understand. Why are you bringing my painting to the opera?"

I could barely make out his half smile through the dim light. "I am lending it to the opera house."

I sat up painfully straight as the air in the carriage grew as stale as a stable.

"I did not know the opera house took amateur pieces on loan," Liza mused, tilting her head. "Whom did you speak to?"

"They have *never* sought amateur pieces," I said. If there was one thing about the opera house I appreciated, it was her artwork.

Mr. Winston looked questioningly between us, neither answering Liza's question nor accepting blame for leading us into a proverbial lion's den.

"I made you a promise," he said, turning toward me. "And after reviewing your list, I thought this item was one you'd have the most difficulty completing on your own. You cannot market yourself as a working artist, nor can you gift a work of art and expect the recipient to hang it in public. My plan is the best you've got."

I crossed my arms. "What exactly *is* your plan?"

"If I tell you now, neither of you will go through with it. But I assure you, we will be perfectly invisible in the crush. No harm shall come to either of you. And by the end of the night, Miss Newbury will have a third item crossed off her list."

Liza reared back. "Third? What have I missed?"

My eyes flicked to Mr. Winston, who mouthed "Sorry" with a feigned grimace and sat back, all too happy to have vindicated himself for a time. He knew we could not tell Liza *those* details either.

I cleared my throat, avoiding her gaze, and with feigned nonchalance said, "Numbers one and five on my list."

She waited, watching me with growing impatience. "Which are?"

I wanted to swipe that happy look right off Mr. Winston's face. I forced a laugh and waved my hand carelessly in the air. "For number five, I followed Benjamin on some silly adventure, and the other is of such little consequence, really. So silly. I went for a quick swim in the pond."

"Where she nearly drowned," Mr. Winston added. "*I* saved her life."

I shot him an exasperated look. Every attempt on his part to clear his name indicted me.

Liza's chest rose and fell, her jaw dropped as she stared at her cousin, and she went pale.

"You did *what*?"

I spent the better part of the drive convincing Liza that I'd never again attempt swimming, that I'd never risk my life, nor do anything else on the list alone. Even writing in my journal.

I also promised to keep Mr. Winston in line and to take whatever blame was necessary should any of this end poorly.

When we turned onto the half-circle drive where carriages and coaches waited, I was out of breath. Liza's eyes were closed as she took steadying breaths through her nose, muttering continuously about how her dearest friend had nearly drowned. Somehow, Mr. Winston had come out entirely unscathed, despite being the brains behind this disastrous evening.

How he planned to accomplish so great a thing as hanging an unnamed artist's painting in an opera house was still a mystery. But we were here. And he was right. What other chance would I have?

Our horses slowed their pace, the carriage gently rolling toward the grandiose building with six pillars lining its front.

The opera house. My heart picked up its pace. We were nearly there.

"What inspired you?" Mr. Winston asked me, his words cutting through the impending darkness and Liza's audible breathing. He held the cylinder carrying my painting in his hands. "When you painted this."

I shifted in my spot, picking at my skirts nervously. "The grove of trees that separates my father's estate from Ivy Manor—but of course you know it well. A patch of wildflowers grows there every year. You see remnants here and there in summertime, but in spring, there are hundreds of them."

Liza shifted in her seat, but I didn't dare look for her reaction.

"Liza and I used to make crowns from the flowers. The

grove was a refuge for us as children. We could stay hidden there for hours."

"From our governesses, to be specific," Liza said, still gazing out the window. "Mine was a tyrannical, dream-crushing devil woman. Remember her eyebrows, Ros?"

"Eye*brow*, you mean?" I could not help but laugh. My own governess had been equally terrifying. She once tied a thin board to my neck that would prick the underside of my chin if I let my posture fall during tea.

I shook my head at the memory and then nodded to the cylinder again. "I love those white daisies and blue forget-me-nots. I suppose I wanted to immortalize that feeling of freedom, and the naïve hope that one's responsibilities could be forgotten for a time."

"I do not think that is naïve," Mr. Winston said.

"But of course it is. You cannot run from life."

There was a moment of silence, then he shifted in his seat. "I like how you painted the sky," he said.

"Blue?" I smiled, feeling clever.

"Sunny." He narrowed his eyes for a moment, then leaned in, filling the air between us with the scent of fresh soap and bergamot. "It's open, and there's not a cloud in sight."

"It is a metaphor for our friendship," Liza said. "Or was. When we were open and honest with each other."

I winced. I deserved her rebuke. "Liza, please forgive me. I promise to never hide a thing from you again. With Mr. Winston as my witness."

Mr. Winston held a hand to his heart as though to pledge his promise as well.

She swatted at his arm. "And you have been sneaking out

of the house every morning? Must I sleep outside your door from now on?"

He winced. "Please, do not."

Liza leaned back and huffed.

He poked her knee. "Would you ever have known had we not told you ourselves?"

"I *promised* I'd look after you and keep you out of trouble."

"Then trust me," he said. "I am as good at staying out of trouble as I am getting into it. And I promise we will have no trouble tonight."

I squeezed her arm, and Liza finally gave in, leaning her back to my shoulder.

Mr. Winston looked out his window. Light from the lantern hanging just outside lit his face, and I caught myself studying him. He was handsome in an obvious sort of way, but there was something more. Something that was starting to feel familiar.

I watched as his lips turned down. His eyes faded, and his shoulders drooped. He harbored more than he let on, but he rarely let it show. Whether I approved of his hobbies or how he lived his life, he'd come to my aid more than once and without asking for anything in return. Somehow, someday, I would repay him. Even if he never made it back home.

The carriage came to a stop just outside the brick opera house. Stragglers like us hurried up the wide stairway to catch the opera before it started.

Mr. Winston helped Liza down, then me.

Then he reached inside the carriage and tucked my painting under his arm, hidden within his coat.

Chapter Twelve

Mr. Winston hurried us inside the opera house, seeming as cool and collected as any other guest. But he hid his plan literally up his sleeve.

"May I help you to your seats?" an attendant asked as Mr. Winston handed him our tickets.

"No, thank you," he answered with a bow. Liza and I followed closely behind, arm in arm.

"Mr. Winston," I said through my teeth. I flicked my eyes knowingly to where he had hidden my painting.

He winked, then stole around a corner and stopped short. "Now that we trust one another. Here is the plan." He looked between us. "We are going to swap your painting for one already hanging on the walls of the opera house."

"We're *what*?" My voice rose an octave, and Mr. Winston's gloved hand rose as though to shush me.

Liza's jaw had completely unhinged. "Have you lost your mind?"

Mr. Winston continued as though the question were irrelevant. "First, we must find a watercolor of similar size. I brought a few tools to help us unbend the nails in the frame backing. No one will be able to tell yours is not the original where that is concerned."

Liza stared at her cousin. "Uncle is right. Something might truly be wrong with your head."

An older woman and her escort rounded the corner. She wore an ostrich feather as long as my arm. "Pardon," she said as her eyes washed over the three of us huddled together.

"Good evening," Mr. Winston said with a bow of his head.

"This is not mere madness," I whispered to Liza. "This is offensive. Criminal. Criminally offensive."

Mr. Winston adjusted his coat all too casually. "Miss Newbury, do take a breath, or you will end up a complication."

He started walking down the hall, leaving Liza and me no choice but to hurry after him. "Luckily, your watercolor is of average size." His head moved with the passing artwork. Some were canvas that had been fitted for their frames. Others were varying sizes and mediums within various frames.

I clutched tightly to Liza's arm, glancing over my shoulder for anyone following us.

When I turned back, Mr. Winston had unrolled my painting and was holding it up against a similarly sized frame hung on the wall. "Just a hair too big. But we can keep this one in mind if all else fails."

"Rosalind," Liza begged.

"Me? He is *your* cousin!"

She reared back, throwing her hands in the air. "You promised you'd handle him, and he is in earnest. What am I to do? How did *anyone* think me capable of keeping either of you two in order?"

My eyes flicked to Mr. Winston, who was measuring my painting against another a few paces ahead. "Mr. Winston, put that away at once!" My mind was catching up with my feet.

He furrowed his brow. "How else will we determine a decent fit?"

His eyes moved fast from one frame to the next every few paces, his attention split in two directions.

A couple rounded the corner ahead, moving toward us. "Now," I seethed. "Put it away *now*."

Mr. Winston's eyes flashed to mine, confused, then he heard the couple's voices.

His back turned to them, he carefully rolled up my picture. "You are upset."

"This is too reckless," I said, holding out my hand. "You'll be caught, and Liza will never recover from the shame. Give the painting back to me. I shall find another way."

Mr. Winston placed it in my hand as the couple walked past us, whispering closely and laughing together. The gentleman's eyes flicked to mine and seemed to sparkle, though whatever affection they held was not for me but for the handsome woman on his arm.

I lowered my voice. "We cannot cover someone's else's work to display mine. It is unethical."

"I agree," Mr. Winston said. He crossed his arms. "But I thought it through all night. A watercolor done by an unnamed artist won't sell quickly enough—if at all—for your time frame, despite your evident talent. Certainly not to a place where the public might take notice. I see no other option, Miss Newbury, than to create our own path."

Liza moved between us. "What if someone catches you? What, then?"

"They won't."

I blew out a breath. The space between us seemed lit with fire, and any path I took would burn me. Why did everything with Mr. Winston always move so quickly?

"Pardon me," an attendant said, walking toward us. "The opera is about to begin. May I help you to your seats?"

"Yes, thank you," Liza said weakly. She grasped hold of my arm.

"Just a moment," Mr. Winston pressed, staring hard at me. His eyes seemed to beg me to reconsider. But how could I trust him? Liza's happiness depended on our walking away from the whole plan. But my list depended on seeing it through. We could not do both.

I shook my head and handed him my painting, which he quickly tucked into the cylinder within his coat.

Liza pulled me along behind the attendant, and Mr. Winston reluctantly followed.

Ornamented in elegant floral carvings, the walls of the opera house seemed to dance with light from flickering brass candelabras situated at every turn. The orchestra had started warming up, and our attendant quickened his pace. Up the wide staircase we went, past groups of ladies in beautiful gowns and sharply dressed gentlemen, until we arrived at our seats.

The Ollertons' leased box was papered in pea-green stripes with rosy-red curtains and matching carpet but was otherwise surprisingly sparse compared to those across the room from us, which were filled with a dozen or more guests and servants. We were up high, dizzyingly so, and I fought the urge to freeze in my spot. I hated heights. Almost as much as I hated depths. I much preferred a perfect balance of the two. Which I supposed could be thought of as . . . land.

Liza walked around the space, admiring the carvings and rich colors. "Just as we last left it."

Mr. Winston looked out around the seats below us.

"Do be careful," I said on a breath as he teetered against the balcony. "We are quite high."

He looked over his shoulder, unaffected. "Do not tell me you are afraid of heights." He turned around and leaned back. "Why is there nothing on your list about it, then?"

"Because I have no interest in the matter, nor shall I have any regrets keeping my feet firmly planted on level ground. And I am not *that* afraid. I've climbed trees before." Though with trees, there was always something to hold onto. Something steadying. And the promise of more things to grip should I slip.

Mr. Winston raised a playful brow. "Are you certain we should not add an eleventh item to your list? Peering over a cliff, perhaps? That is a life experience you should not miss."

A cliff? Was he utterly mad? Who in their sane mind would willingly walk close enough near the edge of a cliff to see beyond it?

He laughed and stood from his perch. "Are you ill, Miss Newbury? You've gone rather pale."

"Any minute now!" Liza chimed, calling us over with frantic waves of her hands, and we took our seats. Liza, me, then Mr. Winston.

Everywhere I looked, I met watchful eyes. *Duchess,* they all seemed to say. Ladies stared as though they expected me to do something, say something, *be* something. But I felt no different than I always had. If anything, I felt nervous and exposed. How did Marlow fare under the constant attention? The same ladies who stared then hurried to smile, and I remembered to smile back.

"I have an idea," Mr. Winston whispered.

I glanced sideways at him. More cliffs? "Please keep it to yourself," I said, smiling down again at the sea of faces.

He furrowed his brow. "I am in earnest. I think I've bridged our problem."

Liza pulled out her fan. "Do you know what you should have written in your list, Ros?" She pointed down to the curtains. "Taking a tour behind the stage. I have always wondered what things look like back there."

"Let your painting hang in public for two weeks," Mr. Winston said in my other ear. "I'll come back and retrieve it. No one shall be the wiser. And you can finish your list."

"An attendant will catch you. We'll get thrown out. My *painting* will get thrown out." I shook my head, trying not to frown while so many eyes watched from below.

"If you put your faith in a lesser man, perhaps," he whispered. "You must trust me."

The curtain drew back from the stage, and lights shone brightly on two performers. A woman's soprano belted out into the silence, Italian lyrics echoing off the walls. At first, I let my mind translate the dialogue. Something about a woman lost in a forest, awaiting her lover to find her. But all too soon, a dull ache brewed in the back of my head, and I lost interest.

My mind mulled over Mr. Winston's words and his confidence that he could accomplish this great task for me, and that three of my ten items would be checked off by night's end. Three of the most difficult tasks.

How would it feel to have my artwork hanging in a public forum for anyone and everyone to see?

Mr. Winston's gaze flicked to mine with a question.

"I am unwell," I said before my mind had a chance to still the words on my tongue. "I need to take a walk."

Liza's unyielding focus on the stage broke for the barest second. "Is it the vibrato?" She knew how I felt about operas. "Can you not press your ears?"

"Go for a walk, or *go for a walk?*" Mr. Winston's eyes were on mine, serious and hopeful.

I gave him a knowing smile. "*Go for a walk.*"

He nodded, a slow curve lifting his lips.

Liza drew in a breath and took my arm as we stood. "Very well. I'd hate for you to get a headache." We followed Mr. Winston out of the box and into the little hallway. "She spent an entire day in bed the day after our last opera."

"This is better anyway," Mr. Winston drew close to me and whispered, his voice light with enthusiasm. "Everyone will be distracted by the opera. We shall go unseen."

Liza looked longingly over her shoulder. "Just a short walk, right, Ros?"

"As fast as we can," I said more to Mr. Winston than to Liza.

"I kept an eye out earlier as the attendant led us here," he said. "There is a perfect frame about midway from the water closet. And the painting is a watercolor similar to yours."

"I do not want my painting to hang by the water closet," I whined. "Can we not find a better spot?"

"Not *by* the water closet. *On the way.* Which, frankly, will ensure more visibility for your two weeks."

I could not argue him that.

"Who needs the water closet?" Liza asked as she hurried to match our pace.

"There!" He pointed down the hall. "Rosewood frame, I believe, with a very pretty polish."

I followed his direction, catching sight of the frame moments before we reached it. This particular painting was of a still pond surrounded by trees. A large cow drank from the water's edge. The glassy water reflected the trees, giving it a similar look to my own, which would make the switch less noticeable. It was, as Mr. Winston had said, perfect in every way. But was it too perfect?

"My talent is inadequate. Someone will notice mine is not the original, and what happens then?"

Mr. Winston blinked. "Your expectations for yourself continue to astound me. I assure you, no one will question your work."

I pursed my lips, so he continued, "At the very worst, *if* someone notices, the opera house will take yours out. An investigation is unlikely, and since yours is unsigned, nothing shall come of it."

"You are certain?"

He shrugged, then grinned. "As certain as one can be when committing a petty crime."

"Oh, no. No, no. What do I do?" Liza asked shrilly, pressing her fingertips to her temples. "How can I stop this? Why, God, have you placed me here between two of Your most wild and stubborn children?"

I could sacrifice my painting if the worst came true, but I'd never get another chance to fulfill my list. And I wanted to. It was now or never.

I took a last moment to appreciate the artist's work and the cow drinking from the pond. Then I clasped my hands together and said, more to the painter than the cow, "Thank you for lending your space to me. I am so sorry to force your hand, but I promise your sacrifice is well spent on me, and I will not in my lifetime forget it. I give you my word I shall return in two weeks to uncover you."

"Rosalind, I implore you to think about what you are doing," Liza said desperately in my ear. "About what you are risking. What Charlie is risking. What we all could lose."

I glanced at Mr. Winston, who gently lifted the frame from the wall. He knew what he was risking. His cheeks were flushed, his eyes alert and alive. He looked over at me and gave me a warm smile. "Still with me?"

Breathless, I nodded. "Just for two weeks?"

"I shall retrieve it myself." He crouched low and went to work.

Liza drew in a breath and pinched the bridge of her nose. I knew she wanted to keep her family safe, but she could not make their choices for them.

"He knows what he is doing," I told her. "We won't be caught."

Her eyes met mine, so full of fear and vulnerability that she would not speak. Her arms wrapped around her middle. "Quickly. Finish this madness before someone sees." She would not yield completely. But I only needed a few moments more.

"Unfurl your shawls in front of me to hinder the view."

Mr. Winston pulled out a tool from inside his jacket and used it on the back of the frame. My watercolor laid unfurled beside him.

"Shawls. Excellent plan," Liza muttered with heavy sarcasm, unfurling hers all the same.

"What a happy yellow," I said, pretending to admire her shawl.

She blinked at my tone. "Are you not at all concerned what *the duke* would think of you hanging your watercolor in the opera house?"

I'd not considered the duke all day. "We are not yet married. His opinion is irrelevant."

Mr. Winston cleared his throat—was he laughing?—and kept working. He removed the back of the frame and carefully exposed the original work.

"Excuse me." A harsh voice carried from down the hall.

Liza's jaw dropped in tandem with mine, and we spun around. My heart flew into my throat, and we were suddenly as exposed as sheep after a shearing.

"Don't move," Mr. Winston said under his breath.

An attendant dressed in red and white rushed forward. "You three. Is that a wall hanging, sir?"

The air shifted as Mr. Winston rose from his spot behind us. What would he do? We were cornered. Caught. Ruined.

Run, my mind yelled, but my limbs were frozen.

"Sir," the attendant called as he raced toward us. "Sir, you cannot move the wall hangings. The opera house pays a high price for such quality pieces, and I must ask that you kindly refrain from—"

"Forgive me." Mr. Winston stepped beside me with a

cool smile plastered on his face. "So clumsy of me. I tripped and fell against the wall." He reached back and straightened the frame with a light touch.

My eyes fixated on the watercolor inside. *My* watercolor. Hanging in the opera house. It was beautiful and smooth and somehow fit perfectly inside its new frame.

Mr. Winston watched me as he said, "Thank goodness I did not damage this extraordinary work of art."

I could not peel my eyes from the sight of my painting, a vulnerable, real piece of me, on display. My insides tingled with excitement, and I could not hold back my smile despite the guilt that nagged at my conscience. My work should not be here. The painting underneath was the one worthy of this spot, but my heavens, *look at my painting on the wall.*

The attendant frowned and squared his shoulders. Did he notice the painting inside was not the original?

"Shall I call a doctor for you, sir?" he asked, though his voice held no real concern.

A smirk lifted Mr. Winston's lips. "Not necessary, but I thank you. Ladies, shall we return to our box for the second act?"

Liza stood still, and I could hardly find my voice. I cleared my throat and shook my head to bring my attention back to the moment. "The second act! We cannot miss another moment, can we, Miss Ollerton?"

Still staring at the attendant, she mumbled something incoherent.

The attendant's gaze flicked to my painting, and, to my utter astonishment, he seemed satisfied, nodded his head, and let us pass.

Chapter Thirteen

Dancers moved around the stage in a blur. My eyes watched, but my mind remained fixed on only one thing: My painting was hanging on a wall in the opera house.

Liza, Mr. Winston, and I sat in our box for a long moment after the performance finished, not speaking, just watching the crush of people make their way out into the halls. Would they see my watercolor? Would they care? Perhaps their eyes would wander over it mindlessly. Perhaps someone—the lady with the ostrich feather hat, for example—might stop and point it out. One, two, three sets of eyes might appreciate the colors. Or maybe no one would. Maybe, like the couple who'd passed us in the hall, all eyes would be otherwise engaged. Either way, a part of me hung for anyone and everyone to see.

And I could not have been happier.

Back home, lanterns welcomed me on either side of the entry door as the carriage rolled to a stop. A servant opened the door, and Mr. Winston descended first.

"Brilliant," he said as he reached up for my hand. "You were absolutely brilliant tonight."

"Me?" I took his hand and stepped down. "Mr. *I have fallen into the wall and loosed this extraordinary work of art.*"

He took a dramatic bow. "You are most welcome."

"Truly," I said, forcing him to hear my sincerity. "Thank you. Twice now, you have come to my aid."

He started to smile. His eyes watched mine.

Liza leaned her head out the window. She looked as though she could barely hold herself upright. "Come, Charlie. My head is *pounding*," she whined. "Ros, I do hope you are happy. I wish to never see you again. Good night."

Mr. Winston grinned and let out a hearty laugh. "Oh, come now, Liza. Just a bit of fun, and it is over now. Are you not happy for your friend? Three items completed off her list, and only seven to go. When Mother hears how much time I've spent with the soon-to-be duchess, she'll change Father's mind and reinstate my funds, and together we shall find you a husband in London in no time."

"*That* is good news," she said.

I paced toward her, climbed a step, and kissed her cheek. "Thank you for being with me. You won't regret this night."

She grimaced but smiled despite herself. "You are a rotten friend. But I shall hold you to that, Your Grace." She puckered her lips, and I leaned my cheek in so she could return the kiss.

Mr. Winston held out his arm, and I took it as I stepped back down from the carriage.

"Visit us tomorrow." His voice was deep and serious, drawing me in like a comfortable pillow, and there was something new in his gaze. A vulnerable sort of hope, like he'd actually care if I said no.

"I have a dress fitting," I said. I loved my new dress, but for some reason, trying it on tomorrow was the last thing I wanted to do.

"For *the* dress?" Liza asked loudly, leaning out of the carriage.

"Yes. *The dress.* And whatever else Mama needs from town."

Mr. Winston looked at Liza. "I could use a few things myself. We could go."

"You'd take me to town? You hate going into town."

"Perhaps we might run into Miss Newbury and steal her away for the afternoon."

I put a hand to my chest and feigned a swoon. "Mr. Winston, are you planning to rescue me from a horrible day of wedding planning?"

He pursed his lips, but I thought I saw them twitch. "We can check off another item from your list while we're at it."

"How chivalrous of you."

"I thought so."

"I thought we made it clear that Charlie and I should not be a part of that list anymore," Liza said, looking between us. "Perhaps we could play cards or have a picnic instead."

Mr. Winston and I groaned at the same time, then immediately looked to each other and laughed.

"What is left on the list?" he whispered conspiratorially, though he likely knew as well as I.

So far, I'd learned to swim—sort of—and I'd followed Ben on an adventure, and, with Mr. Winston's help, I'd hung my painting in public. Of the seven left, a few were small enough that I could do them on my own, but all of them would be better with friends.

I lowered my voice. "A few options. Recording memories in my journal, painting, eating all the sweets I want in one sitting. We could run away for a day. Or change someone's life for the better. Though the last two might take some planning."

Liza, were it possible, leaned even further out of the carriage. "We are not—let me repeat—*absolutely not* running away tomorrow, or ever."

That one would be tricky, for where would I go? Into the grove for a day? No, someone would find me. Perhaps I'd run away to Liza's and hide away in her room. But how unexciting. Wherever I went, would I go alone? I needed time to ponder that as well.

"Perhaps cards are not a terrible idea." I sighed.

Mr. Winston led me up the stairs to where Mr. Norris waited for me with the entry door open. He watched Mr. Winston with the carefulness and caution of a father.

I released Mr. Winston's arm and curtseyed. "Thank you again for accompanying me tonight."

He bowed low. "Thank you for allowing me the honor. I have not enjoyed myself this fully in some time."

"You exaggerate." His boxing was more exciting than anything on my list.

"I mean it." He clasped his hands behind his back. "I know I spoke ill of your list at first, but what you are doing is incredibly brave. You are facing your future with courage and strength. I envy the balance you've found, not limiting yourself despite the mighty change in your circumstances."

Was I brave? I did not feel it. "I should remind you that I have no control over your father reinstating your funds, Mr. Winston."

"Charlie," he offered. "Please."

My grin turned soft, all humor fading into the serious look he gave me.

"Charlie," I corrected myself. But then I could not remember what I was saying.

"Perhaps, Rosalind,"—he said my name softly, with that gentle look that fit him best—"you have more of an effect than you realize."

I searched his eyes under the dim lanterns overhead. The broken line of his nose. The dimple in his chin. Whatever could he mean?

"Charles Winston!" Liza shrieked, and the moment vanished.

With one last grin and another bow, he was gone.

Chapter Fourteen

I awoke from a dream so vivid, so encompassing, I could still taste it, still feel it tingling on my fingertips. Only my dream had been lived. For the first time in my life, I felt alive. New. Like I could do anything and everything and succeed.

"Have you come into money?" Benjamin asked at breakfast.

"She is in love," Mama said with a happy look.

Was I? I tried to picture the duke, but all I could see was Charlie and the way he'd looked at me last night. Had he already been to the grove this morning?

"*And* about to come into money," Father said as he lifted his cup of tea to his lips.

I spooned a few strawberries onto my plate and took a bite of the egg already there. I laughed. "I am the happiest I have been in some time." The world was mine.

All thanks to Aunt Alice and my list.

In town, Mama and I stopped at the millinery first. Mama's newly trimmed hat was due as was my silk bonnet to match my wedding dress.

Mrs. Prim, the store owner, opened the box lids of both hats and laid them in front of us on the counter. "A straw hat with peach trim, white roses, and green leaves for Mrs. Newbury, and a peach silk bonnet with white lace trim for our soon-to-be duchess."

Mama clasped her hands together. Happiness practically burst from her eyes. "Mrs. Prim, you have outdone yourself. The hat is pretty, but the bonnet . . ." Her eyes met mine expectantly.

"A masterpiece," I added.

Mama smiled widely and sighed, touching the fabric with a gloved finger. Her chest seemed to swell.

I followed her motion, careful not to disrupt the flawless placement of the lace. I took a long breath, but I could not imitate her emotion. That pure adoration deep in my bones. But I still had time.

Mama waved over a servant, who carried our boxes out the door and, I assumed, to our waiting carriage. After paying, she squeezed my arm and led me down the road to the dress shop.

Mrs. Lane, the dressmaker, greeted us as we entered. She was a woman in her forties with ribbons wrapped around her neck and pins in a band around her waist. "Your dress is ready," she said with a kind smile.

Her small shop could not have been more filled. Everything seemed to have its own spot—bolts of the latest fabrics and prints, spools of ribbons in every shade of the rainbow, and jars of buttons and needles and thread. I could spend an entire day rummaging through it all.

"Here it is," Mrs. Lane said, lifting a long box upon the

counter. "I brought in the sleeves a quarter inch and added three layers of white lace to the hem, sleeves, and around the neckline."

Mama lifted the lid and the paper, then drew in a breath.

Except this time, she frowned. Mama's eyes flicked to mine with evident worry. "But this lace is ivory."

Mrs. Lane pulled the dress out of the box, and the fabric cascaded along the table like waves. She glanced to me. "Forgive me, Mrs. Newbury. This is the white I carry in my shop. The very one we discussed."

I reached out and fingered the buttery fabric. My wedding dress. It was stunningly beautiful. Fit for a queen. For me.

Mama's lips were tighter than a straight line. "My daughter, the future Duchess of Marlow, wanted a peach gown with *white* lace. You will fix this." Mama tapped a sharp finger against the box. "We need white. *White.*"

Mrs. Lane and I exchanged a confused glance. Mama never took such a tone. And in truth, the ivory—or white?—complemented the dress better than I could have hoped.

I tugged at Mama's arm and walked her a few paces away. "Mama, we do not have much time left to make alterations. Indeed, the difference in the lace color is minuscule, and I am content with my dress as it is."

"You should not have to settle for *content*, Rosalind. You should be grinning. You should be *flying*. I see the truth written all over your face. You want white."

I reared back. What on earth was she seeing? Not to say I did not wish to look the part of a glowing bride. But lace was simply lace and had absolutely nothing to do with my wedding day. Mama had gone mad.

"Might I encourage you to try the dress on?" Mrs. Lane called. "You might find the color more pleasing."

"We shall find the color more pleasing when you have fixed it." Mama tightened her lips once more and turned back to the table. "And we expect you to make this your priority."

Mrs. Lane swallowed and nodded. "Of course, Mrs. Newbury."

"The peach taffeta is perfection," I added to soothe them both. What more could I say? If the lace was that important to Mama, after all her hard work preparing the estate and managing the wedding details, she deserved to have it as she wanted. I could certainly not care less.

Mrs. Lane nodded graciously and carefully secured the lid over the box. "I will send word as soon as possible."

"Very well," Mama muttered, then turned and strutted from the shop. Once outside, she pulled me close and said, "Do not fret, Rosalind. Every detail will be perfect. You will be the happiest, most glowing bride."

I closed the door and lengthened my steps to keep her pace. "I am so grateful to you, Mama. Not just for the lace. For all you've done."

She softened on a breath and tucked me into her side. "You will remember your wedding day for the rest of your life. You will recall each moment—the smells, the music, how you felt in your dress, and how your husband complimented you. Such little details might seem insignificant, but they all combine into the memories you will pass down to your children. I will not forfeit nor compromise on a single one. Not for your happiness."

"Mrs. Newbury!"

My ears perked. Liza?

"Dear girl! How delightful to find you here," Mama cooed, and Liza came hurrying forward. Mr. Winston, dressed in an olive-green coat, sauntered close behind. "And Mr. Winston." Her voice fell decidedly flat.

"Good day, Mrs. Newbury." He removed his hat and bowed. His bruises were more prominent in the daylight than they'd been last night, but less so than when we'd first met. He cast a smile just for me. "And Miss Newbury. How do you do?"

Mama huffed and shook her head, speaking to Liza. "The worst has happened. Mrs. Lane has utterly *ruined* Rosalind's gown."

Well, that was a bit severe.

"*No*," Liza responded critically. "Does it not fit?"

"We could not stand to try it on," Mama continued, moving closer. She lowered her voice and prattled on.

But I was focused on something—someone—else. "How chance running into you here," I said, moving by Charlie's side.

His eyes brightened. "What a perfect coincidence. Pity you are so happily engaged with wedding planning. Liza and I were thinking of having a picnic this afternoon."

I raised a brow and tried to suppress a smile. "Were you?"

He grinned. "I would extend an invitation, but I would hate for you to see it as a rescue mission."

"Ivory! Can you believe it?" Mama's voice rang shrilly, and my spine straightened.

I leaned in closer to Charlie. "You are not as sly as you think. But as luck would have it, my fortune has turned. I would indeed appreciate being rescued today."

"—poor Rosalind was pale with worry—"

Charlie's attention flicked from Mama to me and back again. He cleared his throat. "Miss Newbury, you must be weary with worry."

Taking his cue, I said, "I do feel a bit faint."

Liza squeezed my arm. If she knew of our game, she played her part to perfection. "I have just the thing," she said, digging in her reticule. She pulled out a vial of smelling salts and opened the lid. "Take a few deep breaths."

I did as I was told, and Mama rubbed my back. "Everything will come out in order, darling. I shall be sure of it. Perhaps we should get you home to rest."

"When the weather is so agreeable?" Mr. Winston touched Liza's arm. "We've planned a picnic for this afternoon. Perhaps you'd like to join us? Mrs. Newbury?"

"Thank you for the offer, but I have far too much to do," Mama said.

"Miss Newbury?" His eyes fell to mine. "Fresh air is a balm to the mind and spirit. You are most welcome to join us."

"Most welcome, indeed," Liza added.

"Perhaps a picnic *would* calm my nerves." I looked to Mama, who watched me with worry.

Charlie grinned amiably. "With your permission, Mrs.

Newbury, Miss Newbury can join our party now. We were just heading home."

Mama's lips parted as she gathered her thoughts, then closed. "How can I say no when your destination is a stone's throw away from mine?"

"I shall return home before dinner." I leaned in to kiss her cheek. "Thank you, Mama."

She wrinkled her forehead and turned to Liza. "I would not trust her with anyone else, Miss Ollerton. Do see that she rests."

Liza carried on, assuring Mama of this and that while Charlie silently relished in his victory. We walked as slowly as an unwell young lady would until Mama was out of sight.

"By heavens, I am healed," I said, perking up on the spot.

Liza gave me a strange look. "I am not so certain . . ."

"She is well, Liza," Charlie laughed. "Rescuing her proved easier than I thought."

"You are not troubled?"

I laughed. "Not in the least. Though I admit I am confused between the difference in ivory and white lace. They are far too alike to be distinguished in my opinion."

Charlie harrumphed his agreement.

"Ivory is darker," Liza started, shaking her head. "Pure white is bright and almost iridescent."

I shrugged. "If it matters to Mama, I do not mind the change. Though I do hate that she is upset."

"On to our picnic! What shall we have? Fruit, cheeses, salted ham?" Charlie's steps seemed springier than usual, and I felt a sudden urge to keep *his* pace instead of Liza's.

She eyed him, unamused. "Cook prepared a basket."

We stepped out of the street and onto the walking path, under a hanging sign for Mrs. Brandon's Bakery. The idea hit me so suddenly and with such force I stopped as though I'd run straight into the shop wall. Just under the sign was the bakery bow window, displaying loaves of fresh bread and cheesecakes. *Cheesecakes!*

"I've just had the grandest idea."

Liza did not ask, likely because she did not want to know. Charlie, however, indulged me.

He followed my pointing finger to the sign, then back to me. His eyes seemed to glisten in the sun. "Number four?"

I looked to Liza. "We can take them on our picnic and eat as much as we want." I stepped back toward the bakery door.

Liza hesitated, like she wanted to argue but could think of no good reason. She looked up at the sign, then at the bakery window, and swallowed. "I do love cheesecakes."

I bounced on the balls of my feet. Victory, at last! "Yes! You do. And you desperately love me."

She gave me a reproving smile. "But I am relaxing on this picnic," she said, pointing a finger at Charlie's chest. "There will be no mischief of any kind."

His lips twitched. "Agreed."

The bell over the door rang as we entered Mrs. Brandon's little shop. One wooden table was pushed up under a small window. The front counter waited for us at the end of the shop with a large scale sitting beside baskets of yeasty-smelling bread and pastries.

Mrs. Brandon appeared from a narrow doorway behind

the counter. "Good day. Miss Newbury, Miss Ollerton. What can I get you?"

A slow smile crept upon my lips, and I glanced sideways at Charlie. Excitement pulsed through the air like gusts of wind. He didn't have to say anything for me to know he approved of my choice.

"I should like to buy all of your cheesecakes." I raised my chin and set my reticule upon the counter.

Mrs. Brandon's brows raised to her hairline. "All?"

"All."

She rubbed her hands on her apron and blinked. "There must be three dozen. They are my most desired."

"Wonderful. Package them up nicely, if you please." The bread smelled delightful. "And these five loaves of bread, that basket of hot cross buns—and do I smell marzipan?"

Mrs. Brandon's jaw had gone slack. She was younger than she looked, but the shock in her eyes erased a few years. "Y-yes. Just freshly made for the afternoon rush, Miss Newbury."

"I shall take all of that as well."

Charlie coughed behind a hand to cover his humor. Liza shook her head and pursed her lips.

"In fact," I continued, "we shall need some butter for our bread. And something with icing. Do you have any queen cakes?"

Mrs. Brandon nodded.

I raised my pointer finger. "Here's an idea. I shall purchase the entire lot, everything you've made today, for two pounds."

"Two—" Liza blurted, then covered her mouth with a hand.

For a moment I thought Mrs. Brandon might faint. Two pounds was likely more than she made in a week. Charlie stepped closer to Mrs. Brandon as though he'd had the same thought.

She swallowed. "That is much too generous."

"Consider the surplus payment for your speedy packaging. We have a picnic to attend." I offered her a smile, which she returned slowly. In a blink, she'd vanished, and within a quarter hour, I had paid for five large boxes of every delicious thing Mrs. Brandon had made that day.

And I was salivating.

A servant placed the boxes carefully on the floor of the Ollertons' carriage, and Charlie, Liza, and I squished together nearest the door.

"Poor woman. She looked as though she'd seen a ghost when we left with all her goods," Liza said as the carriage rolled out of town.

"Poor?" Charlie chuckled. "She is no longer poor today. That was quite a gallant use of your list, Miss Newbury. I daresay you've changed her life as well." He narrowed his gaze.

"Changing someone's day is not the same as changing their life. That one, I shall have to ponder." I looked out the window and watched the town shrink out of sight. Changing someone's life would not be the fun, exciting sort of work I'd accomplished so far. It would take thought, calculation, care. But for now, I'd focus on chewy bread and sweet cheesecakes.

Liza picked at her glove. "People will talk about this for weeks."

"I suspect it will mean good business for Mrs. Brandon," Charlie added.

I bounced my knees. "Shall we make wagers on how much we each can eat?"

"Relaxing," Liza reminded me with a raised hand.

"I could stomach a loaf of bread." Charlie patted his middle. "But I do not eat sweets."

"What?" I half shouted.

"They inhibit agility. With boxing, if you are not agile, you end up on the floor."

"Good heavens, let us please talk of finer things." Liza leaned her head back and fanned herself with her hand.

I gave Charlie a hard look. "I have just purchased an entire bakery's worth of food. You will at least try the cheesecake."

"I am afraid I cannot. Too much sugar will make me ill."

"Then be ill. For the list."

He tilted his head and shook it.

Frustration hindered rational thought and I frowned. "Then perhaps I shall advise the Ollertons to wake extra early in the morning."

"Now that is cruel."

"What on earth are you two talking about?" Liza asked through a yawn.

"Nothing," we both responded, unblinking and unfazed as we stared each other down. I lowered my chin.

Charlie leaned in. "Fine. I shall have a cheesecake."

"Five."

His voice went shrill. "*Five* cheesecakes? Are you trying to kill me?"

"Oh, you shall keep your agility. And whatever else you think sets you apart from other *gentlemen*."

"You must mean my naturally handsome face and good nature." He winked.

I gave him a half scoff, half laugh. "Think what you will."

"How about a deal?" Charlie looked me up and down. "I shall eat as much as you."

Did he think me akin to a bird picking at seeds in the grass? I leaned back in my seat and crossed my arms. Oh, this would be fun. "If you insist."

"Would that your entire list could be this relaxing, Ros," Liza said. "Though what on earth will we do with all the excess food?"

"Never fear, Liza. Your cousin has no idea what he's just agreed to."

Chapter Fifteen

Nearly drowning had hurt, but not like this.

My stomach ached with fullness, though it had long abandoned trying to dissuade my appetite. The strangest sensation filled my throat—a thickness I could not swallow. But I'd somehow managed to indulge in one last cheesecake, which meant Charlie would too. I motioned for his attention over Liza, who sat between us on our blanket cushioned by soft grass.

"Your turn," I said.

Charlie groaned, but he reached into the box for his next bite. He wore a golden ring with a ruby crested in little diamonds. A family heirloom, I imagined. "Fine ladies are supposed to eat polite portions in front of gentlemen." He took in a long breath before raising the cheesecake to his lips.

I looked toward the wide-open blue sky, where fluffy pillows of white beckoned, and leaned back to stretch out my throbbing stomach. I could smell the sun-heated pond a few paces away and the wind as it blew through the grove and the grass.

The finish line for indulging sweets had come and gone, and I was miserable. "If a woman cannot eat in front of you, she is not worth having. For if she hides her appetite, what else will she keep from you?"

He harrumphed as he took a bite, choking the sweet cheesecake down like a child would an unwelcome vegetable. "What is our total?"

"Each? Seven cheesecakes. Five queen cakes. Two penny buns. And two slices of buttered bread."

"And three marzipan," Liza added, flipping a page in her book. She'd had two cheesecakes and fruit from the picnic. Wise. But she could have indulged a *little* for my sake.

Charlie groaned. "How, pray tell, are we getting home after this?" The carriage had left long ago, still stacked high with boxes full of sweets, despite what we'd taken out for ourselves.

Liza laughed. "Neither of you can walk. You shall both be bedridden for another day at least."

"What choice do we have?" Charlie asked, leaning up on an elbow to swallow down the last of his cheesecake. The motion stirred something within him, and he moaned and laid back down.

Liza sat gracefully on her cushion with her hands in her lap. "Lie back. I think she's finally finished eating." She cast me a conspiratorial smile, which I would have returned if I had any strength left in me.

Silently, we watched a pair of ducks land in the pond for a bath. I shifted from side to side, trying to find a comfortable spot, but the pain in my stomach only grew more severe. Then my throat had that too-full feeling again—like it was getting harder to swallow. Saliva pooled in the back of my throat, and I had no choice but to swallow. Only then did I realize that my body had planned the motion.

My stomach heaved, and I stood and ran toward the pond, away from Liza and Charlie, landing behind a wisp of tall grass near the water's edge. Remnants of every once-delicious thing left me in foul waves of upset.

"What is wrong?" Charlie called from behind me. I hardly had time to be embarrassed, let alone to warn him, before he was upon me, asking, "Are you—"

Then *he* gagged, and the next moment my cruel fate became his somewhere behind me.

"Oh!" Liza called. "Oh, my goodness." Then she was above me with a handkerchief and patting my back.

I dispelled and dispelled until the pain in my stomach eased. It seemed that whenever I took a breath, Charlie heaved, and all the while Liza fussed between us with handkerchiefs and lemonade to wash out our mouths.

"I've made you a bed. Come lie down," she told Charlie.

I eased back from my crouching position, wiping the sweat from my brow with Liza's handkerchief. I felt as though I'd run five miles for how weak and shaky my legs and arms were.

"Drat that list of yours, Ros," Liza whined. Color had drained from her own face. "How will we ever get you two home *now?*"

She tugged on my arm and helped me to my feet. The ground swayed like the sea, and I leaned into Liza's side. We returned to the picnic blanket where she helped me sit down. She'd placed a cushion for my head. "Lie down," she instructed.

Charlie lay on the opposite side of the blanket, just over an arm's reach away. "You have poisoned me," he managed weakly, his face pale.

I rolled on my back. "I am never eating cheesecake again for as long as I live."

"Do *not* say that word."

Liza paced above us. "I could walk home and order them to bring back the carriage, but I cannot leave the two of you out here alone."

Charlie moaned. "I only need a few minutes. Then I can walk."

"Walk?" Her eyes grew as wide as saucers. "Your entire stomach just came out of you."

My muscles had turned to jelly. With what little strength I possessed, I leaned on my side toward Charlie. "Just let her go. The walk back is long, and I want to rest in my bed."

"You think we can survive a carriage ride home from out here? Did you see it wobbling to-and-fro?"

"There is nothing left inside me to object to the motion."

He sighed in defeat, waved Liza off with a hand, and adjusted his cushion under his head. Then he closed his eyes and crossed his arms over his chest. "As long as everyone agrees that I am an innocent victim, merely asleep and enjoying the sunshine."

"How can you enjoy anything after what we just did?"

He peeked out one eye. "You forget I am used to pain."

His boxing. "Well, if this is what losing a fight feels like, I cannot fathom why you continue."

He smiled and slid his hands under his head. "I don't lose."

Before I could so much as scoff at his presumptuousness, Liza was again above us, retying her hat. Somehow, she looked almost as drained as we did. "I shall return as soon as possible. Ros, are you certain about this? As much as we jest, I trust Charlie. And I cannot fathom that anyone should come upon you here, but there is always a risk."

"I am certain Marlow would understand. Go. Quickly. Before your cousin's pride swallows me whole."

With a rush, she was off.

And Charlie and I were suddenly very alone. Our blanket seemed to shrink; the warmth of the day became more prevalent. For a few long moments, we both laid perfectly still, save for our breathing.

I caught Charlie's gaze as it darted from mine. Then he lifted a hand and picked at the grass above his head. "I am confident when I fight. Why must I feign to be less than I am with the one thing that suits me?"

The one thing? Surely he did not believe that. I shifted to my side and bent my knees, then adjusted my skirts over my legs. "You could admit your winning less pompously."

"That is fair, I suppose. Allow me to try again." He cleared his throat and looked up at the clouds. "I could not compare today's illness to losing a mill, because of the many, many, countless fights I have participated in over the past year, I have yet to lose once."

Trying to hold back my derision resulted in a most unladylike snort. "That was far worse. I see why you chose a direct answer."

He smiled and closed his eyes again. "Very good. Why waste time with flowery words when you can just get to the point? Like boxing. There is no need for words. Only your fists, your footwork, and your perseverance."

"But why? Why would you choose such a sport when there are so many other respectable hobbies for a gentleman?"

"Like cards and horse racing?"

"Like horse *riding*. Fox hunting. Fencing." I rubbed my sore stomach.

He harumphed, his eyes still closed. "I see your point. But those hobbies are for men who are content with their lives. Some of us must persuade ourselves that there is light ahead. Boxing is a perfect vessel for expressing frustrations when life has not turned out quite as expected."

"Do you speak of yourself?" I scrunched my nose. Handsome, wealthy, intelligent—what more did a man need to be content? His silence told me I'd asked too intimate a question.

After a moment, he said, "Did Liza tell you about my brother?"

His question caught me off guard. I tried to recall what Liza had told me about Charlie. He'd made poor choices. A lot of them recently. And . . .

"Your father lost a son." The newspaper stories I'd read took on new meaning. That was *Charlie's* family. His father's grief. His brother.

Charlie held my gaze for a moment, then turned his face back to the sky. "Henry. He was three years older than I. My father's heir and my mother's favorite."

I could not help but think of Ben. Father's heir. My

brother who lit up a room with merely his presence. To think of never seeing him again was unfathomable. To lose any of my family members was unfathomable.

"He sounds like quite the son," I said.

"He was quite the brother." Charlie's lips hinted at a smile. "Henry was easy to love. He filled every room with laughter and kindness, intelligence and compassion. But more than that, he was a good man moved by his duty. He *cared* for the estate, looked after the land and its people, and he always knew exactly what needed to be done."

I could not refute his claims, though I wondered if Charlie thought so highly of his brother, why he thought so little of himself. "You must miss him a great deal."

Charlie frowned and turned to face me on his side. He lowered his voice like his words were a secret. "It isn't fair that he died. He was needed. He was necessary. Not just for the estate, but for our entire community. He did more with his two hands, helped more people and changed more lives for the better, than I will do in a lifetime." He swallowed and pressed his lips together like he was closing a door.

I wanted to wedge my foot firmly there and keep it open, keep his secrets spilling out. But his secrets were not mine to carry.

When his eyes met mine, he had bridled the emotion behind them. "I am my father's second son. When Henry lost his life, my whole world upended. I miss him—more than anything, I miss him—but I could never take his place."

I tried to imagine Charlie's grief—surrounded by my brother's memory, missing him so bad I ached, but forced to walk in his footsteps and keep living. I couldn't.

"I'm so sorry, Charlie."

He drew in a long breath, then smiled despite his sorrow. "Liza says you hardly know the Duke of Marlow."

Smooth change of subject. Why did he always do that?

I adjusted my cushion more comfortably. Exhaustion set in, and rightly so. I let my limbs fall heavily upon the blanket.

"Talking about me in your spare time, are you?"

He met my gaze and laughed. "An engaged woman? I know better than that. I was merely curious about your arrangement. How many times have you met this duke?"

"Twice." I stared back with confidence. Anything less would prove his point, and I would never allow *that*.

"Do you find him humorous?"

"He has a quiet humor. Nothing too boisterous or exciting."

He narrowed his gaze and yawned. "You don't seem like the quiet type."

"We shall pair well as opposites."

"And his habits? Does he rise early and retire late?" Mr. Winston's eyelids seemed heavy, and he blinked lazily.

"Those habits will not affect me. We will be in separate rooms."

"Are you certain? I, for one, should like to fall asleep beside my wife."

Heat rose up my neck, and I dropped my gaze to where Charlie's hand rested near his chest, which rose and fell steadily. What would it feel like to sleep beside one's husband? To feel so warm, so comfortable, that our breaths came in tandem and lulled us both to sleep.

To be *so close*.

Charlie's hand fell to the space between us. I could see the lines in his knuckles, count the hand-sewn threads on his sleeve. My skin prickled and heated, and I feared if I moved in the slightest, we would touch, and then what might happen?

Charlie laughed. "Forgive my impertinence. I should not speak so intimately with you, but you feel so much like Liza—so comfortable. I fear my mind is becoming fuzzy."

I cleared my throat. "Emptying one's stomach is cruelly exhausting."

"All thanks to that list of yours."

"To the list!" I called with a laugh, lifting an imaginary glass in the air.

"Hear, hear!" Charlie raised his, and we pretended to touch glasses before settling back. "Believe it or not, I've grown fond of your list," he said. "But still, I wonder . . ."

I waited. "What?"

"What do you expect to happen when you've finished?"

What did I expect? Logically, I knew my list would not change my life, though a little part of me wanted it to. I thought of Aunt Alice's smiling face as she stepped down the church stairs on Uncle Marvin's arm as his wife for the first time.

"I want to feel complete. Like a perfect picture, ready to be hung."

He made a face. "I do not think that is what you want."

"Why not?"

"Perfection means having an expected outcome. Perfect lines, perfect colors, perfect brushstrokes. But perfection is unachievable. Indeed, it is the attempt, the strokes we did not mean to make, that leave us with an unexpected beauty."

His words took hold of me, and as I lay there, facing him, I studied the bruise still lightly framing his eye and cheekbone and the cut almost completely healed on his lip. He, Charles Winston, was entirely unexpected. How did he understand exactly how I saw life? How I *wanted* to see it. Not just how Society told me to.

I wanted to tell him I understood his meaning. That, yes, I wanted a messy, imperfect life, free of pretense and parties and forced smiles. But instead, I said, "'Perfection is unachievable,' says the man who refuses to go home for fear he will fail." I rolled on my back and muttered, "Hypocrite."

He laughed. "Is that how you speak to the man who saved your life? If Henry were here, you'd see why his shoes are too big to fill."

"If Henry were here, we wouldn't be having this conversation."

"Why not?"

"Because I'd be talking to *him*."

Charlie laughed heartily, the sound echoing through the grove, and I grinned.

"Never truer words spoken," he said with reverence, and he closed his eyes again.

I followed suit, letting the sunlight warm my face as my breaths evened. My limbs settled on the blanket like stones, grounding me.

"I don't know why I told you all that." Charlie's voice broke our silence. "My family—we seldom speak of Henry. It feels . . . strange. Talking about him gone. And it's been well over a year." His eyes were closed, but his face was anything but relaxed. "Talking of him makes me miss him more."

If I had to live without Benjamin and be asked to fill his shoes, I'd want to hit something every day too. Perhaps Charlie's boxing wasn't so different than my list. "I cannot imagine. But I am glad you told me."

"Why?"

"Because now I know why you've acted so poorly. And I shall remind you the next time you think of damaging your family name that, although Henry is gone, your legacy reflects his name too. I am certain if he were here, he'd thump you over the head."

"He'd have landed me a facer to rival yours." He peeked at me and imitated a boxing motion. "He loved the sport."

"I'd like to see that," I grinned, returning my face to the sun.

He chuckled. "The sunshine is loosening your tongue too."

True. But it felt so marvelously good. My aches seemed to be healing in the light.

Charlie turned once more on his side. "Can I ask you something? While our tongues are loose."

My senses tingled with the awareness of how near we lay. I could see every detail of his smooth jawline, every freckle, every scar. I wanted to touch him. I wanted to reach out and take his hand, to feel the warmth of his fingers entwined with mine.

I swallowed and shook away the thought. "We should rest." Talking to Charlie made me feel too free. He spoke as though he could see right into me, like he knew the thoughts I'd never considered sharing. As inviting as his conversation was, I was not free. My future was fast approaching, and I preferred those thoughts staying well below the surface.

But he persisted. "What will you do if, after all your efforts, you still feel as you do now?"

Our eyes met, and he watched me carefully. Like he was waiting for me to admit to some great secret revelation. But I had nothing. I had no other plan. I did not need one.

Did I?

Charlie pursed his lips, then laid back. "You're a hypocrite, too, then."

"I beg your pardon?"

"If nothing changes, if you still feel unsteady about marrying the duke, but you marry him anyway, then what was the point? You chide me for not making changes in my life, while you are just as unwilling."

"I have a duty."

His eyes pierced into mine, like he needed me to hear him. "No. *I* have a duty. You have a choice. And if you feel this unsettled, perhaps you ought to reconsider what you want for your life."

I started to tell him that perhaps he ought to consider a profession in the clergy if he wanted to preach, but his eyes closed, and he crossed his arms over his chest again. So instead, I let out a heavy breath through my nose.

Where was Liza with our carriage?

There must have been a rock under my side of the blanket, for I suddenly could not get comfortable in any position. I turned to one side, then the other. If I hadn't nearly perished in Charlie's presence for the second time, I'd be more worried about my reputation. But anyone with eyes could see that he and I were miserable.

I settled on my back, turning my gaze to the treetops in the distance. The leaves swayed and danced in the light breeze, almost yearning to break free and fly away. What they could not know in their haste was that every good thing came to an end. Their flight would result in certain descension, but where they'd land, no one could be sure.

Perhaps Charlie understood that part of me. Perhaps he saw the dreaming girl who wanted to float away on an adventure. I wanted my life to be interesting, but that did not also mean I wanted it to be free of responsibility like he did. A dukedom would give my family unimaginable opportunities. My life would be filled with them.

But I also wanted a family of my own—a husband who loved me, who *I* loved, and children for us both to adore. Could I have that with the duke?

Charlie's breaths evened out, and a light snore escaped him. As did all his mightiness. As much as I wanted to be put out with him for his hypocrisy, and for his declaration of mine, he looked so peaceful and calm asleep. Without sorrow or burden. His lips barely parted, and the breeze brushed through his hair. So handsome, despite his scars; even I had to admit. To think he'd intimidated me at first.

My eyelids grew heavy. I was so warm and comfortable. But I shouldn't give in. One of us had to maintain some semblance of propriety.

Charlie could not care less, obviously.

I blinked, but this time, my eyes stayed shut.

Chapter Sixteen

"Rosalind."

I tried to swallow, but I felt like my throat was full of sand. I blinked once against the sunlight and stretched out an arm. Then I turned on my side and dug my face into my pillow.

Only it wasn't *my* pillow.

"Rosalind! Quickly!" *Charlie.*

I pushed up on my hand and sat up, finding his gaze already on mine. His eyes were frantic. But why? I searched his face. His disheveled hair. A pink spot on his cheek where he'd slept. Why was he crouched in the grass? My heart started to thrum.

"What in the *blazes* is going on?"

Benjamin? I spun around on my knees and froze in place. No, no, no. Charlie and I were on a picnic blanket, with pillows, alone in the middle of the pasture. Ben stomped toward us with purpose, shoulders squared and fire raging in his eyes.

I stood too quickly, and my head swirled. My breaths came fast, and I could not speak; my throat had altogether closed with panic, and my body felt fuzzy from sleep. How could I talk my way out of this? What excuse could we make for this incriminating display?

Charlie jumped up and created distance between us. "Newbury," he said calmly, but his voice was all wrong. Pinched. Guilty. "Good to see you."

Benjamin was already upon us, charging straight for Charlie with fists at the ready. "You right devil. You dirty, bird-witted scoundrel!"

"Benjamin!" I cried, reaching out to stop his pursuit.

But he pushed past my outstretched hand and shoved Charlie's chest so hard he stumbled back.

"She is my *sister*!" Ben growled.

"Newbury, you misunderstand," Charlie hurried to say. He raised his hands in surrender. "I know what this must look like to you, you coming upon us in such a state, but we were ill—"

Benjamin strode to my side and took my shoulders in his hands. "Did he touch you?" His eyes were a fierce storm. His breaths came fast. "Did he hurt you in any way? You told me not to trust him, but I had no idea—"

"Nothing happened between us, Ben." My voice was hoarse, and my face burned hot, but I held his stare, enunciating my words with seriousness. "You must believe me."

Charlie's face fell. He looked pained, as though he'd betrayed a true friend. "I give you my word, I would never harm your sister. What you saw looked far worse than it actually was. I fell asleep—"

"You are shockingly loose in the haft!"

"But so did I!" I interjected, stepping between them.

Ben raised a hand. "It is *his* duty to protect you at all costs. And *my* responsibility to defend you otherwise."

"We were sick," I pleaded for his understanding. He needed to breathe and see things clearly. "We ate too many sweets and expelled everything. Neither of us could walk. Liza left on *my* request to fetch a carriage to bring us home."

"And? Where is she?"

I looked ahead, begging, pleading for Liza and her carriage to come into view. But the fields remained empty. My shoulders sank, as did my pride. All I had at present were my words to defend the truth.

"She should have returned by now," I started to explain. "She was here."

"Well, she isn't now, is she?" He threw out his hands, then paced between us, grasping clumps of his hair. "You think me some fool."

Charlie rubbed his hands over his face. *He* would be the one to take the blame.

"You are not a fool," I insisted. "But you are mistaken in where you set your blame."

"You tell me to be more responsible." Ben lifted his hands in the air and stared hard at me. "Here I am." He shifted his stare to Charlie. "And you have left me no choice."

"No choice for what?" I breathed. He could not tell Father. Father would never forgive me for such carelessness. He'd keep me in the house until the wedding, and I'd never finish my list. I'd never know if I'd made the right choice in the end. My legs went weak. "Benjamin what are you saying?"

"You do what you must for your sister. I would do the

same." Charlie looked down; his hands hung loose at his sides. "I will not protest."

Benjamin's eyes widened. Had he expected something different? Then he swallowed hard and seemed to strengthen his resolve. "She is my *sister*," he seethed once more. "She is engaged to the Duke of Marlow. What if someone else saw you? Can you imagine our family's shame should he find out? Especially if I let you go free?"

Were they talking about a duel? My senses sobered instantly.

"Benjamin, we are leaving. Now." My voice was harsh, but I didn't care. I grabbed my brother's arm and pulled. "This is all a massive misunderstanding. You will see. We will go straight to Ivy Manor and speak to Liza. She will tell you how sick we were."

But Ben was looking at Charlie, who said, "Regardless of my poor judgment in the past, I would never dishonor your sister, nor would I betray your friendship. I respect you both far too much to risk your good opinion." Charlie hesitated, looked down, then met Ben's stare. "I understand that you are bound by duty. Should you truly wish to call me out, I will not object."

"You most certainly will object!" I shrieked. "You will both object! We will go home and act as though none of this has happened."

We'd only slept near each other. We had not even *touched*. Could a man talk of killing another over so little? I wrung my hands together, trying to breathe evenly through my nose. What could I do?

"I see no other way," Benjamin said flatly. His eyes were wide with fear.

I looked to Charlie, my eyes pleading for him to see the absurdity of Ben's decision. This entire conversation was out of hand. "Do something."

Charlie held up a hand. "Before you demand satisfaction," he said to Ben, "think of what that will mean for your sister. If we use pistols and one of us is killed, everyone will learn what happened here today."

Ben's eyes were fire. "Coward."

"I think only of your sister. As I know you do."

Ben shook his head. His hands were fists at his sides. "You think only of yourself," he growled.

In a flash, he'd grasped Charlie's shoulder, then thrust his fist hard into his stomach.

Charlie grunted and fell to his knee.

"Benjamin!" I cried, rushing forward to place myself between them.

"Go home." The words were Charlie's. His pained eyes seemed to beg my compliance. "Please."

"You cannot do this," I pleaded with Ben. "Let us take a walk, Benjamin. Let us talk this through before—"

"Go home," Ben said icily. "Or I shall tell Father everything I've seen, and we can let him be the judge over you."

I took a step back. How had this happened? We were happy and full one moment, and now . . .

"Stand up, Winston," Ben growled. "On your feet."

Charlie stood and, at Ben's insistence, lifted his fists. But it was a lazy effort. Half-hearted. Charlie would never hurt

Ben, but he'd take the wrongful blame in bruises. Ben would put Charlie right back where he'd started.

"*Go now*, Rosalind." Ben pointed toward home. He raised his fists, and he started to round on Charlie, who blocked his every advance. One hit, and then another, until Ben shouted in frustration, "Fight back, you scoundrel!"

Charlie swung out, but even I could see he'd given Ben the opportunity.

Ben rang out and hit him straight on. His fists were relentless, pummeling at Charlie's chest, his side, his stomach.

I turned, my vision blurry, and started to run.

I refused dinner. My stomach ached so much I could hardly bear to sit up straight or move at all. I'd shaken so terribly from sickness and then fear, every muscle I possessed was weary.

Ben had come home only long enough to change his clothes, which, per Molly's information, were only slightly tinged with blood. I was consumed with the vision of his fists raised. Consumed with worry for Charlie.

Just after I had dressed in my nightclothes, Molly arrived with a letter from Liza.

> *Ros,*
>
> *Forgive me for abandoning you. Charlie assures me you made it home safely not long after, though I feel dreadful for never making it back.*

Charlie. He was home. My eyes flew down the page.

Before you panic, I told no one of you and Charlie being alone. But I fell victim to my own sickness, and Mama sent me straight to bed. I could not stop thinking about you hunched over so, and Charlie, and then, just as I climbed the stairs to the house . . .

Forgive me. Even writing about it turns my stomach. I must retire early, but I could not sleep without first sending you a most fervent apology. I worried if I asked Mama to send the carriage, she would have gone as well, and I could not risk it.

The doctor is certain I was simply overset. After resting, I am much improved, but I cannot say the same for Charlie. He did not come home until late in the afternoon, and he has a swollen eye and a fresh cut in his lip. He claims he tripped and fell on a rock. A boulder, if you ask me, and apparently straight on his face. I am unconvinced. Mama and Papa are concerned he is back to his old habits, though I cannot say how he has managed it. I am only glad there is no evidence to refute his claim.

I worry for him, Ros. He has so much potential, but I fear he will squander his opportunities and live a life full of regret. Help me save him, won't you? I wish I could show him what his future could look like, if only he'd give it a chance.

I hope you are feeling much improved.

Write back tomorrow.

Yours, etc.,

As horrible as I felt for her sickness, I was relieved knowing Liza did not know the truth, and that Charlie had no serious wounds. But now the Ollertons assumed Charlie had resorted to old habits. Did those habits even exist? As far as I could tell, Charlie seemed to find himself in the wrong place at the wrong time. He'd had my best interests at heart since I'd first met him.

But what had I done to help him? I'd only gotten him in more and more trouble. I was the one who'd nearly drowned, who'd followed Ben into the grove. I was the one who'd made Charlie eat all those sweets, so if anything, I was to blame for this current misunderstanding.

I sunk into bed with a greater guilt than I'd ever felt before. After all he'd endured, Charlie deserved better. He deserved happiness.

And I would help him find it.

Chapter Seventeen

Ben was not at breakfast. Nor in his study. Father had left for a meeting in town with our solicitor, and Mama had left to oversee the progress on my wedding dress.

I'd claimed a headache to get out of that task.

Sitting upright was still a chore, so I spent the morning back in my bedroom, thinking about Ben. His fight with Charlie stayed vividly at the forefront of my mind. I could not forgive my brother for what he had done, though neither could I reprimand him for defending my honor.

Instead, when my stomach was healed enough to hold down a light luncheon, I gathered my abandoned notebook, still unwritten in since the day Charlie taught me how to box, and a pen and ink, and sat at my desk, which faced the double windows in my room. Bright sunlight hit my notebook, beckoning back thoughts of my favorite childhood memories. And I let myself get lost in them.

Times when laughter came as plentifully as raindrops in spring. When I still had years ahead of me before worrying about protection and money or about leaving home and starting a new family with someone else. My whole life could be reduced to frames of memory, and while I could not remember every detail, in every memory I felt the same.

Safe.

Happy.

Perhaps that was why I loved painting so much. I wanted to remember moments, scenes, people—forever.

The only sound in the room was my pen sliding across pages. Ben and I floating boats down the stream. Playing spillikins until our fingers ached. Playing duets on the pianoforte and violin. Time had changed us, but at the core, I was still that girl with long brown curls, and Ben was my fluffy-haired, big-toothed little brother. And now, thanks to Aunt Alice and my list, I would have these memories to share forever.

I had just closed my journal, when my door swung open and Mama came through with Molly on her heels.

"Dress quickly," Mama said. "We shall dine at the Ollertons' home this evening."

"The Ollertons?" I stood from my chair.

"Benjamin has befriended their nephew, and Mrs. Ollerton wishes to encourage the connection. I wouldn't have accepted on such short notice, but hearing her admit our Ben is such a good influence . . ."

"On Mr. Winston?" He could not be in the same room as Ben after their fight. But Mama did not know about their secret duel, and clearly neither did Mrs. Ollerton. Could the boys be civil? I doubted anything but shreds were left of their friendship after yesterday.

"Yes. Apparently, not long after his brother died, Mr.

Winston left University, fought with his father, and threw a terrible fit. He said he had no intention of taking over their estate in his brother's stead and even threatened to see it go to ruin after his two younger sisters married. Can you imagine the shame?"

Charlie hadn't told me about his sisters. Nor his ill intentions toward his family home. I could hardly believe Mama; her words did not sound like my friend at all. "But where did he go?"

Molly pulled out an evening gown and moved around me to untie my day dress.

Mama continued, "From what Mrs. Ollerton told me, he left, rented an apartment in London, and has spent most of his time doing heaven knows what. They gave him a year to come round, and when he did not, when he got into a terrible row with an earl, they cut him off altogether. Waited far too long in my opinion. Apparently, his mother hopes having nothing will teach him gratitude."

Pieces that had not quite fit now fell into place. Grief over losing his brother must have truly driven Charlie mad. All his ugly bruises and cuts and faded scars from when we'd first met—had he felt that same pain *inside*?

"I can hardly believe Mr. Winston to be such a selfish man. Our interactions have been pleasant," I said as Molly helped me into my new dress.

"There is always more beyond what the eye can see," Mama said. "Quickly now. We are waiting downstairs."

Mama left, and Molly led me to a chair so she could arrange my hair. But my thoughts were hooked on these new revelations about Charlie. Thinking back over our conversations, I knew he'd not once lied to me about his past, nor that he'd made mistakes. He'd shared his struggles, his grief, even his fears. I may not know his family well enough for their perspective, but I knew Charles Winston.

He'd made mistakes, but he was a good man.

I descended the stairs to where Mama and Father stood by the entry. I had no more than turned before Benjamin was there, dressed and proper, with a bland expression more fit for card tables than dinner. His face was decidedly without bruises.

It was almost laughable, for had Charlie fought back, my brother would have been in a foul state. Ben avoided my gaze, but I latched onto his side as we followed our parents outside to the carriage.

"Where have you been?" I whispered, squeezing his arm.

"Out," he muttered in a dark tone.

I tugged his arm back to slow his quick pace. Before we met the Ollertons, I wanted to understand what had happened after I left the grove. I needed to know what to expect. "Have you settled things?"

"Settled?" He scoffed. "Not until the man has left town."

"Benjamin, you have misplaced your judgment."

He frowned down at me. "He got what he deserved. And I won't have you interacting with him alone ever again."

"Then I suppose it's lucky we won't be alone."

Mr. Derricks greeted us at Ivy Manor. This time he permitted me entrance, though still with a bit of hesitation that only I would notice.

Mrs. Ollerton hurried over as we walked in. She was dressed in red with lips to match and immediately embraced

Mama. They began a hushed conversation about some woman who'd fallen over on the streets in town.

I curtseyed to Mrs. Ollerton and followed Mama, Father, and Ben into the drawing room. Liza was at the pianoforte, only briefly glancing up to smile as she continued to play. Father moved to the back of the room to converse with Mr. Ollerton.

Ben stopped in the center of the room. I looked to my left and found Charlie sitting by the window with a book.

Charlie looked up and stood, bowing at Ben and me. I could not catch his eye, so I stepped even with Ben, whose glare was so severe and so pointed, it could have made a lion cower.

"We are guests," I reminded my brother on a low breath. "You must be civil."

He sniffed and puffed out his chest, obviously determined to intimidate Charlie. "I think I'll stand right here and remind him where he belongs."

Charlie had settled back into the window seat, slouching his shoulders. Instead of reading his book, though, he'd turned a heavy gaze out the window at the last shades of light in the evening sky. My heart could not bear to see him alone and so full of sorrow.

"He is my friend and was once yours," I said, giving Ben a sidelong glance. "We cannot snub him, unless you wish to upset our parents and the Ollertons over lack of care."

Ben pressed his lips together.

"With your permission, brother."

He looked away as Liza's song slowed. I had to make a

choice. Join her at the pianoforte and ensure she had recovered from her fall or join Charlie at the window.

I knew where I wanted to be, but where I wanted was not the same as where I should be. My feet carried me to him anyway. Upon closer inspection, I saw that his right eye was bruised, though not as darkly as the first time I'd met him. And just as Liza had said, there was a fresh cut in his lower lip.

"You are alive," I said playfully as I drew nearer.

His eyes flicked to mine with surprise. He looked behind me, so I sidestepped to block his view of Ben. Charlie's lips twitched, and he closed his book and scooted to one side of the window seat.

"Are you certain you wish to tempt fate this evening with my wounds so fresh?" he said in a low voice as I sat down beside him. "I am under strict orders to keep away from you."

I lowered my voice to a whisper. "What happened after I left?"

Charlie grimaced. "If your brother did not tell you, then I shouldn't."

I looked over my shoulder. Ben stood unmoved. Mama and the rest of our company laughed delightedly at something Mr. Ollerton had procured from his pocket.

"What did he say to you?" I asked.

Charlie raised his brows thoughtfully and let out a heavy breath. "More of the same. I'm to never look at you or so much as blink in your direction."

I looked heavenward and took a long breath through my nose. "You are practically an Ollerton. And we were deathly ill, for heaven's sake. And far apart."

"Well," Charlie started with a remorseful look, rubbing the back of his neck.

"What?" I narrowed my eyes.

His smile was warm, but hesitant. The kind a mother gives her favorite obstinate child. "You like to roll around in your sleep." He bit his lip. "You stole my pillow."

His *what?* "I did not."

Oh, but I had. That split second before Ben's voice rumbled in the air, I'd awoken on a pillow that was not my own. I covered my mouth with a hand. My neck, my face, my ears all heated.

Charlie laughed with that same hesitancy and looked strangely at me, in a familiar sort of way. A way that made my heart stir.

His cheeks pinked, and he suppressed a smile, looking down at his hands. "That is, after I convinced you that my pillow was more comfortable than my arm."

My jaw went slack, and I shook my head slowly, unthinkingly. Me, asleep on Charlie's arm?

This time I buried my face into both of my hands. I would never move from this spot. And no one would ever see my face again.

"I do not think your brother had arrived yet. I'm quite certain I'd be dead if he had." His voice turned serious, but I could not be sure. I would never know because I would never look at him again.

I breathed in and out of my nose, utterly and completely burning with mortification. What must Charlie think of me? A wanton woman quite literally accosting him.

Two warm hands gently tugged at mine, pulling them

away from my face. I looked down at the blue-and-hazelnut-brown carpet at our feet.

Then Charlie's finger lifted my chin. "You have nothing to be embarrassed about. You were a perfect lady. The only sounds you made were sounds of protest when I rolled away."

My eyes widened and met his. "I would never have—"

His eyes brightened as he struggled to keep from smiling. "And I had to return your wandering hands a few times as well."

"Enough," I begged, burying my face in my hands again and curling over my lap. I could take no more. The man could say whatever he wanted to embarrass me, and I'd never know if he spoke the truth because I'd let it all happen willingly. And Benjamin had almost seen!

Charlie chuckled, then cleared his throat. "Your brother is looking at us."

I jerked upright, patting my hair and my assuredly pink cheeks and plastered a grin on my face so Ben would not think me overset. He turned his gaze back to Liza and the pianoforte.

"You are a rotten liar, Charles Winston," I whispered through my false composure, half hoping he'd admit to exaggerating, half thinking back on his claims.

Had I actually reached out for him while sleeping? I peeked sideways through my lashes. Where had I touched him? His broad shoulder? His chest? His neck?

"Either way, I paid the price, did I not?"

His words sobered me. "I should never have let Liza leave. I cannot apologize enough for my part in this. For your pain."

He shrugged. "I'd be lying if I said it was not worth it."

Our knees brushed, and my heart thrummed roughly against my chest. "You don't mean that." Not in the way it sounded.

But instead of agreeing or denying my claim, he smiled to himself in private thought. "About our conversation," he mused, "before we fell asleep—"

"I shall forget it all," I hurried to say. The stories he confided in me about his brother, Henry, were his to tell, and I would never share them. Though the more he gave, the more I wanted. I wanted more of his past. I wanted it all.

But I *needed* to forget that Charlie had a heart. That he could be more the handsome gentleman and less the brooding boxer. That he was kind and insightful. That he somehow, without even trying, saw more of me than I allowed anyone else to see.

The only person who had that right was Marlow. He only needed the opportunity.

Charlie rubbed his jaw and the new bruise Ben had marked on him. "Speaking so intimately isn't proper, I know, but—"

"We were both in quite a vulnerable state."

He watched me under a furrowed brow. "We were."

Was there something else he was trying to say? Did he wish for a different reaction? "But, of course, my engagement does not mean we cannot be friends."

He crossed his arms and leaned back in his seat. "Friends, yes. Of course."

Friends? Why was I so utterly daft? And childish? What grown adult offered friendship? I could feel him watching me, and I cringed. Here I was, blubbering on like a fool. "If you wish it."

His eyes were set on mine. "I do."

Could it be so easy to move forward pretending we hadn't exchanged our hearts so willingly only the day before? Should I? I was engaged to be married in less than two weeks. My heart spoke before my mind could catch up. "As do I." As though nothing and no one could stand in the way of our new devoted friendship.

Charlie nodded and returned his gaze to the window. His eyes were heavy, unsatisfied. But why?

"And thank you," I said. "For taking Ben's hits and not retaliating."

"I have had much, much worse, so do not give it another thought. Your brother did what he thought was right according to duty and in response to your honor. I will not fault him for that." Charlie gave me a little smile as though to prove himself amiable and unharmed. "Indeed, this entire trip has been much more eventful than I anticipated. I really believed I'd be stuck in the house all this time. Liza and I get on, but she was quite angry with me when things came to light."

I listened to Liza's gentle Mozart, a new melody than before, and asked, "Lord Langdon's broken arm?"

"I did not mean to break his arm. I only meant to knock him off, but the man's bones are more fragile than a China plate."

"The break was an accident?"

"Do not spread that around. I have a reputation at the Club." He gave me a sideways glance, but I didn't think it was very funny. Why would Charlie let Society go on thinking he'd broken a man's arm? There were too many holes in his story. And I needed to fill them.

"Then why did your father cut you off?" I winced. *Too forward, Rosalind.*

But Charlie seemed unaffected by my prodding. "Well, for one, I did not tell *him* it was an accident."

"Charlie," I reprimanded, shifting in my seat. "What *did* you tell your father?"

"That I liked fighting. It makes me feel successful and fulfilled."

"And he said?"

"That if I gave our estate as much notice as I did the Club, I could feel just as successful and fulfilled there."

I watched him carefully. Did he hear the wisdom in his father's words? "That is interesting advice."

He pursed his lips. "He does not understand."

"Understand what?"

Charlie only shook his head. We sat in silence for a time, save for the gentle hum of our family's voices and Liza's melodies in the air. I waited. Waited for him to decide to tell me whatever he was keeping locked inside. I wanted him to share his fears and secrets as openly as I had.

He cleared his throat and forced a smile. "What is next on your list?"

I rounded on him, unsatisfied. "I thought we were supposed to be friends." I gave him a face that said, *If you think you can hide from me, you are mistaken.*

He drew in a breath. "My life is complicated."

"And mine is not?" I almost snorted.

He swallowed and looked down, and I felt instantly contrite for pushing him to confide in me. "Forgive me."

His eyes met mine, and he held them, willing me to hear his words. "I am not a perfect man."

"I know."

He nodded, then fiddled with his sleeve. "They all expect me to fail. And they are not wrong. I'll never be as good for the estate as Henry would have been. I shall make a mess of everything."

"A mess that you shall fix with practice."

He looked at me for a long moment, then frowned. "I have already disappointed them. The pain I have caused by abandoning them, and so soon after Henry's death, is unforgivable. I neglected my family and wasted too much time. My mother, my sisters, even my father deserve better."

"Then *be better*."

He looked heavenward with obvious disbelief and perhaps a little annoyance. "It is not that simple."

"It *is* that simple."

"Perhaps for someone like you." He stared out the window. Frustration seemed to overpower him, but the fear in his eyes remained. He feared failure. The strong man in the grove who never lost a mill feared disappointing his family most of all. "All you must do to please your family is marry the man they present to you."

I reared back at the bite in his tone. "You think that such an easy feat?"

"Why wouldn't I? Your family is in raptures over the match. *You* speak only of how wonderful the duke is, as though the man was without flaw. I daresay the entire town envies how perfect and *easy* this must be for you, but if anyone stopped and looked closely enough, they'd see the truth."

My heart fell to my toes. "What truth?"

Charlie's posture changed from forlorn to tense and angry. "That you are *miserable*. You do not want to marry the duke. Perhaps you are aiding your family, but you are failing yourself. And you're a fool to not forecast what that might mean for you in years to come."

His words were a slap to my face. The pain from their truth choked me, but I would not let him see he'd wounded me by speaking the very words I feared to expose the most, the fears I would never claim out loud.

He blinked and swallowed, his face turning rosy with each passing moment of silence between us. "I did not—what I meant to say, was—"

I stood suddenly. "Our lives may not turn out how either of us expected them to, but at least I am trying to make the best of mine. That is more than anyone can say of you."

Without a second glance, I strode to Liza at the pianoforte and pulled up a chair beside her.

"What is wrong?" Liza asked, her fingers dropping from the keys to her lap. "Why does Charlie look so upset?"

"I wouldn't know," I said as nonchalantly as I could. I adjusted the pages of music on the pianoforte, then played from where Liza left off. I let my fingers glide along the keys, filling the air with music to drown out Charlie's words in my head.

Mozart. Smooth, measured Mozart.

Dinner was called shortly after. Propriety required Ben to take Liza in, but I didn't give Charlie the satisfaction of a glance as he stood above me, offering his arm. I barely held on as he walked me to my seat, which was, unfortunately, directly beside his. After he'd helped me settle, Ben stood to push me in a little more comfortably, as though to show Charlie how it should be done. I grinned at my brother. He might not always make the most reasonable decisions, but he certainly and thankfully prioritized loyalty to his family.

Liza sat directly across from me and indulged me in more than enough conversation. And any time Charlie spoke to the table, I took a mouth full of something so he would not direct his conversation at me.

After dinner, Mrs. Ollerton led Mama out, with Liza and I close behind. But halfway out in the hall, a hand took my arm.

"Miss Newbury, you dropped this," Charlie said.

I touched my neck, but I hadn't worn any jewelry to lose.

Liza continued to follow her mother, but I turned to face Charlie with a look of reproach.

His gaze dropped, and he swallowed. He held something in his hand.

"What is it?" My voice came out harsh. Did Ben know he'd followed me?

Charlie bit his bottom lip and handed me a handkerchief. *His* handkerchief. Stitched with the initials *C. W.*

I took it from him, examining it to be sure. "But this is yours."

He tucked his hands behind his back and gave me a pained smile. "I am not good at making excuses, but I wanted to speak with you."

My brow furrowed. Is that why he had pretended the handkerchief was mine?

Charlie's eyes held mine like he wished I would save him from his misery. But I would not. I would make him say every word.

He bit his bottom lip. "You are angry with me. And I find I like that very little."

A lump wedged firmly in my throat.

He took a small step closer. "I should not have spoken to you so harshly earlier. I let my fear guide my tongue, and I wounded you. Can you forgive me?" His eyes were pleading, earnest. "Please."

Never had I heard such sincere words from a gentleman. And so soon after a quarrel.

"I should not have pressed you," I added. He was not solely to blame.

"Why shouldn't you press your friend when he needs to hear what you are saying? Is that not what friends are for?"

I looked at his crisp neckcloth, focusing on the red-and-gold-spotted design he clearly preferred. "Your life is yours, not mine. You are free to choose your own happiness regardless of my opinions. If you wish to live apart from your family, who am I to discourage you?"

He gave me a half smile. "I thought that is what I wanted. I thought I could continue with my life as I had planned it. Pretending like nothing had changed. But the problem is, I do not wish to be free of my family. I simply wish I could escape how painful it is to love them so dearly. Perhaps then I would not care about how inadequate I am to step into such an important role in their lives—in Henry's. Disappointing them when they are already so broken is a pain I cannot bear."

I hesitated, unsure of what to say that might help. "I

wonder what your mother would say to that. I imagine I would tell my son that there is nothing worse he could do than give up before he'd even started."

He rubbed his jaw with his hand, seeming to ponder my words as much as he studied the floor. "I should never have chided you for offering me advice when it is granted with such wisdom. I must apologize again."

I started to laugh; I was anything but wise. "You are forgiven." I handed him back his handkerchief. "We are quite a pair, are we not?"

I hesitated. There was more I wanted to say, but once I spoke the words, I could not take them back. But Charlie had been so open with me about his brother's death. He'd been true to his feelings, even the ugly ones, and he'd inspired me. I wanted to be that honest.

"I do not wish to marry the duke," I said slowly. The words spilled from my lips and took wings. I was equal parts anxious and pleased by the stunned expression on his face. But even the truth would not keep me, or Charlie, from accepting our fates. "And you do not wish to accept your family's estate."

Charlie stood incredibly still. "How ungrateful of us." He teased, but his eyes were serious and searching.

"How selfish," I agreed. "How very unreasonable of us to want to create our own futures."

Charlie nodded. "We could run away." He raised his brows, half serious, half in jest, and I laughed.

"Together? I am currently forbidden from speaking with you without a proper chaperone."

Charlie made a show of looking around, knowing as well

as I that no such chaperone currently existed, and yet here we were. I swatted his arm playfully. "Go back to looking contrite. It suits you better."

He grinned and tucked his hands behind his back, chin down. "Truly, though. Thank you. For including me in your quest, and—"

"I seem to remember begging you—"

"—for indulging my ridiculous notions—"

"You did save my life."

"—and for being a better friend than I deserve."

Emotion welled in my throat, but I swallowed it back and instead raised my chin with a tease in my voice. "You are correct. You do not deserve me."

He tilted his head and seemed to study my face in the candlelit hallway. "I cannot think of any man who ever will."

I held my head high and let him examine me, warming under his attention.

What did he see when he looked at me like that? So unabashedly and tender. I wanted his thoughts, all of them, but especially the ones just under the surface. So close but yet unspoken.

His eyes met mine, and he smiled, then looked down. "I should . . ."

"Of course," I hurried to agree. "Go, repair your friendship with Benjamin. He looks up to you, and whether he will admit it or not, he dearly wishes he did not have to hate you."

"I haven't the faintest idea how to approach him," Charlie said with his palms up.

I made a fist and gently hit his open hand. "I assume there is more to pugilism than hitting a heavy bag. Critique him. Tell him how he could have really hurt you yesterday. Teach him all your boxing tricks, how to truly protect his sister and his future wife, and you shall have him back in the grove in no time."

Charlie nodded and rubbed his jaw.

"And Charlie?" I wavered.

He looked up.

"Tell him again that he was right to protect me, though perhaps next time he should control his anger. And praise his loyalty to his family. Tell him it is the most admirable and honorable trait he could have."

Charlie watched me carefully, and I realized too late what I had said.

"I shall tell him," Charlie said. Then he bowed low, too respectfully for a woman without yet a title, and left.

Chapter Eighteen

For the next several days I ate, drank, and breathed my list. In little more than a week the duke would arrive, and ready or not, my life would change. Duty would take precedence over desire.

I did not even protest when Mama rushed me to and from town, as we tended to endless wedding details and finally brought home my peach dress with decidedly white lace.

But in every moment, I thought of memories to write in my journal. I recorded them between Mama's appointments and late every night by candlelight. I wrote every day until my fingers were sore and all of my memories were in ink.

Over tea one afternoon, Charlie pressed his lips together as Liza examined my fingers. He had sent over a special salve he used for his knuckles and instructed me to try it. It had worked miracles on my sore fingers.

The next day, after staring far too long at my reflection in a mirror, I had a clear vision for my self-portrait. I spent two early mornings of endless work on my easel in the garden under the soft morning light. At first, Charlie and Liza were content to lounge nearby. But Charlie grew restless. He could not sit still with a book like Liza could, so instead, he followed the gardener around, returning later with a barn cat and a host of information about which plants in the grove were edible. Eventually, both my friends agreed that my final piece was a satisfactory likeness, so we left it to dry and then sent it with Molly to be framed. I planned to give it to Mama as a gift before my wedding.

Liza warmed to the idea of helping me complete my list. Or perhaps she worried less about Charlie and things she could not control and more about simply living. So, the next day, when she paid me a call at home, I had the perfect idea already in mind.

"I've been thinking," I said, tugging her into the drawing room. I waited a beat, but no one else entered. "Where is Charlie?"

"Your brother took off with him. Something about missing their morning routine. He's been visiting Charlie more often this week, talking about honor and duty and . . ." She shuddered. "Manly things."

"Missing their morning routine?" Realization struck. Charlie was boxing again. With Ben! "I know where they are. Let me grab my hat."

"What? No!" Liza threw her hands in the air. "We are finally free of him! Let us live as we always have. Just the two of us. We can even do something natural and harmless off your list!"

I snatched my bonnet from where I'd laid it on the settee. "I need him," I said, tying the ribbons under my chin. "And he promised to help me complete my list."

I moved toward the door, but Liza grabbed my arm and spun me around. "Ros, forgive me for asking this, but I must. And you must answer me plainly."

Her eyes were serious and strained, and her grip held strong.

"Of course. Anything. What is wrong?"

She pressed her lips together, then huffed and straightened her shoulders. "Have you fallen in love with my cousin?"

I reared back. "Of course not," I blurted. It felt like the right thing, but the wheels in my mind churned. Fallen in love with Charlie?

Love. Charlie.

She watched me like I might change my mind. "I should hope not." She paused, then took a breath. "But sometimes it feels as though you care more for his company than mine."

Did I? Charlie had become a comfortable friend. But had I neglected Liza? "If that is true, then I must beg your forgiveness. Charlie is a good friend, but you are more a sister, and the only one I have. No one will ever replace you, Liza." I pulled her into an embrace. "But, dearest, unless you are willing to dig a hole, I shall need Charlie for an hour or so."

Liza pulled back with a frightened look.

"Which reminds me," I said, releasing her. "What, out of everything you possess, do you treasure most?"

"Liza and I are here!" I called out to the *pat-pat-boom* within the grove. "Make yourselves presentable and come out. We need your assistance."

The boxing sounds were exchanged with low murmurs, and within a short time, both Charlie and Ben emerged from the trees.

"What are you doing in there?" Liza asked, clearly confused as to why they both were drenched with sweat and Charlie was buttoning his waistcoat.

"Nothing," Ben said quickly, eyeing me like a rabbit caught in a trap.

Charlie dug a hand through his hair, fluffing it out. "What do you need?" he asked, looking to me.

I held up a spade. "I need a hole. Deep enough to fit a box for a very long time."

"Rosalind, can this not wait? Winston and I are busy," Ben said, enunciating the words with knowing eyes.

But a half smile lifted the corner of Charlie's mouth. "Dug where?"

"Under the flowers?" I motioned to a cluster of wild daisies to my right.

He strode close and took the spade from my hand, then said in a low voice, "After this, only two left."

"A hole for what?" Ben narrowed his gaze at me.

"I am burying treasure. Like old times." I nudged his side with my elbow. "Join us."

"Have I finally been invited to play with Ros and Liza?" he asked Liza, who took his arm and laughed.

"Never," she teased. "Now be a good little lad and go home to your lessons."

"I think I'd rather play teacher. And today's lesson," he mused, all too willing to engage with Liza's jests, "is on reptiles and amphibians. Shall we?" He motioned to the pond, then lowered his voice to a whisper in her ear. Then he pulled back. "Ros," he said, eyeing Mr. Winston at my side. He'd reverted to his adult self again. "I will be close, just by the pond, should you need me."

I wanted to look heavenward and scoff. Should I need him! But my little brother was intent on being responsible, and regardless of whether I needed his protection or not, I was proud. "Thank you, Ben."

Charlie knelt by the flowers and seemed to be measuring where to dig his spade first. "In my experience, it is best to dig wide and deep if we wish to save the flowers. Believe it or not, I learned a thing or two from the gardener the other day." He dragged the tip of his spade backward a touch, then pressed it hard into the earth. "Where is your treasure?"

"In here," I said proudly, patting my satchel.

"Do I get to add anything?" he asked. He did not look up, so I could not gauge his seriousness.

"If you wish. But you cannot expect to retrieve it any time soon."

"Or ever?" He looked up and smiled. He lifted the large clump of dirt and flowers out of the ground and set them aside.

"Perhaps."

He continued digging, while Liza and Ben ventured toward the pond. I made a note to keep an eye on whatever they were scheming.

"How deep?" Charlie asked, wiping his brow.

I bent down beside him, tugged off my lace gloves, and reached my hand down into the hole, which was not quite up to my shoulder.

"A little more."

He leaned inside, scraping dirt from all four sides of the square hole he'd created, then farther down, adding the excavated soil to a pile by the flowers. His firm back and shoulders tensed beneath his shirt as he worked, every inch of him focused and determined. All for me. He pushed the spade deeper into the earth, and he must have felt my gaze, for his eyes flicked to mine. He gave me a soft smile, a knowing one that said he understood what this meant to me. That he cared. Then he went back to work.

I looked over my shoulder to make sure Ben wasn't creeping up behind me, but when I turned back to the hole, dirt smacked me in the face.

I sputtered and wiped my face and lips with my hands.

"Drat," Charlie chuckled, rising up on his knees. He started to reach out to me but seemed to think better of it. "Forgive me, Rosalind, I hit a root."

I squinted and licked my teeth, shuddering from the subtle taste of dirt that had managed to find its way in.

Charlie bit back his smile and dug his spade into the hole.

Liza shrieked in laughter from behind us, and I whipped around to find Ben chasing after something hopping along the ground. Some things never changed.

"Finished." Charlie sat back on his heels and let out a heavy breath. "Does this depth suit you?"

I peered in. Then I pulled my box from my satchel and settled it deep inside the hole. "Perfect. Thank you."

Charlie gave me a funny look, so I gave him one back.

"You still have dirt on your face." He pointed to my cheek.

Or at least that is where I thought he indicated. I rubbed around my face. "What?"

"No." He started to laugh. I held still as he reached out. "Just . . . there." His thumb brushed my chin, just below my lip, sending heat and sparks to my chest.

His eyes met mine, and I forgot to breathe. I forgot that we were in the middle of a field, that we were anything but alone, and that mere days had passed since we had laid on our blanket, practically a sick bed, sharing our secrets across the pond from where he'd saved my life.

His thumb was still on my chin, tracing the outline of my bottom lip, and his gaze turned serious and contemplative. My knees went weak, and I started to lean into his touch.

Charlie.

How could something as simple as a touch make me feel like a different person? Maybe not different, but whole. Real and fearless. What was this feeling? And how could I keep it forever?

"Get. It. Away. From. *Me*!" Liza shrieked, and Charlie pulled back, straightening. "Rosalind!"

I jumped to my feet, my chin still tingling from Charlie's touch.

Ben chased Liza with something in his hands, while she ran toward us with her skirts hiked up in a run. He stopped short, bent over laughing, while Liza sprinted around me and behind her cousin. "I *hate* snakes!"

"Ben. Leave her be," I called, though my lips quirked.

He set the thing down close to the pond and rubbed his

hands on his breeches. "Have you finished that blasted hole yet, Winston?"

Charlie cleared his throat and tugged on his glove. "Only just."

"Ladies, if you have no further need of us," Ben said with a dismissive bow.

I held up a hand. "Wait a moment. Are you not going to bury my treasure with me? Ben, you used to love this."

"Surely you can cover the box yourself, Ros. Take off your gloves and use the spade to transfer the dirt. It is exactly like gardening." Ben threw an annoyed glance to Charlie, who laughed. It seemed the two men had decided to forget all about defending both my honor and my feelings.

Charlie turned to me. "I want to see your treasure."

I knelt again with Liza at my side and pulled out the box. I held it close and opened the lid toward me, so only I could see inside. "I collected five treasures," I said, glancing up at my three friends.

Ben looked mildly interested, just enough not to argue; Liza, more supportive than interested; and Charlie, truly curious.

"The first is an old paintbrush that Grandmama gave to me when I was a little girl. It was the first one I used when I realized how much I loved to watercolor."

The brown wooden handle was worn and chipped, and almost all the pig's hairs had fallen out of the head. Still, I laid it softly on the grass for display. "Second, a pair of lace gloves I wore to Aunt Alice's wedding."

Liza gushed over them. "Look how pretty! The lace!"

"Third," I continued, "a family portrait I drew. Fourth,

a journal entry I wrote detailing the last few weeks that shall stay private until this treasure is unearthed one day in the very distant future." I raised a brow until they all nodded their heads in agreement. "And fifth, a handful of halfpennies, which used to be enough wealth to tempt my ornery little brothers to undertake their own search for treasure."

Everyone murmured their approval, and I felt Charlie's eyes on me as I tucked each piece back into the box.

"Liza?" I prompted her. Her mission before we walked to the grove together was to find and bring a treasure of her own.

"Oh!" she startled, reaching behind her head and unclasping the chain around her neck. From the chain, she pulled off a little ivory heart. "Father brought this charm back from India. I'm adding it because I treasure all the places I've been and all the people I've met along the way."

I squeezed her arm. "That is a treasure indeed." I placed the little, smooth heart on top of my family portrait.

Ben straightened, puffing out his chest. "I have something, too."

"No," Liza shook her head. "No snake's skin. No bugs."

But Ben reached inside his coat and pulled out a pretty purple flower. "I treasure the outdoors. And all our adventures, Ros."

"Oh, Ben!" I stood and wrapped my arms around his neck. "You do love me."

"Enough, enough." He laughed and pushed me off. "Just add the thing before I take it back."

Laughing, I knelt and pressed the flower inside the journal entry I'd written.

"Charlie?" Liza asked. "Do you have something to add? Something for Ros to remember you by in ten or so years when her children dig up her treasure."

Charlie stared at my little box. Something had changed in his countenance. Frustration? Anger?

"You do not have to," I muttered. Burying treasure was silly, really. But it was on the list. "You dug the hole for me, after all."

"Ben added a flower," Liza prompted.

I shot her a warning glance. Something told me not to press Charlie.

Without a word, he slowly unwound the red-and-gold-spotted cravat from around his neck. "I shall add this."

"But you wear that all the time," I argued. He would miss it. "You can add anything. A stick from the grove. A rock from the pond." Anything that might remind him of our time together.

"This is my favorite neckcloth," he told me as he folded it. "It's called a Belcher, inspired by James Belcher, a famous pugilist who gave everything to improving his craft and helping others succeed. I respect and admire him. Much like I respect and admire you."

He held the cloth out to me, a piece of him that he wanted me to have, while willfully refusing to meet my eyes. Our fingers brushed as I took the folded neckcloth from his hand, and I felt Liza's stare measuring my reaction. Carefully, I laid it atop the other treasures. My little box had grown infinitely more valuable.

"Thank you," I said. But it wasn't enough. I wished I could embrace him and tell him exactly what he meant to me. I wished I could pull his hand back to my face and let it linger there along with his gaze and his unspoken thoughts.

My *own* thoughts were turning decidedly less friendly and decidedly more something else. Liza's question about my feelings for Charlie crept into my thoughts, but I squeezed it out just as quickly.

"It's getting late," Charlie said to Ben. "Shall we resume tomorrow morning?"

"Very well," Ben practically whined.

Charlie was abandoning the grove? Without complaint? "Certainly we could find some sort of adventure to occupy our afternoon," I countered.

"Not *this* afternoon," Charlie said. "I shall grab the satchels."

"I can get mine," Ben added, following Charlie into the grove.

"Do not take it personally, Ros. Charlie is still angry about this morning," Liza said, sinking with me to her knees as the men disappeared behind the trees.

"What happened this morning?" Something must have made him miss his usual early-morning lesson with Ben, which explained why they were out so late in the day. With my bare hand, I carefully placed my closed box into the hole Charlie had dug.

"He got a letter from his mother." She handed me the spade. "They are reinstating his funds and letting him live in a separate house nearby. They also promised not to interfere in his hobbies, but only if he comes round and engages in part-time work on the estate."

My heart stopped beating and fell into my stomach. Charlie was leaving. "Now?"

"He may leave at first light. But he refuses."

Sudden relief blew through me. But I should not be relieved. I should be upset. Home is where he needed to be. Where he should be.

I scooped the dirt and covered the box. "Why would he refuse?"

She shrugged. "Charlie was not keen on discussing it further. Papa lectured him on honor and duty and told him that regardless of his feelings, he needed to step into his role for the sake of his family."

I gave up on the spade and pushed the cool dirt into the hole with my hands. "What did Charlie say to that?"

"I should not repeat it."

I could all too easily imagine his lips set in a line and the conflicted crease along his brow. I tried not to think on his response.

We filled the hole and replanted the flowers, and when we were finished, no one would have guessed a treasure was buried beneath.

Liza let out a heavy sigh. "He knows what he needs to do. And I imagine it is hard. He loved Henry so much."

"Perhaps he needs a few days to mull it over." I replaced my glove on my hand.

"Ros, he's had plenty of time to mull things over." Liza tilted her head as we stood and dusted off our skirts.

"He'll come round," I said. "I know he will."

A little while later, Ben and Charlie emerged from the grove with satchels hung over their shoulders. Liza, Ben, and

I set off toward the bend where we'd part ways for home. I noticed Charlie lagging behind, digging through his satchel, so I held back.

"You are deep in thought," I said as he secured his bag and walked toward me. "I hesitate to engage you."

His lips twitched. "I have had a difficult day."

"Impossible. I am here," I teased. "And we have checked yet another thing off our list."

"*Our* list?" He cast me that funny look again.

My cheeks warmed, and I strode beside him, looking out in the distance. "You know what I mean." We walked in silence for a beat. Then, because I could not stop myself, I said, "You can confide in me, Charlie."

He sighed and swallowed hard. "My parents are being unreasonable again."

"Liza told me," I admitted. "I want to feel sorry for you, but I am simply too confident in your future."

His smile finally broke free.

"Speaking of which, you still have not told me what your original plans were for yourself. What did you study at university?"

My question seemed to take him off guard. He blinked and looked over his shoulder as though whatever he had to say was a closely guarded secret. Then he looked back at me. "I wanted to be an architect."

"You?"

"I wanted to design and build things."

"I know what an architect is, Charlie."

He grinned at my dry tone and tugged my arm through his. My stomach tightened, and my heart picked up its pace.

All in one swooping rush, there was only us. Charlie and Rosalind.

"My professor thought me quite skilled," he admitted proudly.

I squeezed his arm. I had no doubt. "Did you have any commissions?"

"I never got far enough along, but I'd have liked to."

"I should like to see your work. Do you have any sketches?"

He seemed both surprised and pleased. "I do. My mother sent me to her parents' estate one summer, and I helped my grandfather design an addition to his stables."

"I've met your grandparents. They came to visit Ivy Manor long ago. Their estate is in Dover, is it not?"

"Yes, not too far from here." He looked down at me, and I swore his eyes rested on my lips.

"It must be a half day's drive." I watched his lips, mesmerized by some new and unfamiliar pull. Charlie was my friend. But he was also a man. A very attractive, very compelling man.

He turned his head and looked forward. "A little less."

I shook my head to clear it. Dover. We were speaking of Dover.

That would be a perfect place to visit, so close to the sea.

I sucked in a little breath.

Oh, but I couldn't. Mama needed me here to continue preparations for the wedding. *My* wedding. Not to mention the issue of propriety and the risk of leaving home with a handsome, unattached man, even if he came with a domineering cousin.

Then again, I was nearly of age. Months away, really. And Charlie was just a friend. *Just a friend* because I was engaged to the duke. And friends could travel together, could they not?

"I've just had the grandest idea," I said.

Charlie furrowed his brow. "I am afraid to ask."

I mentally checked my schedule to be certain. The duke would not arrive for another five days. This one would be risky, but I'd known as much when I'd written it on my list.

"Charles Winston, would you like to run away with me tomorrow?"

Chapter Nineteen

Charlie looked as though he were facing down the barrel of a loaded gun. "We? You mean, *us*. Together?"

"And with Liza, *of course*."

He let out a heavy breath and placed his hands on his hips. "Of course." He cleared his throat and shook his head, and I pinched my lips to keep from laughing. "But where shall we go?"

"To your grandparents. We shall be perfectly safe there."

His face grew serious. "Ros, I cannot think they will be pleased to see me at present."

I cast him a frown. "Whyever not?"

"We have hardly spoken since we laid Henry to rest. Per their last letter, which I did not return, they are just as disappointed in my neglecting my father's estate as my parents are."

"Then what a perfect opportunity for you to make amends. You shall need to prepare the carriage here, or else Mama will know and stop us before we've even begun." Distracted by my thoughts, I quickened my pace.

"Rosalind," Charlie called. "As much as I support your list, this idea will not suit me."

"Are you afraid?" I taunted.

He drew back and swallowed. "Of course not. After everything that happened at the picnic, I question the propriety of myself as a companion for you . . . and Liza. Not to mention the fact that your brother said—"

I waved a hand in the air. "I shall manage Benjamin."

"I have only just earned back his trust," Charlie argued. "Perhaps we should tell him about the list. He could come along."

"I love Ben, but he is my little brother. If I tell him about my list, he'll ruin it with ridicule. Besides, he has too many responsibilities on the estate to run away." And I simply did not want him there.

"But I *promised* him—"

"He does not want us to be alone, and we shan't be," I said. "Liza is of age, and I am not far behind. It is perfectly reasonable. Pack for overnight. I shall leave a letter for Ben, and he will tell my parents."

"—such short notice—" Charlie muttered.

"Running away is thrilling, is it not?" I smiled.

But Charlie frowned back, stopping me in my tracks. "You expect Liza will come willingly? And that your brother will not have my head upon our return?"

"Why would Liza not want to visit your grandparents? Besides, the two of *you* do not have to tiptoe around to get yourselves there. Make your arrangements, and I shall simply sneak inside your carriage as you set your course. No harm will come from it. I promise, Charlie."

He licked his lips. "You could go anywhere. Choose any-thing. Why my grandparents' estate?"

Well, I wanted to see Charlie amongst his family, for one. I wanted to help him heal his family relationships. I wanted to *give* him something after he had given me so much. I could stand beside him while he faced his fears. It would be a small step forward—incredibly small—but it was something.

"I simply wish to be with my friends for a time."

He looked heavenward and back down to me. "How can I say no to that?"

"You cannot," I said matter-of-factly.

"All right then. Let us go and convince my cousin."

I held my candle up to the glass to read the clock; it was nearly four in the morning. The Ollertons' carriage would be waiting at the end of the drive for me.

I left a note addressed to Ben on my bed for Molly to deliver when she discovered my absence. I'd only written the barest details, saying that I'd gone with Liza and Charlie for an overnight stay in an unnamed, safe location with family, and that, seeing as we'd moved past the events of the after-noon picnic, I hoped he could grant me enough trust for this last wish.

I'd be back before he had time to worry.

Then I grabbed my rather heavy bag, packed with exactly a day's worth of necessities, and my satchel with anything else I thought I might need, and blew out my candle.

I tiptoed down the dark hall, straining my ears for any

sound of movement around me. It was too early for anyone else to be awake, but Ben had surprised me once before.

I'd just reached the stairs when I heard a cough echo from somewhere behind me. Frozen with one hand on the banister, I looked back. A moment stretched out into a lifetime with a thousand silent breaths, but nothing more.

I was halfway there. Stealing away like a thief, but with only my list and my dreams to take with me.

I took a slow step down the first stair. Then another, and another, until I was sure I could continue without drawing attention. Somehow, I managed to make my way to the entry. My feet glided silently across the wide-open space with haste, for I feared someone might jump out and discover me.

But I was quite alone. I stopped with my hand on the doorknob.

Was I risking too much? Would Mama and Father lose their heads when they discovered me gone? Would they rush to retrieve me? It would all be over then, this sense of independence I'd found through my list. This quest for something more from my life, for happiness and wholeness that every woman needed before stepping forward into the rest of her life.

I only had this moment, this one last chance, to create that feeling for myself.

I pushed through the door and into the darkness of a new morning. I stopped on the step and drew fresh air into my lungs as I closed the door behind me.

I'd be back tomorrow. Indeed, I would hardly miss my bed, and yet, as I gave the house one last backward glance, I felt an unexpected sense of freedom.

Down a few stairs, then gravel crunched beneath my footsteps, and the morning chill bit at my cheeks as I hurried down the drive. I could barely make out the lanterns from the Ollertons' carriage and the figure descending from the cab as I approached.

Charlie.

He yawned and covered his mouth, sidestepping for the coachman to place a step for me. I thanked him for the extra work he oversaw as the only servant on the journey.

"Morning," Charlie said behind his hand. His eyes were tired and still swollen from sleep, and everything about him was utterly endearing.

"Good morning," I replied with a grin. My own exhaustion begged me to draw nearer to him. I imagined curling into his warmth, burying my face in the soft space where his neck met his shoulder and falling asleep to leather and woods and *Charlie*. It would be heaven.

"What?" Charlie watched me closely.

"Nothing," I said, turning my head and shaking the thought away. Nothing I could say aloud.

The coachman took my bag and moved around to the back of the carriage to secure it with the others already there. Liza had likely packed for a week. When we'd asked her about a visit to her grandparents, she'd enthusiastically agreed. But when I'd mentioned the list, and the secrecy it required, I had to also promise her my undying servitude and a rich husband and to never ask another thing of her ever again in this lifetime before she'd agreed to come. Even then, I worried she might change her mind.

Charlie offered me a hand up into the carriage.

Liza leaned back in her corner, motioning for me to sit beside her. "Remind me again why we chose to leave so early."

"We are maximizing our time," Charlie said as he entered, taking the bench opposite us. Judging from his tone, his opinions sided more with Liza's.

"Cheer up, you two," I chided. "This is exciting. I have never done anything so bold. We shall be at your grandmother's house in six hours, where we shall sea bathe and sightsee and picnic."

"No more swimming, no more picnicking," Liza muttered as she leaned her head against the wall of the carriage. "I've kept you two out of trouble thus far"—she squinted at us in turn—"at least from Society. And I intend on getting us back home unscathed."

I nodded obediently and covered my yawn.

Charlie shifted in his seat. "If I am permitted to stay, there is a walking path I want to show you, Ros."

Liza snorted. "You must be permitted into your own grandparents' house, Charlie? If that does not encourage you to change, I cannot think of what would."

He frowned, so I offered him an encouraging smile, and said, "I shall look forward to it."

With morning light still yet to break the horizon, and a swaying carriage, we each took turns dozing for the first hour before stopping to rest our horses. By then, the sun had risen, and the air seemed clearer the closer we got to the sea.

Outside my window, tall grass swayed in distant fields against an endless blue sky. Green mixed with yellow met blue speckled with white. My fingers itched for my brush. I could feel the air changing. It made my heart pound faster, and a giddy excitement created knots in my stomach.

Charlie read his paper, distracted occasionally by my bouncing knees, and Liza worked on embroidering a red rose on a pillowcase she'd brought along. Halfway through the drive, we stopped again to switch horses, and Charlie took a short walk in the woods to stretch his legs. When he came back, he had six daisies for each of us.

"Save them for Grandmama," Liza had said. "She is the one you need to impress."

And so, when we finally arrived at Teague House, a square brick house with three rows of windows lining the front and four columns at its entrance, the hour was half past ten.

Charlie glanced out the window at the perfectly pruned, round green bushes that lined the drive. He gathered his flowers, and I gave him a ribbon from my satchel to tie them with.

"You look nervous," I said when Charlie stepped out and offered me his hand.

"He is shaking," Liza added, though she seemed to take pleasure in the idea.

Charlie rolled his shoulders. "I am not."

"What, do you think she will rap you with her cane?" Liza's lips quirked up. "Or pluck your tongue out?"

I tried not to laugh, but the horror on Charlie's face was far too rich.

"Rosalind?" He held his hand up higher, clearly wishing for me to descend so he would not have to face his grandparents alone.

"It is about time!" A shrill, old voice called from ahead.

I glanced up to find Mrs. Harrelson waiting at the door. She was as finely dressed and with as much exuberance as one could have at her age. "Your letter arrived an hour ago, and the whole house has been in shambles preparing. It is not good form to give such little notice, Eliza."

"Forgive us, Grandmama," Liza called, skipping ahead to greet her. "We wanted to escape Ivy Manor and could think of no better place to visit."

I looked over my shoulder to where Charlie walked a few paces behind. His hands were behind his back, and his face had turned serious and brooding.

Liza embraced her grandmama, and I slowed to walk beside Charlie. He looked like he was trudging up to the gallows.

"Chin up, friend," I said. "Go and embrace your grandmama."

He gave me a sideways glance, hesitant but hopeful.

"And who have you brought?" Mrs. Harrelson asked Liza, though she kept her eyes on Charlie.

He drew in a long breath, then took off his topper. "Grandmother. I have missed you."

"Charles?" Her eyes widened, and Liza stepped back to make room on the square veranda. He climbed the few stairs and hesitated as he approached her. Our collective breath seemed to stall, and I prayed with every fiber in my being for her to receive him kindly.

"You are alive," she said, though it sounded more like a question. "And you look well."

"Thank you, Grandmother," Charlie replied. "As do you."

She stared at him for a moment, and I swallowed. Surely

she would invite him in? I moved beside Liza, who wrapped her hand around my arm. We waited and watched with bated breath.

"Well, then," his grandmother said, raising her chin. "I do not see what all the fuss back home is about."

Charlie swallowed. "I have made some poor choices, Grandmother."

A touch of grace lifted her lips. "You have indeed."

"And I am sorry for the pain and disappointment I have caused you and Grandfather."

"Very good." She held out her arms and drew him near, until she embraced him fully. "Let us not waste any more time discussing the matter, then."

Charlie's shoulders relaxed, and he bent into her embrace, his chin dropping to her shoulder. He almost looked like a freshly reprimanded little boy, but that could not be right. Mrs. Harrelson had wasted no time forgiving him for his past wrongdoings. Indeed, the love I'd just witnessed was perhaps the purest form a person could give.

Charlie sniffed, and a slightest smile lit up his face.

No, it was not sadness he bore.

It was humility. Never before had I seen as strong a man as Charlie humbled by so fragile a woman.

Mrs. Harrelson turned to me. "Miss Newbury, welcome to Teague House. And might I congratulate you on a match well made."

Surprised to be so suddenly addressed, I stumbled forward in some semblance of a curtsey. "Thank you, Mrs. Harrelson."

"Eliza, you've the same room as always. I trust you and

Miss Newbury can find your way there to freshen up. I shall ring for tea."

Liza nodded and pulled me toward the house. We'd made it. We were here. I had run away from home, and no one had stopped me yet.

Had Benjamin discovered my letter? Had he told Mama? Surely she would speak with Mrs. Ollerton, confirm my departure, but there would be little more for her to do except wait for my return.

Before we entered the house, I tugged back on Liza's hold just long enough to hear Mrs. Harrelson say to Charlie, "I do not ever again want to hear of your living in some ratty apartment. No matter what you do, you will always be welcome here."

Chapter Twenty

Our empty teacups clinked as we placed them back on the tray. Mr. Harrelson arrived home from an early-morning ride soon after our arrival, and, after a brief conversation with Charlie in his study, seemed as pleased as Mrs. Harrelson was to have us visiting.

Although, they had no idea I had stowed away without permission from my parents. Honestly, I had thought I would feel more guilty on the matter, but I was having so much fun with Liza and Charlie and the Harrelsons, I had no time to waste on worrying. Mama's fleeting anger would be an easy price to pay for two days of fun. And with Mrs. Harrelson, we already had more than enough opportunities to fill our time.

"The masquerade is this evening. When I received your letter, I sent a servant to purchase your tickets and secure proper masks."

"Grandmama!" Liza sounded surprised, but her eyes were alight with interest. A ball of any sort meant connections. "A masquerade?"

Charlie cast me a look. "How scandalous." He was thinking the same thing as I was. Number ten.

"We do not masquerade as they do in London, dear. Though still public, this will be a smaller event. Your evening clothes will have to suffice."

Liza clasped her hands together and grinned. "Actually, I prepared for just such an occasion. I brought two gowns, Ros! You can wear the red."

"The young earl of Langdon will also be in attendance, Charles, as his country home is just north of town." Mrs. Harrelson looked down her nose. "You will have a perfect chance to apologize for breaking his arm, should you find him amongst the crush."

Charlie nodded solemnly, and I gave him a smile of encouragement.

"But for now, I am certain you wish to explore the estate." Her eyes seemed to sparkle toward Liza and me.

"There is no finer place," Liza said.

Mrs. Harrelson smiled. "It seems like just yesterday I had to pry both you girls out of the trees at Ivy Manor." Her eyes held a faraway look. "You were searching for birds' nests to see if any of their eggs had hatched."

Liza and I exchanged a glance, then covered our respective laughs.

"I should like to see your gardens, Grandmama," Liza said. "Mama and I cannot for our lives get our roses to bloom as full as yours do."

"Perhaps you are overcrowding them, dear. Neither of my daughters, neither your mama nor Charlie's, has any sense with botany." She started to stand, and Charlie rose to her aid. "Come, let me show you what can be done."

"I think I shall take Miss Newbury on a walk, Grandmother," Charlie said, and my eyes flew to his. Did he mean to sound so bold? "With your permission, of course."

"My permission?" Mrs. Harrelson raised a brow. "I should think it is *her* permission you require."

"Alone?" Liza wrinkled her forehead, and I could not tell if she was more unhappy or confused.

"What do you say, Miss Newbury? I think you will enjoy the sight." Charlie seemed as carefree as usual, and I saw no harm in the matter.

I shrugged. "A walk sounds delightful."

"Perfect." He smiled. He handed his grandmother off to Liza and strode to my side.

"Not too far, Charles," Mrs. Harrelson said as she moved slowly toward the door with Liza. "Stay within sight of the house or take a chaperone."

"We shall remain visible," he said, placing his hat atop his head. With land so flat, it was almost hard *not* to be visible.

We followed Liza and Mrs. Harrelson outside along the exterior of the house, parting ways at the garden, which was colored in all shades of green with the most stunning flowers. As Liza drew in a breath and bent over each bush to examine them, Charlie nodded sideways to me, and we turned toward an open space in the distance.

Everything was green, until Charlie led me down a beaten dirt path, where the same tall, yellowing grass I'd seen from the carriage swayed on either side of our path. A cool, salty breeze enlivened our lungs and drew us forward.

Out here, without the watchful eyes of Society and Mama's relentless planning and perfecting, I was free.

"We could not have asked for a lovelier day," I said, tilting back my hat to feel the warm sun on my face.

Charlie walked beside me with a new bounce to his step. "No, indeed."

"Nor a happier welcoming."

Charlie grinned. "Nor better company."

I laughed. "You are in a rather good mood."

"Forgiveness changes a person, Rosalind," he said like a vicar to his congregation. "I am a changed man."

I stole ahead of him and cut him off. "Never to do wrong again?"

"Never," he declared, taking a step toward me. His eyes were playful and bright.

"Shall I test you?" I pursed my lips to keep from smiling. "Just to be certain the old Charlie is not hidden away somewhere in there."

I looked down at his chest, which was a grand mistake. A sudden flame ignited all through me.

"Be my guest," he said, his eyes traveling my face with a measure of humor. Did he know how handsome he was?

"All right. Perhaps we should travel a little farther from the house than we'd planned. Out of sight?" I teased. Then I flushed. I hadn't meant to sound so flirtatious; I was engaged, for heaven's sake! My gaze flew to Charlie's, and the slow curve of his lips. He laughed and wiped a hand over his mouth.

"Rosalind Newbury, are you trying to scandalize me? We have the masquerade for that."

Heat seeped from my cheeks. "What? No, that is not at all—"

"I mean I am flattered," he continued, straightening his jacket. "And in truth, you are a Prime Article. But, darling, you are engaged. And you are not the type to play a man's heart and leave him moon-eyed and alone."

"No," I said in a flat, sarcastic voice as though we were truly discussing the matter. "I am not."

"So, under these circumstances"—he tried to look put out—"my answer is no. As I am now a changed man."

"I see." Try as I might not to smile, his cocky attitude fit him like a glove, and it was either concede or slap him straight on.

"Now, had you asked me a few days ago . . ."

"Charles Winston!" I shoved him sideways, and he laughed.

"What? I am only a man."

"An annoying, nonsensical man. I was *jesting*."

He regained his footing, moving closer to my side. "No, you were not," he muttered.

I caught his laughing eyes and huffed. Of course I was joking. He and I would never suit.

"Can you taste the sea yet?" he asked. The terrain had become rocky and rough. "We are nearly there."

"Does the walking path run all the way down?" We shouldn't climb down. The house was already too far away.

He looked instantly contrite. "No. But the view ahead is incredible."

I furrowed my brow. "Charlie, where exactly are you taking me?"

He kept to my pace and stole a sideways glance. "There is a cliff—"

"A cliff?" My heart stuttered, and I stopped walking altogether. "Heights are not on the list, Charlie. As you are well aware."

"Please?" He ducked his chin. "I want you to experience this, and I promise to keep you safe. Let this view be my gift to you."

"For what?" I narrowed my eyes.

He shrugged. "For being *you*."

His words were so simple, so plain, but the earnestness in his eyes somehow cut through my fears, warming me through.

I wanted to oblige him, to make him happy. I wanted, despite my fears, to share a memory, a view, that was just ours. I took a few steps. "Well, then, this better be good," I called over my shoulder.

He chuckled and followed closely.

More of the sky came into sight the longer we walked, and my thinly stretched nerves shredded into pieces. Charlie had seen me at my worst before, but still I wanted my dignity. Perhaps the drop would not be as dizzying as I feared. But if it was, I would not let Charlie see my terror. I paced faster, hurrying ahead.

"Be careful," Charlie called from behind. "The cliffs are incredibly steep. Stay far back, Rosalind. I mean it."

I believed him, but I had no idea how true his words were until, at last, the sea came into view. Spreading out as endlessly as the sky, more and more blue appeared far down below where I stood. I sensed the edge before I realized how close it was, and the awareness of danger prickled at my skin. Wind from the sea pushed me back as fear spread into every muscle, every limb, and I trembled, paralyzed with the thought that one single gust might tip me over.

"It is beautiful, is it not?" Charlie said when he reached my side, watching the edge all the while. Then he saw my face, and his excitement turned to worry.

"Rosalind? Are you breathing?"

"I cannot move," I managed. My body shook with tremors. "I cannot move, Charlie."

His eyes locked with mine, and his hands held my arms. "You can, Ros. I am here."

I nodded, but my jaw was shaking too much for a response.

"Did you look over the edge?"

I shook my head. I could not even if I wanted to.

"Will you? If I help you?"

"I shall c-certainly fall," I said. "Please, Charlie, take me back home. This is not safe."

"You won't fall." He almost laughed but seemed to think better of it. "I will take you back home if you wish it, but I do not want you to miss this. Will you trust me?"

His eyes bored into mine. When we first met, I'd thought him anything but safe. But now? He'd been my most trusted companion these past weeks.

"Of course I trust you."

"Then take my hand. I promise to keep you safe."

His hand slid down my arm and wrapped around my fingers. I grasped hold of him, leaning against his side. His warmth was a welcome distraction. I concentrated on my breath, holding tightly to both his hand and his arm. With every half step we took, the sea reached closer, but my eyes focused on the grass at my feet. My legs felt like jelly.

"T-terrifying. Just as I thought," I said through a shaking jaw before pressing my face into his shoulder.

"Now, look straight down," Charlie said, his voice steady. "I have you."

I glanced up to his face and was met with an encouraging smile. I could smell leather and woods and the freshness of his shave; then I pulled back and leaned ever so slightly forward.

The view took my breath away.

White foam from the incoming sea crested the sandy shore. We were higher than the trees. Higher than crashing waves and flying birds.

We were limitless. Infinite. A part of something so big, so wide, so all-encompassing, we mattered about as much as a single blade of grass. A piece of the most beautiful landscape in the world breathed with life right in front of us.

"Charlie." I covered my mouth with a hand. My fear seemed to wash away with the rolling waves far below us. "Oh my goodness, Charlie. Look at that."

He laughed. "You see?"

"I have never seen anything so beautiful in all my life," I said, taking a single step closer. Charlie kept firm hold of my hand.

"Look at the sea hitting those rocks, how the water soars and sprays," he said as he pointed out in the distance.

I watched the sea rise in and out with each wave, heard the roar of the water. Birds flew above, seeking fish and a drink. Life moved and grew and changed.

Charlie and I stood on the edge of the cliff in silent appreciation, connected by our hands and our thoughts. Time seemed to stop, and I forgot to be afraid.

We walked a few paces for a different view. I pointed out something swimming far in the distance, and Charlie noted a couple of birds fighting on the shore.

"How do you feel?" he asked.

"I do not want you to let go of my hand," I said, tightening my grip.

He grinned. "But you are happy?"

I nodded. "I am very happy."

He started to move behind me. "What if—"

"Charlie." I tightened my hold. "Charles Winston, don't you dare leave me here alone."

"What if I just moved behind you?"

I turned with him, but then I realized my back faced the cliff and I could step off and fall at any moment. I reached out for Charlie, who took my hands but kept me at a distance.

"I will be right behind you."

"No," I begged. What would happen if I slipped? He'd never reach me in time. "No, no. I cannot do this. I am too afraid."

He held my hands between us. "I disagree. You are, without a doubt, the bravest woman I have ever met. You do not need my hand, nor anyone else's, to stand tall and face your fears. You have proven that since the day I met you."

Emotion tightened my throat, and I raised my chin. I did not believe him, but I wanted to. I wanted to prove I was as brave as he thought I was. I wanted to be the woman Charlie saw when he looked at me.

He placed his hand on my shoulder, and gently, slowly, he turned me around to face the cliff. The waves crashed tumultuously against rock and sand, rising higher on the shore. Charlie released my arms, and I took a step forward to steady myself against a sudden, fervent wind that took my breath away. I froze, unsteady and rife with anxiety, but I pushed air through my nose, trying to focus on the beauty and endlessness of the scene in front of me.

I hadn't realized how tightly I held my middle until Charlie's voice sounded near my ear. "See?" His voice was filled with pride. "Now let your shoulders relax. Let go, completely."

His arms wrapped around me, and my stomach clenched as heat and thrills swirled inside me at his touch. He unwound my arms and carefully placed them at my sides.

I resisted the urge to draw back my arms and hold myself tight. Instead, I fisted my hands and dug my feet into the ground to keep from feeling like I was falling—or floating—away.

"Close your eyes and feel the wind."

My mind screamed in opposition. My very nature begged for me to step backward, not to test fate or push the limits of safety. Then again, I had not moved any closer to the cliff's edge. I uncurled my fingers and stretched out my arms, and, after a few steady breaths, when I was certain my feet were on safe ground, I closed my eyes and lifted my face to the sky.

The wind brushed through me, over and under and around, untamed and free. My hair tangled and flew into my face, my skirts fluttered recklessly in every direction, and, to my surprise, I laughed. I felt like I could lie back and float away just as I had in the pond.

I opened my eyes and found Charlie, who stood beside me, watching me with his arms across his wide chest. He grinned, and I reached for him and pulled him close to my side. We both stood with our arms outstretched, open and vulnerable, feeling as close to the heavens as a person on land could.

In time, my arms tired, and I let them fall, but I did not cower in fear. This sight was special, sacred even, enough to change a person's view of life forever.

"Thank you," I said, trying to infuse everything I felt into the words. "For bringing me here."

We both looked once more at the sea before turning back toward the path that led home.

"Thank *you*," he responded. His smile turned serious. "You—and that list of yours—are the reason we are here. I do not think I believe in fate, but meeting you feels so inspired, I almost wonder if such a thing exists."

I kept hold of his arm, and he did not seem to mind. "I could not have done any of this without you. I'd have surely drowned in the pond or been caught trying to hang my own painting."

"Or died of too many sweets." Charlie laughed.

"Yes, or that," I agreed on a laugh. "I am in your debt."

His humor slowly faded. "Then I suppose it is lucky for you that I am a changed man, or else I might call upon you for payment."

Heaven knew I owed the man. "Oh? And what does the great Charles Winston dream of?"

He glanced sideways at me. "Many things."

I studied his profile and the cut on his brow that had almost completely healed. His old bruises were long gone. With time, the shadows left by Ben's hand would be even less apparent than they were now. Distant memories. My gaze fell to his parted lips, and I swallowed hard.

"Such as?"

"A wife," Charlie said, looking me straight on. "I want a wife. And a family of my own."

It was my turn to look ahead. "Surely not. You like to live alone. It is why you left home in the first place."

"I left home because I did not know what else to do. I thought that if I lived for myself, I could determine the outcome of *my* future and forsake those around me. But you have reminded me that life does not work that way."

"So you will go home?" I asked.

Why did the thought give me pause? I should be thrilled for him, ecstatic for his claim to the happiness he deserved. But the source of my enthusiasm felt like a flickering flame instead of a burning fire.

"I will make a home out of the future I have been given. And I will be grateful that I have the opportunity at all."

I wanted to tell him how right his choice was, and how happy I was for him, but knowing he was ready to go home meant he was ready to leave me, and the words got stuck in my throat.

"You *have* changed," I said instead.

"Don't go looking all smug. You cannot claim me for your list."

I laughed. "You would not fit anyway. You've not *really* changed. You've just found yourself again."

Charlie nodded and smiled. "I might allow myself one last night without responsibility."

"Ah, yes. The masquerade. Where anyone is anyone, and no one will be the wiser for it."

"Who will you choose to be?"

Our pace had slowed, and I looked up at his watchful eyes. I finally knew who I wanted to be. But that girl could not marry the duke. That girl would break promises and duty and cause disappointment and grief to her family.

So I said the only thing I could: "I do not know."

Chapter Twenty-One

Liza's red gown was indeed a little tight, but not uncomfortably so. After attending to Liza, Mrs. Harrelson's lady's maid pinned back my hair and left curls dangling down my temples. When she finished, I held a gold mask up to my face. It covered my eyes and hid the upper half of my face. Liza helped me tie it on, then fluffed out the glittering golden feathers on one side.

Covered in gold, I could hardly recognize myself.

Liza's mask was similar, but in silver, and she wore a pale-pink gown. She was all business, looking in the mirror to apply rouge to her lips.

"We will all stay together," she said for the tenth time. "At the masquerade I attended in London, there were too many people to count. Even the gardens were full of unrecognizables."

I nodded. "I forget you survived an entire Season in London."

"Yet you're the one with the perfect engagement." She

pressed her lips together and made a hopeless face in the mirror.

I joined her and spoke to her reflection. "One day soon your time will come. Then your cousin and I shall have to keep *you* out of trouble."

She smiled, stood from her seat, and turned to face me. "I shall give you the greatest headache of your life after all you've put me through."

"I promise to make it up to you. Tonight we shall find you a second son to dance with," I said in jest. "Or perhaps even a *first*."

She huffed as though such a thing was a chore. "Tonight, let us enjoy ourselves without worrying about love or our futures," she said. Then she lowered her voice despite our being quite alone. "But do *not* let anyone drag you off into an alcove. I learned in London that men who hide away in alcoves only want one thing, Ros."

"Absolutely not. I am engaged," I said. But "engaged" had become a word with little meaning. It was more an adjective, a happy word that one could take or leave when attached to a noun, and it was definitely less attached to me than it had once been.

I tried to concern myself with what that meant, with why, despite my nearly completed list and ever-growing happiness, I cared less and less for my intended.

And more and more for someone else entirely.

But at present, my mind was filled with one thing: What *did* men want to do in alcoves?

"Not to worry," I assured her. "Charlie will be with us."

She frowned. "It is him I worry about the most. Amongst light-skirts and commonplace minds."

"*Liza*!" I laughed. "You should not speak with such a tongue. Charlie is rubbing off on you."

She had the decency to flush. "You know it as well as I."

"He would be the first to admit his faults. That is the difference between him and the commonplace minds you speak of. He will keep us safe."

She pursed her lips and took one last look in the mirror, patting her hair with a hand. "Let us hope no one comes to ruin tonight."

Oh, but I wanted to witness such a scandal. The excitement! The intrigue! Would the masquerade alone be enough to fulfill that wish?

I followed her out the door and to the staircase, where she stopped short. "Oh, Charlie! You look so handsome," she said, rushing down the stairs.

I stopped at the top, and then I saw him. Charlie's hair was brushed back, his clothes sleek and sharp, and he wore a simple black-fabric mask across his eyes. He grinned as he received her, talking low and out of earshot. Mr. and Mrs. Harrelson entered the small entry space, eagerly complimenting their granddaughter.

I started my descent, glad to be overshadowed by Liza for a change. But when I looked back up, I had Charlie's full attention. His lips were parted as his gaze washed over me—my face, my hair, down my neck and to my dress, which swayed as I slowly took each step. He let out a puff of air, then his eyes met mine and he chewed his lower lip.

"You are vision, Miss Newbury." His voice was raspy as he gave me his hand.

"Is she not?" Liza said, stepping between us, forcing Charlie to drop my hand. She threaded one arm through his, and one through mine. "Are you sure you cannot join us, Grandmama?"

Mrs. Harrelson batted her eyes at her granddaughter. "I am old, dearest. Tired. I will be much happier hearing of your fun in the morning."

"Charles," Mr. Harrelson said gruffly.

Charlie stood a little taller. "I shall keep watch over them all evening, Grandfather."

He pursed his lips but gave a smile and a nod. "See that you do."

"Shall we?" Liza looked between us.

Instead of sitting beside me in the carriage like she usually did, she sat on Charlie's bench. After we'd arrived at the masquerade, she took both our arms in the same fashion, separating us again. Charlie looked amused, but I grew frustrated at her obvious attempt to separate Charlie and me.

What harm did she see in our friendship? Perhaps I was imagining things. Perhaps Liza simply felt excluded.

I mulled over these thoughts, which weighed so heavily in my mind that I did not look up until we were already at the building.

Women roamed the terrace dressed in Grecian and Egyptian costumes, and the men wore domino robes, or false beards and beast-like masks, all while sipping their drinks and laughing boisterously with their company.

"There's a pretty one," one man said pointedly as we passed.

For a moment, I thought Charlie might lose all sense and hurl himself at the man, but Liza tugged us both forward until we found the ballroom. A small orchestra played the waltz, and couples danced together in the center of the room.

"Thank heavens we missed the waltz," Liza said.

Charlie looked at me with an apologetic gaze. "Scandalous, to be sure."

Then a man in a domino mask and cloak approached us, bowing. "Good evening, friends. This set is almost through. Might I have the pleasure of the next with"—his gaze landed on Liza—"you, *ma cherie?*"

Liza cast me a worried look, but to decline would mean she'd have to sit out the entire evening, so she nodded her acceptance. "Do not leave this room," she ordered us in a whisper as the domino led her out to the dance floor.

Charlie and I were an arm's-length apart, and neither of us knew quite what to say with Liza gone. She'd worked hard to keep us separated since we'd left Teague House, and all I knew was I had not liked it one bit.

"Her strings are wound much too tightly this evening," I teased. "We must find a way to help her relax."

Charlie laughed. "I think I have one more nefarious notion up my sleeve. But for now, could I tempt you to dance with me?"

I took his hand in answer and let him lead me to our spot for the dance. We were of the minority who'd forgone a full costume, wearing only our evening dress clothes and simple masks. Others had dressed to the nines and were, if I were wagering a guess, completely unrecognizable.

Music filled the room once more, and Charlie and I danced ourselves silly. My stomach ached from laughter as we flew around the room, meeting in passing and exchanging jokes in between. I did not have to tell him that I thought the gentleman beside me looked more like a rat than a horse for him to guess my thoughts and laugh alongside me.

Breathless, Charlie asked for another set, and I happily agreed.

Our conversation flowed, even as interrupted as it was, and when the second set came to an end, I found I did not wish to leave the ballroom.

My wish came true when I saw Liza take the hand of a handsome-looking gentleman dressed in expensive wool in lieu of a costume. She waved us off with a happier smile than she'd had when dancing with the domino.

Charlie left me near the wall to fetch some drinks.

"You are a saint," I said when he returned. I took a long, unladylike gulp.

He grinned, gulping down his own. "I'd ask you to dance again, but others might wonder about my intentions, and I do not think you wish to be a part of that type of scandal."

I bit my lip. "Three sets with the same partner is not as scandalous as four."

"Still, Liza would not like it."

"Liza seems quite distracted, Charlie."

He clearly was trying to hold back his smile, as though he did not want me to see how happy the idea made him. He held out his hand.

Another round of dancing, and my feet were killing me. Empty seats in the corner offered a welcome respite, and Charlie gave me his handkerchief to dab my face with. Then he stood and perused the room for Liza. We found her with a lemonade in her hand, laughing happily with the same well-dressed gentleman she'd been dancing with in full view of the party.

"What shall we do with that girl?" I asked, shaking my head like an old mama.

"Marry her off," Charlie said. He crossed his leg and tilted his head toward mine. "But what shall we do with ourselves? Shall I ask one of those potentially handsome women to dance the next set?"

We looked at each other and shared a private thought. I did not want him to dance with anyone else, despite that being the polite thing to do. In truth, this would be my last ball without my title. I wanted to have Charlie all to myself, checking off my list like we always did. After all, I was not quite finished.

"I think your grandmother was right. This party is not as improper as I expected. Where are the couples escaping to the gardens?"

"Hidden," Charlie laughed. "Dover or not, a masked identity is the perfect opportunity for making choices you wish to remain a secret."

I chewed my lips, glancing around the room. If scandal would not show itself, then I'd have to find it. "Come, then. Let us discover them all."

Charlie obliged all too easily, and with one last glance to Liza, we snuck out of the ballroom. We were not alone, for the spaces were busy with ordinary people in ordinary conversation. But they were not who we sought.

Charlie led me through the other rooms in the building as though he'd been there before. Casually, he pointed to which doors would likely lead to the gardens, or the back of the house, or hidden balconies. But we did not find a soul out of place.

"Where are all the *scandals*?" I whined, placing my hands on my hips. "There is nothing untoward going on here."

Couples meandered here and there, but they walked arm in arm with chaperones and ever-watchful onlookers.

"The night is still young," Charlie said.

I shook my head in disappointment. "I'd even settle for *half* a scandal. The mere intent of a scandal. Anything."

I huffed like a child, then caught Charlie staring hard at me. His throat bobbed, then he blinked away. "The mere intent, hmm? Are you certain?"

"Yes," I said in exasperation. "Anything."

Then all I'd have to do to finish my list was change someone's life for the better. The list was working, too. I had never felt so alive and happy in all my life.

Charlie looked up and down the hallway as people walked in and out of the ballroom, a card room, and others. Then he took my hand and said, "Come with me."

In a flash, he tugged me along, and I struggled to match his quick pace.

"Where are we going?" I whispered, confused by his quick turns.

We headed down a dimly lit, vacant hallway that led to more rooms, when suddenly Charlie tugged me to the side and pulled me into a hidden space. My back hit the wall, and I laughed from the thrill of it.

"What is this?" I whispered, though we were far from anyone who might overhear.

He stepped inside the space, the warmth of his body filling it, and my heart skipped to an uneven beat. He had to know there wasn't enough space for both of us. Then our eyes met, and I realized he *did* know.

He took a half step closer, not speaking, and his fingers brushed my hair as he untied my mask, then his. He tucked them away behind him.

"What are you doing?" My voice came out breathless, and he smiled. Without our masks, all pretense faded. We were suddenly bare before each other, vulnerable in a way we'd never been before. "Where are we?"

"We are in an alcove." His voice was low and raspy. "And this is what a near-scandal feels like."

My eyes fell to his parted lips. An *alcove*. Where couples hid away. Charlie and I were not a couple, and yet, my entire body gravitated toward him. I did not protest when he rested his hand on the wall at my back. Nor when he gently rubbed my arm with his free hand.

"Ros," he whispered. "Do not ever let a man make you feel uncomfortable."

"I am not uncomfortable," I said. Or breathed, really. What was wrong with my voice? And what had I just said? I should most certainly be uncomfortable here!

Charlie's eyes flashed with some deep emotion, but only for a second. His thumb brushed my cheek, sending sparks into my chest that tightened my stomach. "This is the part when a gentleman would lean in closer."

"Closer?"

He placed a hand on my waist, and said, "Closer."

I swallowed hard. I could feel my pulse racing, hear it in my ears. Could he?

"And then?"

Charlie grinned in response. He was teasing me, but I did not care. This was exactly what I wanted. "Then he would whisper something in your ear about how perfectly beautiful you are, though if he was first-rate, he'd know you well enough to make you laugh first." He winked, and the stupidest giggle bubbled in my throat.

"Then," he continued, his voice still raspy and deep. "He'd test the waters by moving even closer."

Another half step, and my back was flush against the wall. His knees brushed against mine.

I thought I might faint, and he must have sensed it, for he tightened his hold on my waist. I looked up, trying to breathe evenly, and he leaned in. I could feel the heat of his breath and a palpable tension I wanted so badly to break. I wanted his lips, his touch, all of it closer.

This did not feel like a near-scandal anymore, nor mere friendship. It felt comfortable. Too comfortable. And I wanted it to be real.

Slowly, I lifted my hands and rested them on the buttons of his waistcoat. They were cool and smooth and heavy as I traced them, each one higher than the last.

Charlie's eyes were dark and serious. His chest rose and

fell faster with each passing moment, but he said nothing. Did he want this as badly as I did?

I slid my fingertips up under his lapels to his shoulders. Why did he not speak? I did not dare read his face. But I could not keep my hands from wandering over his strong shoulders.

"And then?" I asked. I knew he watched me, but I could not meet his gaze.

"Ros," he whispered. His voice was husky and thick.

I tilted my face up and brushed my nose against his. He closed his eyes, moving his hand around my waist to my neck, trailing up to my cheek.

"I am not this man," he whispered so near my lips I could almost taste his breath. But he was leaning in, and his other hand moved from the wall to my waist, teasing up my side. The alcove was warm, so deliciously warm, and I felt like a pool of lava under his touch.

"What man?" I breathed. My fingers curled into the nape of his neck.

"Not a man to kiss a woman engaged."

Slowly, tenderly, he pulled back, and our eyes met. His lips closed, and he swallowed hard. His hands released me and fell limp at his sides.

My stomach clenched. I felt suddenly sick. This had all been a ruse. A near-scandal intended only to check off a number on my list. Charlie had promised to help me see things through, and, I, foolish and naïve, had completely lost my head.

My hands were still wrapped around his shoulders. What in heaven's name was I doing? All at once, the faraway music and laughter grounded me back in the present, and I jerked back my hands and stumbled against the side wall.

"Well done, Charlie." There was a painful lump in my throat. "That was incredibly convincing."

"Ros—"

The space seemed to spin. I could not stop the tingling in my fingertips, the tightness in my chest, or the burning behind my eyes. My words spilled out without restraint. "You are really too good at scandalizing. I can only assume you've been in many alcoves before."

"No." He stepped back, scrunching his brows together. "Not at all. Ros, forgive me. I did not expect . . . I mean I certainly *wanted* . . ." He averted his gaze, looking anywhere but my face. His cheeks were rosy with embarrassment.

What did I think would happen? Charlie would kiss me, and we'd fall in love, and suddenly he'd grow a title as good as the duke's so we could truly run away together?

What utter nonsense. No. Charlie would go home. And I would marry Marlow. Anything less would ruin my family. It would break their hearts, their expectations, their *dreams*.

I could not stay in that small space with Charlie's unspoken words any longer. I ducked around him and, without a second glance, raced into the empty hall. Cool air brushed past my hot cheeks as I careened wildly around corners, not bothering to apologize when I cut off two men dressed as highlanders.

When I found the ballroom, I slowed my run to a fast walk, looking for Liza. I found her in the exact spot I'd left her.

She looked up as I approached and jerked up straight. "Rosalind, are you unwell?"

"There you are," I said, catching my breath with my hands on my hips.

"Oh, do not fret over me." She laughed, swiping a playful hand at her companion. "Mr. Cox has me quite entertained."

The man gave me a smile with teeth as white as clouds. "Is that Mr. Charles Winston?" he asked suddenly, looking over my shoulder.

I stiffened and lifted my chin. I was not ready to face him—*us*.

"Rosalind, where is your mask?" Liza furrowed her brow.

Drat. I'd completely forgotten. "Liza, I must speak with you."

"There you are," Charlie said from behind me, though I could not know if he spoke to me or Liza.

"Pardon me," Mr. Cox said, rising tall. "I must attend to a friend." Then he left before any of us could be introduced.

"The earl?" Liza called after him. But he'd already disappeared within the crush.

"Who was that?" Charlie asked Liza. "He seemed a bit . . . skittish."

"The two of you fell upon us like the plague," she chided. "Good heavens, put your masks on. People are starting to stare." Liza stood and straightened her dress. Then she took my mask from Charlie and secured it over my face. Charlie did the same with his own.

Liza took her place between us, and I was grateful. I could not face him. I would've rather faced a hundred cliffs alone than look at Charlie after I'd dashed off like a thief. I'd practically begged him to kiss me, but true to form, he'd been an honorable companion yet again.

But the way he'd held me, the way his hands had traced my sides and cupped my face, how he'd brushed his fingers along my neck . . . How could he do all those things if he did not feel as I did?

And I *did* feel them. With Charlie, I was exactly myself and completely undone all at the same time. This unexpected feeling that had been growing since we'd met now demanded recognition. It demanded a name.

Affection. Care. Devotion.

Love.

I loved Charlie Winston.

Did he feel it too? Did it matter if he did? I was engaged, and I'd be married in six days to a man I barely knew.

"I think I am ready to retire," I told Liza.

"Now? The night is young, Ros. Let's have a few more sets, shall we?"

"I am quite tired myself," Charlie said, and I could feel his gaze burning into the side of my face.

"Honestly? Both of you? The two people in the world who enjoy making a mess cannot manage to get through a masquerade?" She huffed a breath. "Fine. We have an early drive in the morning anyway."

We navigated through the crowd, all the way to the entry.

We were a few paces from the door when an unfamiliar man sharply dressed all in black and holding a long, polished cane rounded the corner and stood tall in front of our exit. His right arm was in a sling. His hair dark as night. Then he took off his mask. A sheen of sweat touched his brow. His hazel eyes were narrowed over a round nose and thin, taut lips.

This was the Earl of Langdon.

He looked down at us. "Mr. Charles Winston."

"Lord Langdon." Charlie bowed. I followed his gaze to the man's arm. "I heard you'd be among the crush. I meant to seek you out to apologize—"

"Let us not trifle with one another. You wronged me, then fled the city, and I have every intention of paying back the favor."

Liza puffed up her chest and stepped between the men. "Mr. Winston has been visiting family. He most certainly did not flee London. We were just on our way out. If you'll excuse us, my lord."

But the man did not budge. His eyes hardened with the fiercest scowl, and I realized that he had not removed his mask for recognition. He wanted Charlie to see his anger, to hear it in his voice as he said, "One day soon, Winston, you will find yourself at your lowest."

Charlie pulled Liza behind him and stood tall, but silent.

"Remember me then," Lord Langdon said.

Before Charlie had a chance to speak, he brushed past him and into the ballroom.

"Devilish man," Liza muttered, lacing her arm through Charlie's. "Do not fret. His intention is merely to frighten you."

Charlie frowned, and his jaw ticked. He looked straight ahead. Whatever he thought or felt or feared, he buried. "We should go."

Liza glanced at me questioningly, and I furrowed my

brows. What could we say to comfort him? To reassure him that one man's ill opinion did not mark his character for worse?

There was no tiptoeing around what had just happened. Charlie had attempted an apology, but Lord Langdon had threatened him in return. Angry feelings were one thing, but a threat was entirely another. There was nothing to say, nor anything to be done about it now.

We rode in the carriage for a quarter hour before Liza's body went limp from sleep. Her head rested on Charlie's shoulder. There were still hours yet before the sun would rise, but the lanterns and moonlight shone enough light to cast our outlines in the cab.

Charlie sat tall as he watched out his window. My instinct was to comfort him, though I could not be certain he wanted me to. If he cared about me—my stomach sank; what if he did not?—he was too good a man to say it. Too good a man to tempt me away from my commitment to the duke and to my family.

I sat across from him helplessly, unsure of what to do next.

I closed my eyes and leaned my head against my window. My mind was a mess, but my skin remembered the way Charlie's touch had driven me to distraction. We were halfway to Mrs. Harrelson's, but I was exhausted. I wanted nothing more than an empty mind, so I drew in even breaths, one after another.

For a moment, I forgot everything.

Chapter Twenty-Two

I awoke with a jacket covering me.

Charlie's jacket. His hand was patting my arm, his voice gently calling my name. "We are home, Ros."

Somehow, I stumbled inside the house and into my bed in the dark. But it seemed as soon as I'd fallen onto my pillow, a maid was pressing my shoulder. We had to leave early to make it back to Ivy Manor and home, but early had come far too soon. My mind swam through a fog of last evening's events. My memories weren't as sharp, but they were just as piercing.

We made quick time of dressing, and by the time we descended, our things had already been packed into the carriage.

"We must be off," Liza said to her grandparents. "We are on a strict schedule, unfortunately. But it was so wonderful seeing you both."

Charlie's glance met mine for the twentieth time since we'd risen, though neither of us had said a word to the other.

"Oh, do come again soon," her grandmother said, patting each of us on an arm. "None of you visit me enough."

"Thank you for your kindness, and for accepting us into your home with such short notice," I said as I embraced her. I felt as though we'd just arrived.

"Good luck, dear. And congratulations again on such a fortuitous match. I hope the wedding is as lovely as you deserve."

I flinched, and she gave me an odd look. My wedding. It seemed like such a faraway thing, but it was real, and coming closer every day.

Charlie embraced his grandmother. She whispered something in his ear and squeezed him tighter than she had Liza and me. She walked us out to the carriage, and then we were off. Headed home at last.

"Well, you two are very quiet," Liza said. She pulled out her pillowcase and began stitching another rose. Her eyes jumped between Charlie and me. "You've barely said a word to each other since we awoke."

Charlie flipped a page in his newspaper without looking up. "How are you this morning, Rosalind?"

"Very well, thank you, Charles," I replied, trying to appear as unaffected as I could.

"I trust you slept well?"

"Indeed. And you?"

"I tossed and turned all night," he said.

My heart wedged in my throat as he folded his paper.

Liza raised a brow and looked between us, still stitching away.

"But I have been wondering . . . " Charlie continued,

"you have but one point left on your list. How are you feeling about marrying the duke?"

I choked on air and coughed, raising a hand to my neck. Of all the things to say. For once, I knew exactly what Charlie was thinking about. Me, engaged. The problem was, I did not know how to answer him. And I could not ask him the burning question I'd thought of ceaselessly: How was he feeling about me?

"I—well." I fiddled through my satchel for anything that might aid my fumbling tongue.

"That list," muttered Liza. "As though one little thing would change your mind. The wedding is in five days. Ready or not, Ros, you are marrying Marlow."

Charlie frowned and looked out his window with the same pained look he'd had when I first met him.

"Actually, I am not certain," I said.

The carriage hit a bump in the road, and Liza's embroidery went flying. Her hands hung empty in the air, and she stared at me with wide eyes and an open mouth.

"What?" Her voice climbed an octave. "You are not seriously considering crying off."

"I hardly know him, Liza. It would not be unreasonable."

Charlie straightened in his seat.

Liza's face had gone pale. "Your family would be *mortified*. To cry off at all is embarrassing. Worse, it is harmful to your prospects." She shook her head as though she could not comprehend the idea. "You are engaged to a *duke* who wants to marry you and connect your family to his title. You'd have to be mad to abandon him."

"I disagree," Charlie said.

My gaze flew to his face to measure his sincerity.

Charlie looked at me, *really* looked at me for the first time all day, and said, "There is more to life than status."

My heart readily agreed and pounded wildly in my chest. But status meant everything to my family. And everything Liza had said was true. Agreeing with Charlie would be the greatest risk I'd ever taken.

A risk I had not planned for.

I nodded. "I am starting to see that too."

His serious expression turned smug. Only this time it didn't seem so flippant. His gaze was careful, cautious, like he did not want to give himself away. But why? What was he thinking? We needed a moment alone to speak before I made any rash decisions. I clasped my hands and rubbed my fingers together.

What if we spoke, and he *did* feel the same? I looked up at him.

"Good morning," Charlie mouthed through a smile.

I bit my lip. "Good morning," I mouthed back.

Liza, oblivious, recovered her embroidery and pulled her needle through the fabric. "There is certainly not more to life when you have a duke."

Charlie raised a brow and rolled his eyes, and I laughed. He shook out his paper and leaned back.

A few more hours, and we'd be home. We would speak soon.

We drove through Dover, then stopped to let our horses rest. As we journeyed closer to home, I busied myself with sketching Teague House in a notebook. My legs bounced and Charlie's crossed and uncrossed, and all the while, we exchanged stolen glances beneath Liza's notice.

We stopped a final time to rest the horses, and I was desperate to move. We'd just discovered a dirt footpath when our driver called Charlie back.

"My legs are so stiff," Liza whined, pulling me along for a walk before the final ride home.

I looked over my shoulder and found Charlie facing the driver, who spoke wildly with his hands. I wondered if something had broken on the carriage, but when we returned, both men were ready to receive us.

We'd driven for another half hour or more, when suddenly the driver shouted, and our carriage jerked to a stop.

Charlie peered out the window, his expression growing tight.

"What is wrong?" I asked, exchanging a worried glance with Liza.

Angry voices sounded from behind the carriage, and a chill ran down my spine. Something was wrong.

Charlie closed the curtains on the window. "Stay inside. Do not, under any circumstances, leave this carriage. Am I clear?"

"Highwaymen?" Liza's voice wavered despite her obvious attempt to sound calm.

"No. But I shall handle them."

Charlie burst through the door and slammed it closed, and his voice rang out in the still air. "Be gone," he bellowed. "I will warn you only once."

His anger frightened me. If not highwaymen, who were those men? Did they wish to hurt us? I peeled back the curtain and peeked out. Three men with black handkerchiefs covering their faces stood at the side of the road. Their horses they'd left to wander. Whoever they were, they had an agenda.

Something banged hard against the carriage, jolting it sideways, and I held fast to the walls to keep steady.

"Get off me," a man's voice yelled.

Another jolt and another harsh yell. The door swung open, and a hidden face with beady black eyes jeered at us. "Two women inside, just as expected," he growled over his shoulder. "Does he want them to pay regrets as well?"

"We have no money." My voice shook. "Nor have we traveled with jewelry."

"We do not want your money," he spat. "Langdon wants anything that makes *him* suffer."

Charlie.

These were Lord Langdon's men. The man grabbed my arm and yanked me out. My feet caught on the carriage floor, and though he held me up, I fell hard on my knees to the road.

I cried out as pain shot up my legs.

"Get up," he sneered, tossing me aside. Then he reached inside for Liza. She screamed, and I stood, ignoring the searing pain and every sense that told me to run.

On instinct, I kicked behind the man's knees in the same fashion I'd seen Ben fight with Jasper and Nicholas. Then I made a proper fist and beat upon the man's shoulder and his side with every ounce of strength I could muster.

Liza must have seen me, for she used her feet to advantage and kicked, pushing the man backward. I slid to the side, and our driver appeared from behind the carriage.

He grasped the man's shirt and heaved him back, away from Liza and me, and the two of them wrestled for control.

Liza's sobs were uncontrollable.

"Stay here," I pleaded. "I'll find Charlie." I shut the door and spun around.

My feet took control, and I raced around the carriage. Eyes wild and searching, I stopped short.

Charlie stood a distance away, his bare fists raised against a man twice his size. They rounded one another with quick steps, locked in a dance. One would move and the other would dodge or block, like they were toying with one another. Charlie twitched his left arm, but in a flash, he threw a blow to the right and knocked the man's head sideways.

I sucked in a breath and covered my mouth. But I could not look away.

The hit hadn't stopped the man from moving, and he rounded even faster on Charlie, ready to retaliate. He thrashed out, but Charlie dodged low, narrowly avoiding the hit.

I recognized the movements as the same ones Charlie had taught me in the grove. I could hear his voice in my head: *"Can you anticipate his moves? Where will he aim?"*

Charlie faked right, then threw left, connecting his bare fist with the man's jaw.

But the beast only shook his head, blood spraying in the air, and again raised his fists. He turned wise and guarded every hit Charlie attempted.

I saw no end. Only two men, and one would surely tire soon.

He never loses. I could hardly breathe. *Charlie never loses.*

They danced and blocked and tricked one another until the man, in evident frustration, barreled forward with all his weight and threw an earnest fist, striking Charlie so hard on his left side that he stumbled back.

My stomach bottomed out, and I spun around, helpless and alone. I had no weapon. Nor aid to call upon.

The man drew closer, forcing Charlie back another few steps, for he had not yet recovered. Both men held their fists at the ready.

Movement from my peripheral caught my attention. Another man had crept up behind Charlie's back, but *his* fists were not raised. Instead, he crouched low and reached inside his boot. A long, sharp knife glistened in the sunlight.

Charlie seemed to sense him, and he sidestepped to round with both men. I knew the instant he saw the knife, for he hesitated.

He could not fight them both.

I made my decision in an instant, the same way a person chooses to breathe. I started to run—to throw myself between them; to do something, *anything*—but someone pulled me back. I kicked wildly and threw out my arms.

"No, Miss Newbury," my driver said, tightening his grip as I thrashed. His face was bloodied and bruised, his wide eyes shocked and terrified. "You'll be killed."

My head jerked back to Charlie.

The first man swung at his head, and Charlie leaned back.

Then the knifeman took his opportunity, stabbing his blade into Charlie's side.

"No!" I screamed.

Charlie grimaced and a guttural sound escaped him.

Instead of falling, he wavered for a moment, then threw his fist into the knifeman's jaw.

The driver's hold slacked, his expression one of pure shock.

"Help him," I cried in a broken sob.

His eyes looked wildly between the two men still circling Charlie and then back to mine. He bolted forward.

Charlie yelled out in anguish as the knifeman struck again, burying the blade into his stomach.

I felt the sound in my heart, clawing up my throat, taking my knees out from under me. My entire world, my hopes, my dreams, my very insides were being ripped out of me, like an antelope under a lion, and I could do nothing. I could not save the man I loved.

Then a bullet fired, and I shrunk into myself, falling back against the carriage window.

I smelled smoke, and suddenly four men on horseback were upon us, shouting and waving their pistols. In their midst was a man I recognized.

He sat tall in his saddle, his long arm raised above his head with a smoking pistol in his hand. Blond hair rustled under a black top hat, and a gray tailcoat flew behind him in the wind. His ice-blue eyes were set on mine, a fierce expression on his face.

The Duke of Marlow.

Chapter Twenty-Three

How had he found us? How had he known?

Our foes scattered like rats, jumping onto their horses, and taking flight into the tree line.

"Go after them!" Marlow called, and two of his men darted off like lightning. As the duke steadied his horse and dismounted, our driver ran to meet him.

My eyes flew back to Charlie, whose chest heaved as he stood alone in the distance. His shoulders slumped, and I could see him falling.

Without thought, I bolted toward him, knowing I wouldn't make it in time. I ran as fast as my legs could carry me.

I fell to my knees beside him. My whole body shook with tremors as I tried to make sense of what I was seeing.

Charlie's eyes were closed, his lips parted and pale.

There was blood everywhere. This was all my fault. Had I not insisted we run away, we'd have been safely at home. He would be safe.

"Charlie, what have they done?" I cried, swallowing down

the painful throb in my throat. "Charlie, look at me." His hands were covered in red, but I took them anyway. Blood soaked through his clothes.

A shadow fell over us. It was Marlow and another one of his men. "He's bleeding badly. Fetch the surgeon at once." His final companion wasted no time racing off to obey the duke's orders. "Miss Newbury," Marlow said, softening his voice. "You must come with me."

"Don't you see this man?" I could hardly speak. "He needs attention."

A muscle twitched in Marlow's jaw, and I realized I did not know him at all. Was he angry? Offended? "His driver will transport him home."

"Alone?" I put my hand on Charlie's arm, and Marlow's eyes followed.

"My carriage is here," he clipped. "Miss Ollerton is already safe inside. I must ride ahead on horseback and alert your family. Please, do as I say and join her."

Marlow wasn't thinking. He was angry with me, but I could not let him punish Charlie for my mistakes. "I must insist—"

"I *said*—"

"He needs me!" I shouted.

Marlow swore under his breath, clearly more at me than at our predicament. But how could I even listen to him when his recommendation might cost Charlie his life? How could he ask me to leave right now?

Charlie shifted, moaning and writhing in pain. He'd fainted, but he was coming to.

"Charlie," I breathed. "You're hurt. Do not move."

But of course he did not listen. "It's not so bad," he slurred, his voice pained and weak.

"It *is* bad. You must come with me. Can you stand?"

He groaned, and I took that as my answer. But what could I do? I had not the strength to lift a man alone.

The Ollertons' carriage rolled to a stop near us, and the coachman hopped down.

"She is erratic. Illogical," Marlow said to him. "I cannot get her away from this man. Get him in your carriage *now* and set off."

I stood, seething with anger and pain and frustration, and faced Marlow directly. We were running out of time. "Your Grace, I am not asking for your permission. Mr. Winston just saved my life, and I intend on saving his. I am riding in *his* carriage."

Marlow surveyed Charlie, then searched my face. At first glance, he was cold and unwelcoming, frustrated and understandably so, but there was something else too. I hoped it was compassion.

"Please," I begged. "I swear I shall do whatever you ask of me when we return home."

Jaw clenched, he motioned for help. He and the driver heaved Charlie up and carried him over. His middle swam with blood as they laid him on the carriage seat.

"He'll slide off as soon as we start moving, miss, but I don't see how he can sit upright either," the driver said.

"Then I shall sit on the floor and hold him up."

The driver nodded solemnly, moving out of my way.

I climbed into the carriage and knelt beside Charlie. His face was white, his breathing shallow.

Marlow reached in from behind me and handed me his cravat. "Apply hard pressure to his stomach if you can. And hold him steady. I'll ride ahead to prepare Ivy Manor, and my carriage with Miss Ollerton will lead you home."

I nodded, blinking back my tears, and he closed the door behind him.

"Rosalind," Charlie whispered, swallowing hard. "This isn't proper." He spoke each word slowly.

I smiled despite myself and wiped away the moisture in my eyes. I summoned all my courage. "Now I know you aren't in a right state of mind. I can think of many times where you and I have thrown propriety to the wind."

The carriage jolted forward, and his body rolled toward me. Already the cabin bench and walls were stained with his blood. I pressed my hands and all my weight against him, and he moaned.

"I've got you, Charlie," I whispered as he settled backward. I folded Marlow's cravat and pressed the already drenched cloth against his stomach, trying not to focus on the sharp metallic scent of his blood.

"Thank you, Ros," he grunted, meeting my gaze.

I pressed harder into his stomach. "I thought you said you were good at fighting," I teased. "You're in terrible shape."

Charlie grimaced and looked up about the cabin, at the brown-and-white papered trim, the blue curtains, and the brown cushioned benches that had transported us to the opera, to our picnic, to Dover . . . seemingly anywhere but at my face. He drew in a shallow breath. "I put you in danger. I shall never forgive myself."

"You saved my life," I countered as I held him steady. His

hair had fallen near his eye, so I gently pushed it back. "Are you in terrible pain?"

He closed his eyes and steadied his breathing. "A bit."

"I shall fix you right up when the surgeon comes." I lifted my chin. "And we can eat unlimited cheesecakes and sweets until you've recovered."

He opened his eyes only to squint them. "Just let me perish."

I sucked in a breath dramatically. "Oh no, not when I have created the perfect gentleman out of you."

He adjusted his head on the seat and, whether he intended to or not, moved closer to me. "A perfect gentleman?"

I flushed. I hadn't meant to speak so honestly. "You'll forget I said that."

His lips lifted into a weak grin, and my heart took flight. I hoped he would never forget my words. Indeed, I wished I could speak more plainly.

Then he shuddered, and I realized he'd been stabbed more than once. I started to unbutton his jacket.

"What are you doing?" He tried to sit up but fell back. His bare hand grasped mine to stop me, sending waves of tingling sensation through my chest.

"I am examining you." I squeezed his hand. "You were stabbed in the side as well as the stomach."

"Let the surgeon—"

"Charlie, this is serious. You are bleeding terribly." His entire countenance drained of color with each passing moment.

"Ros," he said. He swallowed as though saying my name caused him some other sort of pain, and he lifted his hand to my cheek. "You are good to help me. But the sight will stay with you."

I let his hand linger on my cheek, his touch burning into my skin, as I finished unbuttoning his jacket, revealing his waistcoat soaked in blood. A tear was evident in his stomach, and another higher up on his side. When I touched the spot with my bare fingers, blood gushed out.

"What is it?" he asked, thumbing my chin to get my attention.

"Nothing," I said, feigning a smile.

I left the folded cloth at his stomach and shimmied out of my pelisse. After tightening it into a firm ball, I hesitated, trying to decide which wound needed the most attention. Marlow's cravat was doing little to stop Charlie's bleeding stomach, so I exchanged it with my bundled pelisse, holding it firmly in place. Then I wedged Marlow's cravat between Charlie's bleeding side and the bench. There was too much blood and not enough fabric, but, if nothing else, the pressure would help slow the bleeding. I swallowed hard and steadied him once more.

His hand had fallen to my waist, and I took it, holding it against my cheek with my free hand. "There. That is better," I said in as reassuring a voice as I could muster.

His eyes bored into mine, and we stared at each other for a moment.

"Almost there," I said, but I hadn't the faintest idea where we were. Close to home, but not nearly close enough.

"Tell me something," he said, thumbing my cheek. "Anything."

I shifted, relying on my knees to hold me up. "Anything?"

I thought for a moment. Charlie already knew about my family, my home, my hobbies. He already knew so much about me. "You know I like the bakery," I said.

"*Love* the bakery," he agreed. I'd have swatted him if he weren't so injured.

I mused. "I used to chase butterflies as a girl."

"Why?" His other hand slid forward, holding mine that put pressure on his wound. Was he scared? Would he die from his wounds?

I shook away the thought. "Because they are beautiful, and I wanted them all for myself."

He closed his eyes. "I understand that sentiment."

"Do you?"

The carriage hit a bump in the road, and he grunted, again trying to sit up.

"Charlie, lie still."

"It hurts," he whispered, wincing.

"You're a pugilist. Practically a professional." I marked the words with all his smugness. "You know pain."

I let go of his hand and stroked his wavy hair. He closed his eyes. "A strong drink awaits you soon," I whispered.

"I don't deserve it," he said, that solemn look surfacing again. "This is all my fault."

"What are you talking about?"

"Those men. They were on the earl's errand." He lifted a hand, bloodred and wet, and let out a panicked breath. He squeezed his eyes tight like he, too, was fighting back his fear.

"I won't let you feel guilty for someone else's mistakes," I said, enunciating every word. He focused on me, so I grasped his hand and pushed it back down. "No matter what you've done, Lord Langdon alone is to blame for what happened today. Do you understand?"

"Ros, you are too . . ." he said on a shallow breath.

"Good a friend?" I supplied with a smile that I hoped masked my ever-mounting fear.

"That, yes." He swallowed hard again. "And smart. And generous. Talented." He laid his head back. "Absolutely beautiful."

My heart was in my throat, and tears filled my eyes. I should think of Marlow. He had saved us too. And I had made a promise to him. Indeed, I owed him my life—and Charlie's and Liza's. But none of that mattered now. Not with Charlie lying like this and looking at me for the first time with truth on his lips.

I did not want Marlow. I wanted Charlie.

"Well, don't stop there," I whispered. My voice was raw and faltering.

He looked up at me, and I blinked back my tears.

"I should have kissed you when I had the chance," he whispered back.

I touched the corner of his mouth with my thumb. "Then what are you waiting for?"

He watched me for a moment, letting me brush my fingers over his cheeks and forehead and neck. Every scar, every line, every dimple—I adored them all.

He shook his head. "I will disappoint you."

"I highly doubt that. I have never been kissed, and you are rather appealing, Charlie."

Half his mouth lifted. "You know what I mean."

And I did. Kissing Charlie would be both an ending and

a beginning. I'd have to jilt the duke and destroy my family, but I could also create a new future. The question was not if I wanted to, but if I was brave enough. If *he* was brave enough. And I was terrified.

"I make a mess of everything," he continued. "You deserve better. You deserve someone who has his life together. The duke. A king. You deserve the world, Ros, and I won't keep you from it."

Could I say the words? Could I speak the truth?

It would change everything.

But this was *Charlie*.

I leaned in closer, applying pressure while also settling close to the man who had captured my entire heart. I had finally found my place. And I knew exactly what I had to do to claim it.

"Unfortunately, Charlie, *you* have become my world."

He watched me, seeming to measure the truth behind my eyes, then let out a steady breath. "You think I am dying, so you aim to please me."

"*Are* you pleased?" *Tell me that you feel as I do.*

"I fear I am dreaming." He closed his eyes, wincing at another bump in the road. His face paled further, his arms hung more and more limply at his side.

I gave myself one moment of discomposure, covering my mouth as I forced back a sob. Here we were, quite literally between heaven and earth, and Fate was forcing me to answer the question I feared most: Could I live in a world without Charlie? If he lived, would that even be enough, if I could not have him by my side?

We would get him healed, and then I would convince

him. I'd explain everything to Marlow as soon as Charlie was safe. The duke would be frustrated, but he would understand. And my family . . . I wiped my face with my forearm and readjusted the cravat on Charlie's side. The entire fabric was soaked in blood. Panic swarmed in my mind. We needed to hurry. He needed a surgeon.

I pulled back the shade on the window above my head. We were passing farmland. His hand lay limp in mine, so I tightened my grasp.

"Almost there, Charlie. I see Ivy Manor now."

I glanced out the window, and the sight held true. We were winding down the long drive past the grove, and I thought I saw a flurry of servants outside.

The carriage came to a halt, and the door immediately opened. I released Charlie's hand as Mr. Ollerton stepped inside.

"I need help," he called. "Rosalind, exit out that side."

"I can help," I said, though I did not know how. The door beside me opened.

"Rosalind." Mr. Ollerton's voice was harsh and final, more a father than a neighbor.

I released my pelisse. My knees popped and protested at rising after leaning so heavily upon them for so long. Another man rushed in as I exited the carriage.

Derricks ushered me inside, where Liza waited in the entry. Her horrified expression told me all I needed to know about my appearance. I looked down to my dress. It was stained red from blood, as were my hands.

"Will he live?" she asked as tears streamed down her face.

"He has to," I said. I'd finally found where I belonged,

where I felt whole and complete and myself. My list had worked, only not exactly as I'd planned.

"You must go home," Liza said, wiping her tears. "Mama said—"

"The surgeon is situated," Marlow called from the top of the staircase. He saw me as he descended, his gaze sweeping over my filthy dress.

I hung my head and curtseyed low. "I must beg your forgiveness," I said when he reached us.

He held up a hand. "Go and be cleaned. I will wait for you outside."

I nodded. "Thank you for—"

"Do not thank me," he said harshly. "Not yet."

Chapter Twenty-Four

Grass. Focus on the grass.

My knees ached, my entire body trembled, but somehow, I moved one foot in front of the other.

Molly had come with new clothes and scrubbed every inch of me with hard soap and a towel, but I could still smell Charlie's blood.

I had needed air, so Molly led me through the closest door—a side entrance—and toward the drive, where a figure stood on the front lawn.

Marlow.

He was conversing with two servants, their backs to the house. We were far enough away that I could not hear his voice.

Molly must have sensed my discomfort, for she squeezed my arm, and said, "Everything will come together. Do not fear. I have heard the duke is a kind and forgiving man."

I rubbed my hands over my face. If that were true, I'd brought the worst out in him. Was it wrong that I did not want him to forgive me? Part of me wished he'd leave and never return so that claiming what I wanted would be easy. But I knew what that would do to my family.

I had to face him. But even as I thought the words, my legs went weak.

Molly held fast to my arm, holding me up. "Are you tired? Shall we rest?"

My mind was fuzzy. Tired, yes. All over. But the pain in my chest was encompassing. I needed to be with Charlie. I needed to see him, to care for him. To be certain he would live.

"There was so much blood," I said through my tears. "And Charlie was in so much pain. I could not help him. I could not stop it."

"The surgeon will attend to his wounds." Molly took my face in her hands and brushed away my tears. "Mr. Winston is not your responsibility nor your priority. The duke is."

The duke. No, that would never be right. Marlow was a stranger to me. I did not know anything about his family or his passions or his fears. Charlie, I knew. I did not want to move toward Marlow because the only place I belonged was with Charlie.

But before I could take another step, the door to Ivy Manor opened, and Benjamin walked out, his eyes downcast. He looked to where Marlow stood across the drive but strode the shorter length toward me.

Ben kept his voice low. "Rosalind, what were you thinking, running off to Dover?"

"Is Charlie well? Will he live?" I whispered. "Please, I must know."

"As long as infection does not set in, he will recover," Ben said. His shoulders sagged and he looked like he'd aged ten years, but I felt more relief in that moment than in all my life.

I tried not to cry. He would live. Charlie would live.

Molly took her leave, retracing our steps back to the house.

Ben took my hand and turned me away from Marlow. "Charlie is asleep now, but he asked after you, earlier."

"What did he say? What can I do?" I asked, wiping my eyes and stumbling as I followed him. I was too eager. Too obvious.

Ben cleared his throat, and I instantly regretted the emotion in my voice. But I could not hide the fact that I loved Charlie. Not anymore.

"I told him you were going home. Where you belong. The surgeon wants him in bed for the next few days. Then you may visit him to say goodbye before the wedding."

I stepped back, cursing the swell in my throat and the tears pooling in the corners of my eyes. Ben would be devastated to hear the truth. They all would be. But I had to tell them.

"I cannot do that." My voice came out choked, and I blinked back my tears. "I do not want to marry Marlow."

He stared at me for a long moment as his brow furrowed more and more, and then he forced a laugh. "Of course you do."

"I don't expect you to understand, but I hope you will forgive me in time. I cannot marry the duke, because I wish to marry Charlie."

For a moment, I thought he hadn't heard me. His face relaxed, and his lips parted slowly. "Charlie?"

I nodded solemnly.

"Charles Winston." He wiped his mouth. A muscle jumped in his jaw, and his eyes met mine with a fierce glare. "That picnic."

I hurried to clarify. "I did not realize then—"

"He *swore* to me." Ben's hands shook. His voice rang in

the air, uncontrolled and fierce, but he quickly lowered it. "The man gave me *his word*!"

I stepped back, glancing over my shoulder to where Marlow still stood, talking with the servants. I turned back to Ben. "Whatever do you mean?"

His eyes were daggers. "He swore nothing had happened between you that afternoon."

"Nothing did!" I reached out, but Ben flinched away and shook his head.

He balled his fists. "He admitted attraction, affection, but claimed he would never act upon it. And fool that I am, I believed him."

"He did?" My chest tightened. Charlie loved me. "What else did he say?"

"He told me about your list and all you'd done together, the three of you, and how desperate you were to see it through before marrying the duke. He promised to inform me of your whereabouts and to keep you out of danger. He even told me of your plan to 'run away' to Dover."

Ben laughed mirthlessly. "I told Mother and Father that you went to London so Mother wouldn't worry or try to bring you back before you were finished with that ridiculous list. But then the duke arrived. He apologized for being early and asked to see you." Ben shook his head. "Imagine my mortification when he started to set out for London to meet your party. I had to tell him the truth, apologize for my deceit in *front of Father*, then direct him to Dover instead."

I covered my face with my hands. Charlie had told Ben everything. I should be angry that he'd decided to speak to Ben without my knowledge, but how could I be? He'd ensured my progress would not be stopped because he wanted to keep me safe. Because he loved me.

"I am so sorry, Benjamin."

Ben folded his arms across his chest. "I let you go. *I* lied to Mother and Father, I put my trust in Winston, so I cannot blame him, but I also cannot deny that had he been a responsible man of honor, he wouldn't have found himself in this predicament at all. And with you and Liza in tow."

"How could he have known? What Lord Langdon did is not Charlie's fault."

"But it is. It *is*, Ros. His leaving his family, the choices he's made thus far—it all has accumulated to this. And I cannot support my only sister trying to attach herself to a man like that when she can have a duke. I am sorry." He drew in a shallow, unsteady breath.

My little brother stood tall in front of me, unraveling, then piecing himself back together for my sake.

I swallowed hard, wiping my eyes. There was one piece Ben did not yet understand in his eighteen years of life. One crucial factor *he* had yet to experience.

"I love him." My voice tremored. "Ben, I love *Charlie*."

His eyes searched mine. "You hardly know him. Nor of his past."

"You're wrong." I stepped forward, reaching for his arm. I wanted him to hear me and truly understand that the choice I was making was anchored and deeply rooted, not just a silly whim from a silly list. I wanted Ben to understand that I would not take away a title from our family for anything— nor anyone—less.

"I love who Charlie was before his brother died, and who

he is now because of it. I love what he learned about himself in the time between. He admittedly made poor choices, but he owns them. He looks forward to starting anew. He is a good man. And as wise as you are, perhaps you cannot yet understand how love can change everything."

Ben shook his head again.

He didn't understand. Could anyone, really, without being changed like this firsthand?

He grabbed my arms and gently squeezed. "You didn't get a Season. You have not experienced this sort of attention before. I regret that Winston came before the duke, but I truly believe if you only give Marlow the same chance—"

"I've met him before. Several times. And not once did he make me feel how Charlie makes me feel over and over again. Charlie and I . . . We get on so easily. Our conversation makes me wish to never be out of his company. He understands me, my dreams, my notions as though they are as much a part of him as they are a part of me. And I finally feel *ready* to start a life with someone. We are different, and we have our own struggles, but I choose him."

Ben clenched his jaw in evident frustration. "Has Winston offered for you? Has he hinted at it?"

"No," I admitted. "But he wouldn't. Not while I've committed myself elsewhere. I am more sorry than you know to reject a title for our family. I understand what that means for us. For you. I am truly, truly sorry. I will speak with the duke directly."

Ben glanced behind us as though worried the duke had overheard me. But he was too far away. "Rosalind, have you heard a word I've said? This is utter madness."

"I know, and I'm sorry."

"I do not worry for myself. I will live fine with or without your title, though I'd be lying if I said I wasn't disappointed."

No matter what he said, I knew my brother wanted this connection. He'd depended on it. And who could blame him?

I had wanted it too. When I'd signed the contract, I'd imagined myself as a duchess, married to Marlow and running his home, managing his social engagements, bearing his heir. And yet I could not imagine it anymore. The thought of standing beside any man that wasn't Charlie made me ill.

"I'm thinking of you," Ben said. "Perhaps of things you have not yet considered. Winston is practically estranged from his family. How can you know they will be accepting of him? Of you?"

I thought of Charlie's grandmother. How loving and kind and forgiving she was. She'd understood, and she'd accepted him so easily because there was love between them. Pain, yes. But love and understanding.

"They will be."

His gaze flicked over my shoulder. "The duke is walking this way. Please, Ros, consider with caution. Do not make any rash decisions tonight. As your brother, I *beg* you."

"I love you, Ben," I said, for I could not make a promise I could not keep. "I will consider your words."

Ben pulled out his handkerchief and wiped my cheeks dry. "If you care at all for our family, please, for one night . . ." Ben looked at me as though I might take flight.

I looked down at the grass. Where would I go? Where *could* I go? I'd promised my hand to one man, but I'd given my heart to another. And something had to be done about it.

Chapter Twenty-Five

Gravel crunched, then a soft pattering told me the duke was near. I caught sight of a polished pair of brown Hessian boots that strode around and stopped beside Ben's.

I curtseyed. "Your Grace."

Marlow's gaze fell heavily upon me, but I was too afraid to look up.

"Miss Newbury," he said gruffly. "I trust you are more comfortable now."

Ben stepped sideways, and I took in a slow, steadying breath as I looked up. Marlow wore evergreen velvet coattails over a white shirt and gray vest. Someone had also brought *him* new clothes. A clean cravat, doubly tied, was pinned with a diamond stud as it had been in times past.

Our eyes locked, and for a moment, I remembered how I'd felt when we'd first met. Charmed. Giddy. Like a little girl who'd longed to become a princess.

This time, whatever allure he'd held dissipated. A handsome man stood in front of me, but he was just a man. Everything about him was polished and pressed and perfected. Even his subdued smile and the way he held his hands behind his back.

"I am well, thank you," I said. "Forgive me for keeping you waiting."

Ben looked between us, then said, "Your Grace, is there anything I can do to—"

"Leave us," Marlow said without blinking. "We shall walk home."

Ben's brow furrowed, but he nodded. He bowed, and our eyes met for the slightest second. Just long enough for me to sense his worry.

What would Marlow do? What would he say, now that he had me alone?

A servant approached with Ben's horse, so he strode toward him and mounted.

Marlow, silent and towering, flicked his hand, and his two servants joined us. Then he raised his arm for me to take, and said, "Come."

Slowly, I laced my arm through his. I looked up at Ivy Manor, at the windows high on the building, and pictured Charlie lying in his bed with Liza nearby. My stomach dropped to my toes. I felt more ill than if I'd eaten a hundred cheesecakes, more trapped than I had ever felt alone in my bedchamber, and more dismal than a girl with no prospects at all.

Marlow must have sensed my feelings as we walked down the drive, for he said, "His surgeon is well trained. And your friend, Miss Ollerton, will settle and feel much better by morning."

"Thank you, Your Grace," I said. And I meant it. Marlow did not deserve to be abandoned. But what could I do?

"You are most welcome."

Despite his words, I felt completely out of place. This was wrong. I did not fit here. Rolled gravel crunched beneath our feet.

"Miss Newbury, I was harsh earlier, but I hope you do not mistake my intentions as lack of care. You set out in a very precarious way, and as my intended, as the future duchess, you simply cannot abandon everything and run off as you did."

I chose my words carefully, thoughtfully. "Yes, Your Grace. A future duchess would never do such a thing."

"You are fortunate that I came along in time. I'll admit, I had no intention of surprising you early. But my mother insisted the wedding would seem more natural if we grew accustomed to one another beforehand." He seemed to stand taller, like the trees that lined either side of the road we walked upon.

I swallowed hard. There was silence for several steps. "And what happens if we do not grow accustomed to one another?"

He looked amused by my question. "Then we shall do what all of Society does. We shall pretend."

I nodded slowly. Pretend. For the rest of my life he wanted me to pretend to love him. Perhaps before Charlie I could have. Maybe I still could. But now that I knew the difference, staying with Marlow would be subjecting myself to a life of misery.

His eyes smiled down at me as we rounded the bend. He was hopeful and somehow both gentle and commanding.

After everything that happened, everything I'd done, he was trying to make this arrangement work. That was more than many wives could say of their husbands. For some other woman, he'd make a fine companion.

But not for me. Any moment I spent with the duke was a moment I was missing Charlie. And right now Charlie needed me. Any further conversation would only make the inevitable worse.

The duke led me in silence for a time, seeming to appreciate the view. The sparkling sunlight through hundreds of leaves, the sounds of birdsong, and the rustling of life all around us. I could paint this scene a thousand times and still it would not be right.

"Are you certain this is what you want, Your Grace? We may never suit."

He pursed his lips and looked sideways at me. "We'll suit. One way or another."

"How can you be sure?"

"Because I have seen it time and time again. Marriage is a strategic play. When you calculate well, two people get everything they want, and they start off happily. Of course, there will be bumps along the way, but I shall hazard a guess your newly acquired status will be enough to placate you."

Not anymore. "And if it isn't?"

He slowed his steps and pursed his lips. I was pressing him too hard. He had to sense my intention. He flicked a hand in the air, and his servants jogged ahead, out of earshot. "Miss Newbury—"

"I cannot do this," I interjected. "I am sorry, Your Grace, but I do not want to marry you."

The words were like bricks, and each one spoken took a weight off my usually tense shoulders. And I was free.

I expected him to explode, or at the very least turn red. Instead, he drew in a breath through his nose and examined me. "You and I signed the same contract. I understand having reservations. But I assure you, I will do everything in my power to make you happy."

He took a step closer, holding my arms in his hands. That same citrusy smell I remembered wafted between us. "You will be busy in your new role. You shall make new friends, order around your servants. And you can redecorate and repaper the entire east wing if you wish. I know we do not know each other well, but in time, you will see that I am loyal to my family. I care greatly for their well-being, and I will not bring you into our lives only to toss you aside and make you miserable."

I looked down at his chest, at the diamond stud on his cravat. He could offer me the world, and it would not be enough. "No, Your Grace. I am quite serious."

He forced a laugh, as though this was all some grand jest against him. "Rosalind, we will marry in five days."

My name sounded so insignificant on his tongue. There was no gentleness, no measure of emotion. When Charlie said my name, it felt like an embrace.

"No. We will not." I held his gaze, serious and unyielding, until the barest hint of frustration flared in his nostrils.

He stepped back and shook his head, searching the grass, the sky, the gardens. His jaw ticked, muscles popping as he gritted his teeth and composed himself. Even his silence was powerful.

"I am the Duke of Marlow." His voice was low and devoid of inflection, but still I shivered with fear.

"Please forgive me," I said. "I know all of this will be an embarrassment, canceling the wedding—"

"The *wedding?*" Marlow scrunched his nose at the word. "Do you think I care about the wedding?"

I parted my lips to speak, but nothing came out. I had expected Marlow to be frustrated, even angry, but thwarted?

"No, of course you don't understand," he said. "You have no idea what you so easily toss aside." He drew in a strong breath that seemed to grow him three sizes. "Your father thinks he owns that parcel of land, but it belongs to *my* dukedom."

I puffed up with defense. "Are you insinuating that my father stole your land?"

"Decades ago, it was bartered or traded or sold at some painfully low price thanks to the one weak link in the Marlow line. The one ignorant half-wit who cost us half of our holdings. That land is the final piece of what we lost. You will get your title, and I will have my land."

He looked away and refused to meet my gaze. He was different now, and we both knew it. Gone was the man who offered forgiveness, who used his power to fix instead of to harm, who aimed only for my comfort. He'd been kind and compassionate and welcoming.

But this was the true Duke of Marlow. And he would not be trifled with.

My hands curled into fists, and I blinked back the wetness in my eyes. "I shall never love you. I couldn't."

"Your heart will make room." His words were clipped

and final, his eyes hard. How quickly he constructed stalwart walls around his heart. If he had not offered it to me so willingly only moments ago, I might have believed he did not have a heart at all.

But *I* did. "Your Grace. My heart is already full."

His eyes widened, clear with understanding, and his composure wavered for the slightest moment. "There is someone else." He laughed as though everything now made sense. "Was there always?"

"No," I hurried to say. "I mean yes, but not always."

"If you've met someone over the last month, he will hardly keep. Who is he? Who dares to touch my intended?"

I would not name him. I couldn't.

"Mr. Winston." His flat voice sent a chill down my spine.

"Please, Your Grace. He has respected our engagement; it is I who am not satisfied. Do you see? I know who you are and what you offer, and I know that I am mad to refuse you, but I have fallen in love. Please understand, nothing less would keep me from your offer."

Marlow stood still, facing me but not meeting my gaze. A vein in his temple protruded, but this time, he did not temper his emotions.

"Nothing, in fact, *will* keep you from my offer. Not even your little infatuation. You signed an agreement. You *will* meet me before the vicar, and so help me if I am left standing there alone, your family will spend the rest of their lives regretting the day they bargained with me. Have I made myself quite clear?"

His voice echoed around us with enough power to make me shrink in my spot. With authority. With promise. As though he could create worlds. And yet. His eyes did not match his tone. They were almost . . . fearful. Like I could wound him if only I found the right entrance.

Somewhere hidden under all his threats and evident frustration was just a man. A man desperate to save himself at whatever cost.

My family would pay the price.

I swiped a loose tear from my cheek. "There must be another way." I hated how weak and fragile my voice sounded. "Perhaps my father will sell the land."

"I offered him an outrageous sum. He would not sell." His teeth clenched as he spoke. "And at this point, I'd rather make his sons pay for that mistake before offering to purchase a second time."

"I will speak to him. We could come to a reasonable agreement and cry off amicably." I wrung my hands together. "No one need know the details. We will be in your debt—"

"Enough!" His voice rang harsh and heavy in the air. Then, in an apparent effort to control his temper, he whispered, "Enough."

"You are blackmailing me." My voice wavered.

"What other choice do I have? In fairness, Rosalind, your father forced *my* hand when he offered this union as the only means by which I might purchase his land."

"My father would *never* force your hand like this."

"Your father's ambitions are no more saintly than my own. He gave me a choice, just as I am giving you one now." He stepped closer, towering over me, and spoke in a hushed voice. "Believe me, I have seen the ugliest sides of the world, and they can be much uglier than this."

I stepped back. How could this be happening? How could I finally reach the edge, only to be pushed back the length of my progress. "You are in earnest, then? If I do not marry you, you'll—"

"Do whatever it takes to make you regret it." He lowered his chin. His eyes were set.

I looked down at my hands, at the bunched fabric of my skirts in my fists. The choice was clear: Charlie or my family? If I chose Charlie, the duke would ruin my family. But if I chose my family, I would never see Charlie again.

In a flash of memory, I faced the cliff's edge, the same one he and I had visited in Dover. How free I'd felt. How happy and fearless, infinite and alive.

And yet, I feared heights for good reason. Just beyond the cliff was a sharp and dangerous fall. And *this* time, I stood on the edge not with Charlie, but with Benjamin, Mama, Father, Jasper, and Nicholas. How could I ask them to face the fall with me? How could I lead them toward certain outcast, ridicule, failure, and despair at the expense of following my heart?

I could not have my family *and* Charlie. One would suffer.

Or maybe not.

Maybe only *I* had to suffer.

My family would rise if I married Marlow. Charlie would recover in time. He'd already decided to go home, to live a life Henry would be proud of. Whether he and I created a life together would not change that.

He'd told me he loved me in so many ways and words, but he had not offered for me. He could move on with his life never truly knowing I'd have said yes. He'd mourned and lived again once before.

With a title, I could help my family, but even more than that, I could combat whatever rumors Lord Langdon spit on Charlie's name. I could ensure Charlie lived a happy life.

Far away from the cliff's edge.

I met Marlow's stare. Then lifted my chin. "You will give me time to adjust."

"To mourn your loss," he scoffed.

"And you will not seek out Mr. Winston, nor harm him in any way."

His lips flattened, and he swallowed. "As long as you never see him again. You will be loyal to me. To my family."

The pain in my chest overwhelmed me. I lifted my eyes to his, willing myself to say the words that would seal my fate once and for all. "Yes, Your Grace."

"Very well." His words were clipped. "A happy start. How fortunate we are both so well versed in pretending."

He flicked his hand, and his servants came closer. We walked in silence down the drive until the house came into view.

"Take Miss Newbury inside," Marlow said to his servants. "I shall need a brisk walk alone before returning for dinner."

Chapter Twenty-Six

I couldn't breathe. I could hardly stop crying long enough to wash my face in the basin Molly had brought to my bedroom. She hadn't questioned me, but simply dried my face with a towel and fixed my hair and rubbed my back until I composed myself enough to walk down to the drawing room.

Mama held out her arm to me as I entered. Her lips were smiling, but the rest of her was stiff and still as though she feared moving out of place.

The duchess was thinner and more youthful than I'd imagined, and she regarded me like I was a dress needing alterations. I stopped to curtsey, and she nodded her seeming approval.

The duke walked in shortly after, and stiffly led me to my seat in the dining room.

"Are you comfortable?" he asked without inflection as he tucked in my chair.

"Yes, thank you," I managed, knowing everyone was watching us closely. This would be the rest of my life. Making polite conversation with this man. Avoiding the fact that before we wed, I declared my heart, not for him, but for someone else entirely.

I picked at every dish, including the rosemary lambchops, which I had chosen for the menu myself, knowing they were Marlow's favorite.

After dinner, I played the pianoforte for the duchess and Mama while the men took port and cigars. When the clock at last struck eleven, the men came out to bid us good night.

"Do not expect us back until dinner tomorrow," Father said. "We have business in the morning."

"We?" I asked.

Father's eyes met mine, but I could not hold his gaze. Could he see my misery? My lies and deceit?

"Your father is introducing me to some of his business associates," Marlow answered. "Then we shall finalize the paperwork for my land."

"I can only imagine your excitement," I rallied back.

"It shall be the highlight of my trip."

"But surely the highlight is seeing your bride," his mother whispered, touching his arm.

"Of course." He looked down at me. "She is, thankfully, a handsome sight to behold."

Ben cleared his throat and stepped forward with a furrowed brow. His lips parted to speak, but Mama took hold of his shoulder.

"If there is anything you need . . ." Mama said to the duke and duchess. "Please do not hesitate to ask."

Then Marlow took my hand, his countenance unreadable, and bowed over it. "I shall see you when I return."

I swallowed hard, and curtseyed. His words were not a

question, because he knew I could never leave him. Not with such a serious threat to my family.

Benjamin came around and pulled me aside. "Good night, Ros," he said with a strange look in his eye. When he took my hand, he slipped a folded piece of paper into my palm.

I gave him a confused look but did not ask questions.

Instead, I took slow steps around our party, grabbed a candle from a table, and walked until the darkness on the stairway hid me well enough from watching eyes.

I opened the paper Ben had given me. Using the candle's light, I found Liza's easy scrawl inside.

> *How are you, Ros?*
>
> *I am still quite shaken from this afternoon. I cannot go above a half hour without wondering what could have happened to us. What might have happened had Charlie not fought those men off and the duke not arrived to shoot at them.*
>
> *Charlie is well. Sleeping. The surgeon's work was thorough, and we are confident Charlie will recover.*
>
> *There is news. His Grace's servants came just after dinner to inform us that two of the men have been apprehended. I cannot recall their names, but Papa claims they were hired out by Lord Langdon in revenge toward Charlie. They were told to bruise him up, and Papa thinks that because Charlie is so skilled, they grew angry and . . . Can you believe it? All this over Charlie overestimating his strength and breaking a man's arm. A man who aimed to hurt him in the first place!*

I want to be furious with Charlie for getting tangled up in such a mess, but all I can think about is how some men get all the luck and some do not. Some have power and wealth and influence while others are left with shreds of what they wanted for their future.

Why is life sometimes so unfair?

I hope you are well. You were so brave, and I cannot thank you enough for aiding Charlie. No one will ever know what you did, but I cannot help wishing they would. If nothing else, so they could see you for the fearless girl you are.

I would not have written so late, but I am certain if I cannot sleep, then neither can you, and I made a promise to Charlie before he drifted off that I would send this. Every time he wakes, he asks after you. I do not have the heart to remind him that you are with the duke.

I shall not utter another word on the subject after this, for it would do no good. I forgive you for lying to me on the matter, because I don't believe you realized your feelings until now. I hope, in return, you'll forgive me for being so blinded by my own lacking, that I could not see yours.

I hope you find happiness. Know that no matter what the future holds for you, I am ever so proud to be your friend.

I love you, Ros.

Liza

Molly was waiting for me in my room. She took the candle from my hand, and I folded up the paper. It would do no good to reread Liza's words, nor to linger on the hope and longing that stirred my heart knowing Charlie had asked after me.

That he wanted me there.

Molly moved behind me and started untying my dress, but I stopped her. I could not go through the motions, not tonight. I pulled her around to face me.

Her countenance grew serious. "What is it, Miss Newbury? Are you unwell?"

The tenderness in her voice crumbled my defenses, and my eyes filled with tears. I buried my face in my hands, and Molly's slender arms wrapped around me.

"Oh, Miss Newbury. What has happened? Is it the duke?"

"Molly, I do not love him," I managed as I wiped my wet cheeks. I choked on a sob.

"But that has never bothered you before." She brushed back my hair with her fingers, her thoughts working behind her eyes. "What has changed?"

I could not say it aloud. I trusted Molly, truly I did, but if word reached Mama and Father, what would they say? What might Marlow do to our family?

"You love *him*, don't you?" Molly asked in a quiet voice. "Mr. Winston."

Our eyes met, and mine filled with more tears. I nodded and fell onto her shoulder. Mine was a hopeless case. Owning my heart meant risking the livelihoods of the ones I loved the most. Father could disown me, but even that would not be enough to save our family from the duke's reach.

I cried until Molly's shoulder was wet with my tears. Then she dressed me in my nightclothes and tucked me in with a cup of warm lavender tea and made me promises for tomorrow that she could not keep.

At some point after the moon had sat high in the sky long enough, I drifted off into a deep, dreamless slumber.

Chapter Twenty-Seven

Molly woke me early. She said nothing of our conversation from the night before but gave me special cream to soothe my puffy eyelids and dressed me in a light-yellow dress fit for a duchess.

"Are the men gone?" I asked as she smoothed my hair into an intricate weave of curls.

Molly smiled softly back at me in the mirror. "Yes. Though Mrs. Newbury has been up since dawn. She insists you be seen about the house, or else the duchess shall assume you are a slothful creature. And we cannot have her knowing the truth." Her lips twitched.

"I do not wish to exchange pleasantries with the duchess." I looked down, and Molly squeezed my shoulders.

So instead of attending to my duties, I hid away in the gardens to fill my dulled senses with something sweet. But I was empty still. My heart wept and gnashed its teeth, so I took it through the fields to the grove, despite knowing that Charlie was not well enough to be outside. But my heart had tricked me, for instead of comfort, the trees, the earth, and the pond's edge all brought me infinitely more pain.

Molly brought news of Charlie's continuing recovery, which should have made me happier than it did. I would give anything to visit him, or Liza, even. But doing so would risk the deal I'd struck with Marlow. It was my turn to keep *Charlie* safe. And that required distance between us.

By evening, the men returned from their business in town, and Marlow had cheered to the idea of marriage, or at least of having his land once and for all, enough to look in my direction again.

I slept a few hours that night, and later on into morning, only showing my face downstairs long enough to appease Mama and learn more about Piedmont Castle from the duchess.

On our third day together, while we awaited dinner in the drawing room, the duchess turned to me on the settee and said, "You will need to grow a backbone, dear. You are too quiet. Too malleable. People can sense that."

"Quiet? Ros?" Father chuckled from where he sat facing Marlow by the hearth. "You are mistaken, Your Grace. Our Rosalind is a true leader. When she sets her mind to something, no one can stop her."

"Is that so?" Marlow's eyes flicked to mine. This was no show of care or curiosity. He likely worried that I'd set my mind *against* him and he would lose his precious land.

Would that I could take the risk. That I could call his bluff and risk the chance that he would blot out my family from Society's good graces. But just as he loved his dukedom and his land, I loved my family. They—and Charlie—were everything to me. And I would protect them.

"Normally, I would agree, Father. But I have recently learned that even in the direst of circumstances, one can always be swayed by love and family. Perhaps that is the weakness Her Grace senses."

Marlow frowned. No, he *scowled*.

"How perfectly sweet," the duchess said approvingly.

Ben left Father and Marlow at the hearth and approached me. His expression was tight, bothered. "Ros?"

"Yes?"

"May I speak with you?"

I looked to Mama, who quirked a brow, then shook her head slightly. Then to Father, who raised his chin.

"On second thought," Ben continued. "May I have a word with my family in private? In the study."

Mama held a hand to her chest. "Benjamin, darling, we are entertaining our friends at present. You cannot simply call us away."

"A family meeting," Benjamin persisted. "In the study."

"Now?" Father asked. The question held a greater meaning, as though he sought to trust his son but needed to know whether or not the matter was urgent.

"Now," Ben replied with a single nod of his head.

"Forgive us, Your Grace," Father said, standing. "Just a moment, I am sure."

"But Mr. Newbury," Mama sputtered, following after him. "*Frederick!*"

"Rosalind?" Ben encouraged me.

Had something happened? Was Charlie unwell?

My stomach shrank as I followed my family down the hall.

Mama whispered harshly to Ben. "Do you have *any idea* how embarrassing that was? The *Duke* and *Duchess* of *Marlow*! Rosalind's *intended*."

Father shut the study door behind us as the four of us crowded around Father's desk. He squeezed around to his seat, and Benjamin stood to the right, leaning on the side of the mahogany wood.

Mama stood by the door, clearly impatient to make an exit, and I crossed to the window on the opposite side of the little room on bated breath.

"I have done a disservice to our family," Ben started. "I have kept secrets. I have been blind. I have let my own ambition and selfishness get in the way of what has been right in front of us all along."

Oh, no. This was serious indeed. In all my wallowing and wasting away, what had I missed? "Ben, what has happened?"

Ben looked directly at Father. "You told me once that the most important work a man will do is within his home. Within his family. I did not understand exactly what you meant at the time, but since the duke has arrived, I am starting to."

Father looked solemnly at his son. He placed his hands on the top of his desk. "I have no reason to believe anyone in this family is unhappy. Is there something you wish to tell us, Benjamin? And must it really be said at this precise moment, when our visitors are sitting aimlessly in our drawing room?"

Ben's gaze flicked to mine. He couldn't be talking about . . . me?

"Rosalind is unhappy," he declared. "She does not wish to marry the duke."

My nerves came alive, and my stomach bottomed out. *No.* Ben had no idea what he was doing. Trying to absolve my connection to the duke would hurt him and our family more than he could imagine.

"She has said nothing to me," Father said flatly. Then he looked up, and his eyes widened when they met mine. "Rosalind?"

Tears threatened, and I blinked wordlessly to push them back. What could I do? What could I say? I had kept the truth from my family for so long, but now that it had been spoken aloud, keeping it inside was more painful than a physical blow to the chest.

"Ros?" Ben prompted. "You have asked me time and time again to be a responsible man. To uphold my duty to our family as you have done." He swallowed and looked hard at me. "Sometimes the most responsible thing one can do is to tell the truth."

Mama stood still as a board at the door.

"I only wish to please our family," I said, forcing every ounce of energy into steadying my voice. "I will marry the duke. It will be my contribution to our legacy."

"Yes, but do you *want* to?" Ben spoke low, forcefully. "Do you actually want to marry the duke?"

"Ros?" Mama stepped forward.

All three sets of eyes watched me, and I shrank under their attention. What did they want me to say? If I told them the truth, if they insisted I break the marriage contract, the duke would stop at nothing to ruin them. He could. And he would.

My silence filled the room.

"I see," Mama whispered. Her cheeks turned red, her eyes filling with tears. "Fredrick, what can be done?"

"No." I raced forward, grasping the side of the desk beside Ben. "Do nothing. The duke is a powerful man. I see that now, and I must protect you from him."

"No," Ben said with a shake of his head. He took hold of my arm. "No, Ros. We can protect ourselves."

Mama, Ben, and I crowded around Father. Mama turned to face me. "Rosalind, being a member of a family means our ambitions are the same."

"Yes, Mama, I understand, which is why—"

"*Our* ambitions have always been to bring a title to the family."

"—I will take my place in our family legacy."

"But *yours*, darling, is clearly to love and be loved. And who can fault you for that?" Mama took my free hand in hers. Her eyes were filled with tears. "If you would like to change your course, my love, you need only make yourself clear. Disappointment, we can withstand. Embarrassment will fade. But you will always be our daughter, and our priority. Our greatest ambition in life is to see you happy."

I bit hard on my lip and stifled a sob. Could it be true? Could the people I loved the most truly love me despite my weaknesses and many, many mistakes?

I had wronged them in so many ways. I'd been dishonest. I'd told falsehoods. I'd pretended to be someone I wasn't. But still, they offered me compassion and a type of love I'd only ever imagined. Love that was unconditional. Love only a family could give.

But I loved them—and Charlie—too much to hurt them.

"But Mama, you don't understand. The duke is angry; he will force the marriage or ruin Ben and Jasper and Nicholas in every way."

"He will *what?*" Father stood, his shoulders squared and his jaw set.

"I'll fight him," Ben said as he squeezed in closer, until I was surrounded by my family.

I choked out something between a laugh and a cry. "I apologized and tried to make amends after I told him the truth, but he wants our land so badly."

"That bird-witted—" Ben started.

"Whey-faced—" Father spat.

"Loose in the haft—" Mama said, then covered her mouth with both hands.

I drew in an audible breath, and Ben laughed aloud.

Father's brows touched his hairline. "Darling?"

"Forgive me." Her cheeks pinked. "I must speak a truth of my own. Rosalind, you have polished yourself and endured my lectures for weeks now. I wanted to prepare you to be favored by Her Grace, but the truth is, Her Grace is a miserable, conceited—"

"Mama!" I breathed.

"—horrible tripe of a woman who sees fault in nearly anyone and everything." Then she smiled hesitantly. "In truth, I am relieved to hear you will not proceed. You are perfect in every way that matters, and no amount of further polishing will change that. I thought you were happy and only a bit nervous. I was so focused on making everything perfect that I did not stop to truly see. But I am your mother. I should have known, and I am sorry."

I pulled Mama close. "How could you have known? When I did not even realize myself before it was too late?"

"I will speak to His Grace," Father said brusquely.

"Father, he meant his threats," I said, pulling away from Mama. But she kept hold of my arm.

"His threats are weak. That he made them is a testament to how desperate he is. His father would be ashamed." Father looked at his desk and shook his head. "*I* am ashamed. I thought he saw a greater benefit to your union than merely the acquisition of the land. Had I known his aim was singly guided, I would never have bargained with him. A man with no honor is not worthy of my daughter, titled or not."

"I am sorry, Father. I wanted so badly to bring a title to the family."

He raised a hand. "Why do you think it has taken our family generations to marry into one?"

"Mama said there hasn't been an opportunity before me."

"My younger sister, Alice, had men banging down our door religiously," Father mused. "I remember our father pleading with her to marry a baron. But she'd met Marvin Allen at some dinner party, and before we knew it, he was in Father's study, offering everything he had for a chance at her happiness."

"Aunt Alice?" I asked.

"Aunt Alice." Father nodded. "I now see why Father flipped a table when he learned that Alice had chosen a banker over a baron. But I also see why he smiled when he walked her down the aisle all the same. Because as angry as I want to be, I know I do not have much time left to call you mine."

"Oh, Fredrick," Mama cried.

"Well said." Ben clapped lightly before clasping his hands in front of him. "Now, who wants to go and tell our guests the happy news?"

Chapter Twenty-Eight

I paced the floor of the drawing room while Ben and Mama sat nearby. After our family meeting, Father had walked us out and invited Marlow into his study. The clock on the mantel told me the two men had been conversing—and yelling—for more than an hour now.

Only pieces of conversation carried through the slits in the doorframe. Something about "If your father were still alive" followed by, "You will be in my debt for the rest of your life."

The duchess had vanished into the foyer. Their empty carriage pulled up and waited in the drive. I watched as servants carried bags and luggage down and loaded them onto the carriage. They were leaving, but on what terms?

Then the door to Father's study opened and footsteps sounded down the hall.

Low voices murmured, then the entry door opened and closed. Ben and Mama stood and joined me in the center of the room.

Father walked in. His face was weary. "There will be no

wedding. And he has agreed to part amicably. Though we are being robbed, for I've agreed to sell the land for the same price your great-grandfather purchased it."

Ben blew out a breath. "Robbed, indeed. There goes your pin money and your entire dowry, Ros."

"He is gone?" I could hardly believe it. This had all happened so fast.

Father nodded. "He is gone."

Mama's lips parted in disbelief. "We must write letters to your wedding guests before any further plans are made."

"Yes, Mama." I would do anything she asked. Accomplish any task. Attend any appointment. Sing any aria.

"And we must brace ourselves for a very long summer," she said. "There will be talk. Ceaseless gossip. Our names will be in every paper."

"That should be an exciting life experience, eh, Ros?" Ben elbowed me. "How do you feel?"

I thought back to that not-so-long-ago day when I'd found my list in the bottom of my trunk. When I'd dreamed of Aunt Alice's wedding and longed for one of my own. To my first meeting with Charlie, when he'd frightened me and offended me, only to have him save my life in more ways than one.

I took his arm and said, "I feel *free*."

Mama wiped a tear from her cheek. "I imagine you shall want to go and tell *Liza* the news."

The look in her eyes told me she did not mean *Liza* at all. But I did not wait. After embracing my family, I raced out of the drawing room and out the entry door, down the stairs, and into the endlessly green pastures toward Ivy Manor.

"Derricks." I nodded breathlessly to the footman as he greeted me. "Good day."

"Not today, Miss Newbury. The house is again closed to visitors. And with dinner almost served—"

"We've been through this." I keeled over, begging more air to fill my lungs.

"The family has been through a lot these past few days, as you are well aware, and needs time to recover."

I straightened and searched frantically for any source of inspiration. I looked to the side toward the stables. "Should your horses be roaming freely?"

"What?" Derricks stepped outside, eyes searching the grounds for horses he'd never find, and I took my opportunity. Bounding in the house, I raced straight to the drawing room.

"Miss *Newbury*!" Derricks cried.

"Liza!" I called. The drawing room was empty.

"What is this about?" Their butler, Mr. Hudson, appeared out of the dining room. "Miss Newbury, what is the matter?"

"Rosalind?" Mrs. Ollerton held a hand to her chest as she descended from the upstairs floor with Liza on her heels. "What is the meaning of this?"

"The house"—Derricks's face turned fiery-red up to his ears—"is closed."

"Quite right," Mrs. Ollerton agreed as they met me in the foyer. "And I saw the duke and duchess leave. We assumed you'd have gone with them."

"Not today," I said weakly. "Not ever, actually."

Both women froze.

"You cried off," Liza said with astonishment. "You really did."

The words seemed to sink into Mrs. Ollerton much more slowly. Her chest suddenly puffed up and with a flash of her skirts and a wave of her hands, she said, "Where is your mother? I must go to her at once."

"At home," I said to encourage her.

The front door opened and closed and Mrs. Ollerton was off.

I turned to Liza. "May I please," I started, but I almost lost my breath. "May I please speak with Charlie?"

"Charlie?" Liza's shoulders sank. "His mother came yesterday. They departed early this morning."

I wanted to cry out in despair, but then, I realized what Liza meant. "He went home?"

"Yes." She gave me a sad smile. "He made the decision all on his own. He left you something." She reached out for my hand and tugged me toward the staircase.

Heart in my throat, I followed her to her room with only one thought: Charlie was home. After all his time away, after all his pain both inward and outward, still he chose to face the most painful path in the end. And I was so proud of him.

She let go of my hand and paced to her desk to pick up something. She brought it near, and I recognized it instantly. My painting.

"I'd forgotten completely."

"He didn't. I kept his secret. He built this frame, pieced it together perfectly. Then he went back to the opera a few nights ago, and somehow managed to slip out your watercolor

and sneak it back home. He wanted to give it to you himself."
Liza shook her head. "Well, honestly, he wanted to take it
home with him. But when you never came . . . I think he
thought this was best."

She held out the framed picture and a folded letter. "I'll
fetch us some tea," she said, patting my arm.

She closed the door behind her, and I sank onto her four-
poster bed.

I traced my thumb along the simple carvings Charlie had
made to the picture frame. Ivy, the very same that grew upon
the house and upon the trees in the grove, climbed up the
sides and met with tiny flowers. He must have worked on it
every day. And it fit my painting perfectly.

I set it aside and picked up his letter.

I had no idea what to expect. Charlie had never written me anything before. No man had. My fingers stilled on
the folds. What if inside this letter, instead of what I wanted
to hear, he refuted ever loving me? What if he apologized or
claimed madness and embarrassment from our time together?

Look at this frame, my heart whispered. And carefully I
unwrapped the page.

Dearest Rosalind,

His hand was slanted, but sleek. Perfectly Charlie. I
wanted to laugh and cry all at once.

> *Forgive me for not seeking you out before I left.*
> *I am not certain you would have wanted the inter-*
> *ference.*
> *As promised, I hope this painting finds you well.*

Such a beautiful picture deserves an equally beautiful frame, and while I cannot claim to be perfect, I tried my best to craft something deserving of the honor. I found this wood from a felled tree in the grove, where we so often met, and where I fell utterly and entirely in love with you.

Please do not feel sorry for me. I am happy to have known you at all. Happy to have helped you in some small way in your journey. You certainly inspired me in mine.

And so, I wanted to thank you, dearest Ros, you brilliant, beautiful girl, for being true to who you are. What a list you created! I can only imagine what more you will do and see and become. I do wish I could have withheld my affection only if it meant that you and I could maintain a comfortable friendship.

But that would not allow me to be true to myself. And I am trying. Truly, I am. My mother is here, and she has taken me in her arms and loved me like only a mother can. She has humbled me. And I am going home.

Can you believe it?

I know you will argue me, but I shall say it anyway: You say I do not belong on your list. That I did not change but merely found myself again. Perhaps that much is true. But on the whole, you are wrong, Ros. I have changed. I want to be a braver, kinder, more generous man because of you.

So with a happy heart, I tell you: Rosalind

Newbury, you have checked off every single item on your list. You are ready for whatever life brings you.

Thank you, my dearest friend, for never giving up on me. For giving me even an ounce of your affection. I shall carry it with me always.

Yours,
Charlie

"Lovely, isn't it?"

I wiped my eyes and looked up to find Liza leaning against her doorframe. She scrunched her nose. "I read the whole thing. I could not stand it."

"Liza!" I chided with a surprised laugh, still tearful from the loveliest letter I'd ever received. I was a mess. Entirely.

She strode to the bed and plopped down beside me. "I tried to fold it neatly back so you would not guess, but I don't know why I tried. Of course I'd have to tell you the truth." She took my free hand and pulled it into her lap. "You love him, too, do you not?"

I met her gaze with a weak smile and nodded. "I do."

Liza nodded, and together we sat in silence. Charlie was gone. He'd said goodbye in this letter. Without any offer to take me with him.

"I'll call for the carriage." Liza stood and rang her bell.

"What?"

She paced around her bed and started pulling dresses from her armoire. "I'll send Harriet over to Molly and have her pack your things. We'll have to stop at an inn halfway, but we can be to Whitely by sunrise."

"Liza!" I shrieked.

She sighed. "For heaven's sake, Ros, this is not our first runaway. Nor our first close encounter with death."

"I must be dreaming," I muttered. First the duke leaving, then Charlie's letter, and now, Liza's newfound fearlessness?

"How can you stand to wait?" Her eyes bulged, and I could not help it. I let my smile free.

"I cannot. But there are a few things I must see to first."

Chapter Twenty-Nine

Between the four of us, the carriage was stuffy and hot. Liza monopolized the view out one window, while Molly and Harriett commanded the other. Since I was the reason we were all stuck together in a carriage for so long, I would not make a single complaint. I'd have sat on the floor if I had to.

I rechecked every item on the list I'd made before leaving:

Cancel all wedding plans and help Mama write letters of regret to all attendees.

Donate the flowers and food to our servants and those of Ivy Manor.

Spend an entire day with my family and beg their forgiveness a million times over.

Pack for a fortnight.

Breathe.

"We're here!" Liza crooned, leaning back for me to take in the view. "Whitely is expansive, is it not? Not quite as big as your father's house, but they have an *orangery*, Ros! And their music room has every instrument imaginable. Henry played the viola."

I stared up at the great tall building hovering higher as we drew closer. It was square and stately, modeled elaborately after the Baroque fashion. A white stable stood in the distance, and a round building with tall columns further back. My heart pounded wildly in my chest. Somewhere within these borders was Charlie. And he had no idea I was coming.

The carriage jolted to a stop.

Liza squealed and squeezed my arm.

My smile wobbled from anxiety and eagerness. "Stop. You are frightening me."

She swatted playfully at me and cackled. "Come and meet my aunt and uncle. You will love them. After you marry Charlie, we will be *true sisters* at last!"

"Liza, we won't actually be sisters."

"Close enough!"

"And all this depends upon Charlie desiring what I desire."

She looked heavenward as she descended. "Honestly, Rosalind, we are far beyond all that."

I followed her down the carriage steps. My heart pounded in my ears and in my head, and the door Liza knocked upon seemed to swim in waves.

Do not faint, I told myself.

A servant opened the door, but before he could speak, he moved out of the way for a regal woman who looked so strangely familiar. I was sure we'd never met, but there was something in her eyes.

She looked like Charlie.

"Aunt Edith!" Liza exclaimed.

The woman stepped out with surprise and outstretched arms. She and Liza embraced.

"Eliza, what on earth are you doing here? Is everything well?" She peeked over Liza's shoulder at me and furrowed her brow. "Who is this?"

"Aunt Edith, may I introduce my dearest friend, Miss Rosalind Newbury."

The woman's face fell.

"Ros," Liza continued. "My aunt Edith Winston. Charlie's mother."

I curtseyed as best I could. "A true pleasure to meet you, Mrs. Winston."

She looked between the two of us in silence, with that same almost distraught look upon her face.

Then a girl squeezed her way through the narrow doorframe in between them. "Liza?"

"Eloise!" Liza's delight doubled.

I needed no introduction to Charlie's younger sister. She had his eyes, his coloring in every way, the same bounciness and energy in her step.

"Why have you come?" Mrs. Winston's voice pulled me in. "Forgive me. My son is . . . well, I wonder why you would visit us so soon after your wedding."

Oh. "I am no longer engaged," I said.

"She cried off!" Liza said, throwing her hands in some sort of celebratory fashion. "She has gone mad, but we still adore her."

"You jilted the Duke of Marlow?" Mrs. Winston looked taken aback.

"Yes," I said. Then I waited. For what, I was not sure.

Charlie's sister—Eloise—threaded arms with Liza, her eyes locked on mine. "*Are* you mad? Or wait—" She lowered her voice. "*Are you with child?*"

My face heated instantly. "I—I'm sorry?"

"Eloise Anne Winston," her mother chided. "Into the house at once. You wonder why I cannot let you into decent society. Heaven and earth."

Then I realized we had not been invited in. Mrs. Winston's greeting was less than welcoming, and sudden embarrassment engulfed me. I'd decided against marrying a duke. And she thought me truly mad. "Liza, perhaps we should go."

"Do not be silly," Mrs. Winston waved a hand in the air. "Miss Newbury, when you are older, much older, and your children grow old enough to experience genuine heartbreak, you will understand why I hesitate in this odd, incredibly unique circumstance we find ourselves in."

I nodded, unsure of what to say.

"You will understand why I must ask you to divulge your secrets in such an uncomfortable and direct manner. Before another word is said, I must ask: *Why* did you break your engagement?"

Liza looked tensely at her aunt. Clearly, she too had not expected such a reaction.

I licked my lips. "The truth, Mrs. Winston?"

"Yes, please."

I took a deep breath. "I left the duke because I love your son. And I came here today because I think he loves me too."

She tilted her head and gave me the barest hint of a smile. "Charlie? My Charlie?"

I nodded. Liza swooned and Eloise made a gagging noise, and I bit my lip to keep from laughing. "Is he home?"

"He is finishing work on his new house," Eloise said. "He shall be more than happy to see you. All I've heard since he arrived is 'Rosalind this,' and 'Rosalind that,' and 'Today must be her wedding day, and by tomorrow she'll have forgotten I exist.'"

Mrs. Winston laughed. The sound was musical, and it brightened her whole face. "You horrible girl, do not speak of your brother so. He has been grieving."

The thought, for once, made me soar.

"The house is not far, is it?" Liza asked.

"Shall we all go?" Eloise perked up. "I would love to see the surprise on Charlie's face when he sees Miss Newbury."

All eyes looked to Mrs. Winston, whose thin lips flattened as she considered the display we would most certainly cause together. "Oh, all right, get your bonnet and we'll take her halfway."

"Halfway?" Eloise whined. "At the very least, three-quarters. You cannot even see his eyes *halfway*." She huffed, disappearing into the house with her mother.

Liza grinned and our eyes met. "He is going to fall over when he sees you."

My stomach tightened, and I pressed a suddenly cold hand to my burning cheeks.

"Shall we?" Mrs. Winston said with a crisp bow under her chin and a straw hat decorated with wisteria. She stopped beside me, almost my height exactly, and held out her arm to thread through mine as we walked back to the carriage. "Tell me, Miss Newbury, what was it like growing up as the oldest child with three younger brothers?"

Her eyes had turned kind, encouraging even, with a hint of teasing. She knew about me. And wanted to know more. A footman helped us into the carriage, with Liza and Eloise just behind. Once we were situated on our bench, I said, "I learned quickly to peel my bedcovers back before settling in each night." I narrowed my eyes at her, and she laughed.

"Smart girl."

"Thank heavens I had Liza next door. I would have never survived."

Another laugh, and she squeezed my arm. "I do believe Charlie feels similarly about his sisters, but instead of his bed covers, he worried about waking up covered in rouge."

"He looks rather pretty in red," Eloise added half seriously as she sat across from me. Then she banged on the roof and we were off. "You do know about his nose, right? It will never go back to the way it was."

"Eloise!"

"A woman should know what she's getting into. And, also, while we're on the subject, he spends a ridiculous amount of time in the water closet every evening."

"Heaven and earth." Mrs. Winston clutched her chest.

Eloise prattled on about Charlie's habits and his temper when she aggravated him, and all the while Liza laughed and grinned at me.

Then, after what seemed like moments later, the carriage rolled to a stop. I peeked out my window at a little house in the distance.

"Come, now. Hurry down. He'll have seen us by now."

Liza and Eloise, then Mrs. Winston, descended. And slowly, I took my turn.

They watched me with curious gazes as I descended.

I took in the scene, until I found my focus. A figure standing on the right side of the house. Moving closer, I noted three other men working nearby. One of them *had* to be . . .

"Ros?" Liza touched my arm.

My breaths were coming faster. My heart had long ago bounded free. And there was a tightness in my stomach, a churning that I wanted terribly to cease.

"I cannot stop shaking," I whispered.

"I think he sees us," Eloise said, raising her chin.

Just ahead, in his dark-brown overcoat and tight breeches with faded Hessian boots, was Charlie.

Laborers were plastering stones together to form some sort of barrier a short distance from the little house ahead of us, and it seemed he'd been leading their efforts. We were still too far away for me to read his expression, to know if he recognized me from such a distance.

My stomach flipped over. And under. And around. A tremor shook my whole body. Of their own accord, my feet shuffled to a stop.

"She's going to faint," Eloise said.

"She's fine," Liza argued. "Go and tell him your news, Ros. We'll follow behind."

I met her gaze. Her confidence, her assurance, was everything I needed. I chewed my bottom lip and nodded, then released Liza's arm and took a step forward.

Charlie raised his hand over his forehead to shade his

vision, but he still did not seem to recognize me. His sister waved, and he waved back hesitantly.

I took another step forward. Then another. It was now or never. I had one last item left on my list, and I would see it through.

"Oh, good! Father is with him," Eloise said from a few paces behind.

My shoulders tightened, and I suddenly felt light-headed.

Meeting Charlie's family before we'd even had a chance to discuss our future? Before he'd so much as declared himself? Had I rushed into this?

Perhaps I should have had Ben send him a letter first. Or waited a few weeks for him to settle into his own home. Instead, I was throwing myself at him yet again, and what did I expect him to do? Run to my side and twirl me around and kiss me senseless?

Yes. That was exactly what I had expected.

Somehow, I moved with a steady pace, and I'd drawn close enough that we could see each other's faces. Each other's expressions.

Charlie was frowning. He shifted his weight from one foot to another. Then he straightened.

Then he started to move toward me.

I lifted a hand in a little wave.

A wave? Are you twelve? I chided myself.

I rubbed my cheeks and tried desperately not to gnaw my lips into oblivion.

We met somewhere in the middle, and his face came into focus. He looked exactly as I'd left him. Bruises still healing.

That crooked nose. The little scar on his lower lip. His tousled brown hair and warm chocolate eyes.

"Charlie," I breathed.

His brow pinched, and he stopped an arm's-length away. "R-ros?" He drew a hand through his hair, his expression one of complete surprise. "That is, Your Grace, I assume. I imagine . . ." He looked over my shoulder, then back to me. Then down at his hands. "Forgive me, I did not see your wedding in the papers, although I cannot be certain it would have posted yet."

His sister laughed from somewhere close behind. "He's been watching every day."

He shot her a death-like glare.

I took a step closer. "It did not post."

His eyes flicked to mine. Then back down again. "Right." He frowned. "I shall continue to look for it, then."

"No," I said, wincing. I was botching my explanation, and horribly. "It *won't* post."

Charlie furrowed his brow again. How desperately I wanted to smooth it. He stood still save for the rise and fall of his chest.

I swallowed hard. It was my turn to look away. "I'm terribly sorry to have neglected you after everything that happened."

"You left before the wedding?" His voice was incredulous, and my eyes snapped up to meet his. He looked breathless. Hopeful. "Why would you do such a thing?"

I threw my hands in the air. "Why does everyone keep asking me that?"

His lips twitched.

"I had one last thing to check off my list."

"Change someone's life," he said without pause.

"After running away to Dover, I knew who needed it most."

Charlie chewed on his bottom lip. "The duke."

I waited until his eyes were set on mine. I wanted him to hear me. I wanted him to know that the list I'd finished had worked, but not because I'd completed it. Because I'd found myself in the process.

"No," I said, wrapping my arms around my middle. "I changed mine."

Charlie let out a puff of air and shook his head with a rueful smile on his lips. What on earth was he thinking in that handsome head? And why would he not speak?

"Charles, love," his mother cooed. "Miss Newbury has come all this way, and no one has offered her a tour of the estate."

He grinned at his mother and cleared his throat. "Miss Newbury," he said, biting back his smile. "May I offer you a tour of Whitely?"

"I would like that very much," I said.

"Start here, in this house," his mother instructed. "She'll want to see where you've taken residence. The three of us can wait out here for a time."

"A *short* time," Eloise added.

Charlie looked down at me, studying my face as though looking for my approval. But the question wasn't about propriety, for we'd thrown that to the wind long ago. His question was one I already knew the answer to. He needed only the opportunity to ask.

He held out his arm to me, and I took it. His eyes gleamed.

Our steps flew by in a flash. We said nothing, only watched each other and held fast, perhaps both frightened the other might fly away.

Up five stairs, and Charlie opened the door of his own accord. There would be no butler for so small a house. Perhaps a man of all trades? But not yet.

He closed the door behind us. Its heavy thud reverberated along the walls and up the stairs to what I imagined was three floors. Charlie's arm straightened, and my hand slid down to catch his. He wrapped his fingers around mine and squeezed.

"This," he said with reverence, "is my new home. It's been called Blackstone." He made a funny face, and I laughed.

"And what will *you* call it?"

"I haven't the slightest idea," he admitted as he walked me through the little dining room. Still holding fast to Charlie, I grazed the smooth, polished table, suited for eight, with my free hand. It matched the buffet on the far wall. A vase of flowers was all it needed.

Together we moved into the drawing room, less than half the size of mine at home, with only a settee and four chairs for entertaining. A stack of books sat on a table, and I released Charlie's hand to study them.

Architecture. Framework. Engineering.

"Have you been reading?" I grinned.

He gave me a half smile. "I have indeed."

My gaze stopped on a little notebook left open. It was a drawing of a woman with dark hair and round eyes who looked almost like . . . me?

Charlie snapped it closed and threw it under the settee. His cheeks pinked. "Inspiration," he muttered.

"I should like to see that." I moved to the settee, but he sat on it and splayed out his legs to block me.

"I do have a small library attached to my study." He pointed out of the room. "Shall we?"

"Lead the way," I said innocently.

"I couldn't. You first."

"You are acting strange."

"I am a terrible artist."

I grinned at the ridiculousness of his embarrassment. "You cannot be. You are an architect."

"I can draw buildings, but people? I am learning." He smirked, knowing full well what I wanted to see.

I could not stand it. I wanted to tug him to his feet and kiss that smirk right off his face. "Speaking of building things, the frame you made me is beautiful," I said.

His whole body tensed. Goodbye, smirk. "You saw it."

I paced a few steps away. "And there was this letter attached to it," I said over my shoulder.

"Ah," Charlie said on a breath. He stood from his seat and followed me around the room. "You read it."

I stopped at the mantel, where Charlie had placed his mufflers and a little clock. I looked over my shoulder again and nodded.

He grabbed my wrist, turned me around, and pulled me back a few steps toward the settee. His eyes had changed from teasing to stormy, and his lips were parted and inviting.

"Before I admit to ever writing those words, I must first ask you something."

I threaded my fingers through his. "Anything." I studied his eyes. His wispy hair. His full lips.

"What happened, Ros?" His voice turned soft. "Where is the duke? Where is your family? Did you run away without their permission?"

I should have known he'd worry that I'd left Marlow at the altar and caused a horrible scandal. I shook my head and smiled. "They know exactly where I am."

He let out a breath of relief. His shoulders instantly relaxed.

And then I told him everything. About the duke. About the land. About Marlow's threats to my family.

"Ben called a family meeting and made me confess my feelings. My parents, Charlie . . ." I shook my head, remembering, and fresh emotion raised to the surface. "They saved me."

Charlie nodded in understanding as only he could and thumbed away the loose tears that fell down my cheeks. "Are you happy?" he asked. "Do you regret—?"

"I am happy," I cut him off. "*So* happy."

His smile sent warmth tingling through me. He traced his hands down my sides to my waist. "I've thought of you ceaselessly. I have missed you to distraction."

I laughed with half joy, half shock to finally be exactly where I wanted. "I've missed *you*. How are you?" I glanced at his side and his stomach, where he'd been stabbed. "You should not be out of doors, carrying things around, *lifting*."

"I am much improved." He clasped his hands behind my waist, pulling me closer, and I held his arms. "Eloise has helped me organize my things here. The servants have moved all the heavy things. And soon, so says my new surgeon, I will be cleared for all sorts of lifting." A devilish grin appeared, and he bit his lower lip.

"*Charlie!*" I laughed, leaning back in his steady hold.

"Ros." His smile faded slowly, replaced by a look so serious, so affectionate, so full of radiance that I stopped breathing entirely. "I know you are fresh out of an engagement. Perhaps you need time to recover."

"Charlie," I said his name with great patience. "I have traveled a long way to be exactly where I want to be."

He stared at me for a long moment. "Are you sure?"

Slowly, I traced my fingers up his chest and over his shoulders. Then I wrapped my arms around his neck and pulled his head down until his forehead brushed mine. I nodded against his nose. "Yes."

I wanted nothing, no one, like I wanted Charlie. Our eyes met for the briefest of seconds before his lips pressed firmly against mine.

He held me there, his every movement soft and careful and slow. Affection turned into warmth that flooded me, surrounded me, stopped all time and sense. This feeling was everything I'd been searching for. No list had brought me here. Charlie had. And I belonged to him.

I softened into his hold, and he reacted by pulling me tightly against him. His lips parted mine, devouring, hungry and urgent like he'd been starved, and I realized I'd been too. He tasted like honey and sunshine, and I wanted to live and breathe him. I wanted more of his hands on my sides, trailing up my back, and his fingers tracing my skin and leaving fire in their wake.

My mind, muddled and useless, focused only on him, and I wrapped my arms tighter around his neck. He groaned and kissed me deeper, until we drowned in each other and had to come back up for air.

His lips brushed my jaw, down my neck to my shoulder, and back up again.

My breaths came in wisps. "Charlie," I breathed.

"I love you," he said into my jaw. "Like I've never loved anyone else in all my life. You are the most extraordinary woman I've ever met, and I don't care where I live or what I do as long as I have you."

I swallowed hard and pulled back to see the sincerity in his eyes. He loved me. He wanted me. This incredible man whose broken heart had healed into something more beautiful with its imperfections than in its original form. His hands held my waist, and mine rested on his chest.

I leaned my forehead against his. "I love you, too," I whispered. "Only you, Charlie."

He pulled back with fire and urgency in his eyes. "I have no title to offer you. I am no duke. But what I have is yours to mold however you want it. I have a pond." He kissed my temple. "And I can build you a changing room."

I laughed, and then I realized I was crying.

"Our cook is exceptional. You shall never want for sweets."

"Charlie." I pulled him close and kissed him deep.

"Say you'll marry me. Say yes."

I hesitated just long enough to tease him, then said, "Of course I will."

He growled and laughed and lifted me into the air, spinning me around and laughing more. "Yes?"

"Yes!" I laughed into his neck. But then I realized he was *lifting me.* "Charlie!"

"What?" He stopped abruptly. Quickly enough to trip backward and, in that same breath, we were falling in a heap together onto the settee. He caught me in his lap and pulled me close. His arms again found my waist.

"Are you hurt?" he asked, tightening his hold.

"Me?" I chided him. I wrapped my arms around his neck both to steady myself and to be as close to Charlie as I could. Being in his arms, enveloped in his strength, felt like swimming, so free and so weightless. "You cannot lift me with your wounds so fresh!"

"I can when the woman I love agrees to marry me." He nuzzled my neck, his breath tickling my skin and heating every inch of me.

I sucked in a breath of surprise. "No more lifting."

He pulled back and kissed my cheek. "For one more week." Then my lips. Then the corner of my mouth.

I smiled and leaned into his kiss. "Upon the surgeon's approval."

He moaned, and one hand dropped to my thigh. "And until then?"

"Well, this settee is very nice."

He pulled me, if it were possible, even closer. His lips found my jaw, my neck, and—

"Charlie!" I laughed, half surprised, half driven to utter distraction.

He growled again. "Yes, love?"

My face was hot. *Everything* was hot. But it was Charlie, and it felt so recklessly, wonderfully good. To be safe in his arms, forever.

I pulled back one last time to meet his eyes and be sure I wasn't dreaming.

Had my list led me here? Had it changed me? Helped me face my fears and learn to be brave?

Perhaps.

Or perhaps it was . . .

"Nothing, my love. Nothing at all."

Epilogue

Two Years Later

I crashed into the cool water of the pond, all sound muted beneath its surface, and thrashed my arms and legs in measured movements, up, up until my face broke free into the warm air and sunlight.

A deep breath.

Then, "You cannot make me get in!" Liza's shrill voice rang in the air.

"It is warm enough!" Ben laughed. "We will save you if you sink."

"I've swam before, thank you very much." She poked his chest.

Even from a distance I could see Ben's cheeks grow rosy. He'd reached one and twenty a fortnight ago, and I knew exactly where his mind was.

Liza's prospects had come and gone after three Seasons. She was decidedly through with the anxiety of matchmaking and therefore happily "on the shelf," though I wondered if that would last.

The door to my new changing room creaked open. Its architect stepped out dressed in his bathing costume. A size too big, if you asked my opinion.

"Is she still not in?" He smirked at Liza, then his eyes met mine.

"Toss her overboard!" I called, reaching my arms out to float as Charlie had taught me.

Liza's eyes were as wide as saucers. "Don't you dare. *Please.*"

Charlie nodded toward her, then Ben put a finger to his lips.

"Very well, I'll get in. *Myself.*" She turned quickly to be certain they weren't sneaking up behind her.

Charlie shrugged and ran into the shallow end. When the water hit his waist, he leaned forward, swimming toward me with swift speed. He swiped a hand through his wet hair and tucked his arm around my waist, pulling me closer to the shallows so he could hold me in his arms.

"Not too bad, is it?" He motioned to the square house he'd designed.

I held onto his neck and kissed him soundly. "It is perfect."

He grinned. "Are you certain you can swim so soon after the birth?"

"Four months, Charlie. John Henry is four months old."

"Really?" He drew back. "It seems like just yesterday. Well, our son is asleep. His grandmothers are both perched over his crib in the nursery at Whitely."

"Lucky boy," I said. Our families had gathered for the week at the Winstons' ancestral home to belatedly celebrate John Henry's birth.

A splash, and Liza shrieked. Ben had jumped in the water right in front of her.

"Ah," Ben teased. "So refreshing."

With both hands, Liza swept water into his eyes.

"As it should be," I said to Charlie, in more ways than one. Our son would be heir to all this, and everything more we created together.

We swam until it was time to dress for dinner. Then Charlie and I dressed and drove our gig from our rechristened home, Oak's End, to Whitely, where our families awaited us.

A carriage pulled up in the drive behind us as we descended. A man in his late thirties stepped out, turning to lift his hand for his companion.

"She's here!" I let go of Charlie, racing forward. "Aunt Alice!"

A short woman in a lace-trimmed hat stepped out. Her sandy-blonde hair peeked out in curls, and her head lifted at the sound of my voice and she turned.

"Rosalind?" she called, arms outstretched. "Look at you! You beautiful young mother. You've the start of wrinkles already."

I buried myself in her embrace. "I certainly hope not!"

She laughed, and Uncle Marvin snuck behind her and kissed her cheek. "Let them live in ignorance for what is to come, Alice."

"They have no idea. Look at them." She smiled between us.

Voices sounded from behind. Mama, Father, Mrs. Winston, the elder Mr. Winston, Ben, Liza, Eloise, and Charlie's older sister, Josephine, even Jasper and Nicholas, who were home for a break from school, all surrounded us in greeting. Enveloping us in a love only family could provide. Some by blood. Some by ties alone.

Aunt Alice turned weepy, taking John Henry from Liza and holding him close. "Look at this little man," she cooed, cradling him in her arms and kissing his chubby cheeks.

"It will only get worse." Uncle Marvin grinned and patted Charlie on the back.

"Hush." Aunt Alice laughed. "John Henry is an angel. You will be an angel for your mama, won't you?"

"If his father is any indication . . ." the elder Mr. Winston cut in.

"I'll thank you," Charlie laughed, "I have passed the whims of an unattached man on to Newbury here." He grasped Ben's shoulder with a hand. "How is my old leather bag?"

"Still hanging in the grove. Taking a beating every morning or so." Ben raised his fists in a show of strength.

"Cover your ears, John Henry," Aunt Alice warned.

"Look at those fists. Perfectly up to scratch." Charlie beamed proudly as he watched his son's eyelids fall heavy and close.

We all shared a laugh, inching closer for turns to catch a glimpse of those chubby little fists. Perhaps when he turned twelve, Charlie and I would dig up our treasure box, and I'd tell him all about my list. How it brought me to Charlie. And how it completely changed my life.

"I'm so proud of you," Aunt Alice said with feeling, looking between us. "Look what you've made."

Our families murmured their agreement. Charlie's hand

smoothed down my back, then tucked me into his side. Our eyes met, and we smiled. Already, we'd created beautiful things together.

"I thought I was happy on our wedding day," I whispered to him. "But this. . ." I looked down at our perfect boy, then back to my husband. "*This* is true happiness."

Acknowledgments

This story has been in my head for years, and despite countless beginnings, I'm so proud of the finished product. I have so many thanks to give.

First, a huge thanks to my outstanding publisher, Shadow Mountain Publishing, and the brilliant minds and hearts there. Without their support and encouragement, this book would not be possible. A special thanks to Heidi Gordon, for her endless patience and sincerity; Lisa Mangum, for every second of editorial polish and shine; Heather Ward, for making such a gorgeous cover with detail that makes me weepy; and Troy, Callie, and Haley, the best marketing team, for being excited with me and shouting about my books from the rooftop!

To my darling critique partners, Arlem "Don't put the list in her stays!" Hawks. Joanna "What is this land agreement?" Barker, and Heidi "Give me more emotion *here* and *here* and *here*" Kimball. I love you three more than words. Thank you, thank you, thank you for the laughs, the support, the late-night word choice helps and the early-morning "You've got this!" chants. Writing would be a million times less fun without you.

Thank you to my parents, and my sisters, Chels, Jenn, Erin, and all my family, for cheering me on and always being excited to hear more.

And to my other half, Ted. I couldn't do any of this without your support. Thank you for loving me, dressing up in Regency clothes and dancing with me in public, and for being the one who inspires the most noble traits in all my heroes.

To Soph, Owen, Henry, and Si—I love you more than words.

Endless thanks to my God, who I feel in my daily life, and whose love and guidance continue to humble and amaze me. Life is never perfect, and it's not always fun, but the gift of writing has certainly made mine a happier one to live.

And lastly, thank you, dear reader, for taking this journey with me. I am imperfect, and surely this book and its historical accuracy are as well. I hope you've loved it anyway.

Discussion Questions

1. At first, Liza has to choose between helping Ros with her list or staying by Charlie's side and keeping him from leaving again. Have you ever been torn between helping two people you've loved? How did you decide what to do?

2. Ros is eager to please her family until she falls in love with Charlie and must make some difficult decisions about her future, knowing it will also change her family's future. How can love sometimes change our plans?

3. Ben struggles with tempering his impulsiveness and fulfilling his responsibilities. Have you ever had to balance these two qualities in your own life? What were some things that helped you do so?

4. Charlie is against Rosalind completing her list, at first. Do you agree with his initial opinion? Why do you think he ultimately changed his mind?

5. Mrs. Newbury struggles to make everything perfect for Rosalind and the wedding. Later, she admits it this was because of her feelings about the duchess. Have you ever

felt a driving need for perfection? What might lead a person to want everything to be perfect?

6. Which item on Rosalind's list was your favorite, and why?

7. Charlie uses boxing to deal with his grief. Do you think this is a healthy outlet for his pain? What other ways do we deal with grief, and how can we help others on their own paths to healing?

About the Author

MEGAN WALKER was raised on a berry farm in Poplar Bluff, Missouri, where her imagination took her to times past and worlds away. While earning her degree in Early Childhood Education, she married her one true love and started a family. But her imaginings of Regency England wouldn't leave her alone, so she picked up a pen. And the rest is history. She lives in St. Louis, Missouri, with her husband and three children.